CU00833739

Rightfully Ours

a Novel

by

Carolyn Astfalk

Full Quiver Publishing
Pakenham, ON

Rightfully Ours

copyright 2017 Carolyn Astfalk

Published by Full Quiver Publishing
PO Box 244
Pakenham, Ontario K0A 2X0
www.fullquiverpublishing.com

ISBN Number: 978-1-987970-02-9

Printed and bound in the USA

Cover design: James Hrkach

NATIONAL LIBRARY OF CANADA
CATALOGUING IN PUBLICATION

Published by FQ Publishing

A Division of Innate Productions

To God the Father,
from whom all good things come.

"A faithful friend is a sturdy shelter;
he who finds one finds a treasure." Sirach 6:14

"For where your treasure is,
there also will your heart be." Matthew 6:21

"When a young man or woman recognizes that authentic love is
a precious treasure, they are also enabled to live their sexuality
in accordance with the divine plan, rejecting the false models
which are, unfortunately, all too frequently publicized and very
widespread."

Letter of His Holiness Pope John Paul II
to the Young People of Rome
September 8, 1997

Chapter 1
At Home in Penn's Woods
2011

An unexpected detour left them lost in the dark. Paul had been certain they were heading the right way, but the two-lane country roads they had traveled the last half hour had few markers, and his older brother questioned whether they had missed a junction sign. Paul's grip tightened on the clumsily-folded map as he peered out the window. Maybe Sean should drag his knuckles out of the Stone Age and get a GPS.

Paul had been anxious about this move more than the others, even though it would only be temporary. The claw-like limbs of the barren trees whizzing by his window made the whole ordeal seem even more foreboding. He'd never been through North Central Pennsylvania, but in the daylight, the mountains would probably be beautiful, if a little desolate.

It's only for a few months. By spring, Dad would be home, and things would go back to normal. Normal for them anyway. Besides, maybe he'd like it here.

"We just passed it," Sean said over the acid rock music blaring from the speakers. "I thought you were watching for signs. Some navigator you are." Sean scowled and jerked the wheel to the right, causing the truck to careen onto the berm and Paul to slam into the door.

Paul rubbed his shoulder where it had smacked the door and sat upright. "I'm sorry, okay? I guess my mind wandered." He'd swear "In-A-Gadda-Da-Vida" had been playing for the last half hour. He hoped to God at least one other radio station had a signal strong enough to carry over the mountain they'd crossed.

"Yeah, you'll be sorry when we run out of gas and have to sleep in this truck." Sean sat hunched over the wheel, his strong arms gripping the ten and two-o'clock positions. His left leg, forever encased in worn denim, bounced erratically in a rhythm out of sync with the booming bass rattling the speakers.

He pulled into a narrow gravel drive and backed the truck out onto the main road, completing his three-point turn. The high beams caught a pair of glowing eyes sinking into the underbrush on the opposite side of the road.

"We'll get there, okay? Maybe if you'd get a GPS or something—"

"You want to pay for it, by all means, do like the commercial says and give a Garmin. Otherwise, maybe you should go back to grade school and learn to read a freakin' map."

Paul suddenly felt ten years younger than Sean instead of the four that separated them.

"There it is, on the right." Paul pointed to a road sign obscured by an overgrown sumac tree.

Sean turned right, and in the space of a mile, the road went from desolate rural to brightly-lit business district.

He swung the truck into the hotel parking lot, rolling over a speed bump with a jolt that made Paul glance out the rear window to see if the pickup had lost any critical parts.

The parking lot islands were filled with mounds of clay and not a living thing grew around the building, which looked as if it had been assembled and dropped into place like a giant LEGO creation.

"Well, if it's new, at least the mattresses should be good." Sean killed the engine and shoved his keys in his pocket.

Apparently Sean had chosen to look for the silver lining, like he had when he first told Paul about this move.

"Hey, it'll be cool." Sean had waved a couple of employment and tourism brochures at him. "Just us. A new job for me, and when I'm off work, we can hang out. Maybe do some hiking, hunting, backpacking. Maybe meet some new people."

What he meant, Paul thought, was that he might meet a girl—*the* girl—something that, despite his good looks, he hadn't had any luck with at home in Maryland. Paul recognized he didn't have a choice in the matter and settled for making the best of the situation. Still, he felt uneasy about the whole thing. There was a finality about it. He couldn't put his finger on it, but he sensed that this move wasn't going to be what either of them expected.

***

The frosted grass crunched with each footstep Rachel Mueller took. The November chill in the morning air invigorated her, and she quickened her pace as she strode along the path. She walked this way nearly every morning, and still it seemed new some days. Today, her hood up, head down, she wouldn't have noticed if there were a gleaming pot of gold at the end of the trail. Rachel held her arms close to her body to insulate it from the breeze. She fixed her eyes on the ground beneath her and scanned for roots, rocks, or anything else that could trip her up.

The blast of cold air that had rolled in overnight seemed to have frozen her brain. When she had gone to bed last night, she couldn't stop her mind from ticking through an endless list of chores, worries, assignments, and plans for the future. Or at least for the rest of her freshman year of high school. This morning, a blessed peace had settled over her like the blanket of fog that hung low around the tree line at the southernmost point of her family's land. She concentrated on putting one foot in front of the other, making the loop around the property, and getting back to the warm house where she hoped she'd find a steaming bowl of baked oatmeal waiting for her.

As she stepped over the frosted mud at the wood line, she rounded the northern end of her family's property, the highest elevation on their land. She lifted her gaze from the trail, taking in the spectacular view of her home, the land, and the unsightly fracking equipment and truck path that now dominated the lower, southern end of the property.

What used to be an overgrown meadow of wild grasses that filled an old farm field was now one of many drilling sites around North Central Pennsylvania where gas mining companies had tapped into the rich gases of the Marcellus Shale.

Marcellus Shale. Five years ago, those two words would've sounded to her like a foreign language or a dreaded skin condition. Now they rolled off the tongue and into her ear daily. Rachel didn't get into the science of it the way her eight-year-old brother did. James was fascinated with everything from the types of rock to the drilling process to the heavy equipment. Rachel's take on it was simple. A gaseous gold mine ran beneath their property. Getting at it involved lots of heavy equipment and noise. It was an intrusion on her family's quiet life, but it brought a much-needed boost to the income and lifestyle of pretty much everyone in the neighboring counties.

By this time of morning, the crews already gulped coffee from their big thermoses and smoked their morning cigarettes. Diesel engines sputtered to life, and as morning sunlight melted the frost, the men would take their positions at the rigging and go about extracting natural gas from below the earth's surface.

"Fracking," they called it. Until a couple of years ago, Rachel thought people used the word "fracking" to swear without actually saying an offensive word. She learned that it could also be shorthand for this mechanical process in which the ground was split up—fractured—to get the gases out.

Rachel's school bombarded her with enough environmental impact education for her to know people disagreed about whether or not fracking was wrecking the planet. She figured the truth lay somewhere between the doomsday cries of the "environmental whackos," as her dad called them, and the carefully-crafted sound bites of the corporate spin doctors. It would all be figured out eventually, probably when she was an adult, so why invest time trying to figure it out now? The truth was that their drinking water was fine, the planet seemed to be getting along all right, and the fracking brought more cash into the household. And some of those young guys that came to work with the drilling companies—they were cute. Granted, these guys were at least eighteen years old, and Rachel was only fourteen, but they sure improved the view and made up for the ugly fracking equipment and mud-covered roads.

When she turned the bend at the end of the tree line, Rachel spotted an unfamiliar truck in the driveway. A cloud of exhaust billowed from the tailpipe and hung low in the dense morning air. She quickened her pace, eager to see who visited at this hour.

She couldn't imagine her parents inviting anybody over at this time of day when they were trying to drag James out of bed, her mom was packing lunches, stuffing things in backpacks, and barking out orders and spelling words.

When she reached the back door, she spotted two people inside with her parents: one of the cute drilling company guys she had seen on the property last week and a boy who looked to be about fifteen or sixteen years old. Their features were similar: broad shoulders, short light brown hair, strong jaw, but somehow the boy was not quite as good looking as the older guy, who leaned against the kitchen counter.

She hesitated, trying to recall what she must look like at

this time of the morning. She had yanked her long, uncombed, brown hair into a loose ponytail and smashed it under her hood, and her nose and cheeks probably flamed red from the cold air. Her mismatched, multicolored gloves set off her baggy gray sweatpants and puffy blue winter jacket. Not the look she would have chosen for a first impression, but left with no choice, she put on a slight smile and opened the door.

"Rachel, I'd like you to meet Sean Porter." Her mom's hands tightened around her mug of coffee. "He's been working at the drilling site."

Rachel slipped off her shoes and unzipped her jacket.

Mom turned to the boy, who sat at the claw-footed kitchen table with her. "And this is his brother Paul."

Sean nodded in her direction, and Paul smiled then settled his gaze on his folded hands.

"Nice to meet you." She spared each of them a glance, then stepped around her dad, intent on scooting down the hall to her bedroom. "I, uh, have to get ready for school." She had barely cleared her dad's big feet when Mom's words stopped her dead in her tracks.

"Wait a minute, Rachel. Paul is going to school with you. In fact, he's going to stay with us for several months while Sean is working here."

She hoped they didn't notice her slack-jawed reaction. "He's . . . staying with *us*?"

About twenty-five yards from the house sat what most people called an "in-law cottage." No in-laws ever stayed there, but it resembled a small, freestanding apartment. Her mom, ever hopeful that someone would visit, had fixed it up as a guesthouse. This, she guessed, was where Paul would stay.

Rachel's dad gathered his iPad and lunch box and backed toward the door. He had taken a position as a middle manager at a logistics warehouse last year, and upper management didn't tolerate lateness.

"I'm sorry we're springing this on you when you've got to get ready for school," Dad said, "but Paul can explain it to you on your way to the bus stop. Things happened kind of fast, but, uh, we're glad to have him here." He gave her mom a quick kiss then slipped out the door.

Mom mustered an enthusiastic smile, but Rachel detected a little pleading in her eyes. Since no time remained for either explanations or oatmeal, Rachel excused herself for the second time and dashed to her room. The peaceful brain fog she had enjoyed during her walk had lifted, and her mind raced again as she peeled off her clothes and pulled her white blouse and plaid uniform skirt from the closet. She kept coming back to the same questions: *Why would my parents put up some stranger's younger brother in our house? Where were their parents?*

By the time she slipped on her scuffed, brown Mary Janes, she couldn't wait to get out the door and interrogate Paul.

Unfortunately, Paul seemed rather tight-lipped. He was still intent on his hands, the table, and any other inanimate object that kept him from making eye contact with her. Sean had left. Down to the drilling site, she presumed, and she heard her mom still trying to drag James out of bed.

She grabbed her lunch and backpack and turned to Paul, ready to go. "We'd better get moving if we're going to catch the bus."

Without a word, Paul got up, grabbed his backpack, and traipsed toward the door.

"We're leaving, Mom," she called down the hallway before stepping past Paul, who held the door for her. At least he had decent manners.

Once outside, Rachel fell into her usual quick pace. She hoped that Paul could keep up; her morning schedule didn't allow for dawdling. She knew precisely how long she needed to get to the bus stop in order to maximize her time snuggled under the flannel sheets and blanket in her drafty bedroom.

"So, Paul, what are you doing here?"

As soon as the words left her mouth, she cringed, wishing she'd found a more delicate way to ask. If only her parents had given her a clue as to what was going on. Maybe there hadn't been time to discuss it, but bringing a stranger into your home was a pretty big deal.

Finally, Paul spoke, dispelling her niggling fear that he was mute. "It's only for a few months. Dad's in the Army in Afghanistan, and my brother had to move here for work, so I had to come along." He jerked his backpack higher onto his shoulder and dug his bare hands into his jacket pockets.

"But why are you *here*? I mean, at my house."

Paul slowed his pace, and Rachel matched it. "In a nutshell, I'm a liability, at least according to the corporate lawyer. But they'll only reimburse Sean if he stays at the hotel. He was gonna quit, then the foreman said to talk to your dad . . ." He glanced at her.

If he thought she knew the rest, he was dead wrong. "So, Sean asked your parents about some place for me to stay, and they said I could stay with them . . . with you."

"Oh." It was kind of a strange setup all around. Shouldn't he be with his brother? And he hadn't mentioned his mother, so Rachel presumed she wasn't in the picture. At least one thing was clear: if *his* dad was in the Army, that explained why *her* dad was willing to open up their home. Her dad wasn't a veteran, but almost all of his friends were—or had been—and he had a tremendous respect for the military. "Well, the guesthouse is pretty neat, so I think you'll be comfortable there."

"Yeah. I appreciate it, but to be honest, this is kind of messed up. I should be used to moving from place to place by now, but somehow it's always...tough." He boosted his backpack on his shoulder.

"My mom passed away when I was little, and my dad's career has had us all over the country. It's been hard for him. I try to fit in, get along, and keep my nose clean. Sean's had a lot of extra responsibilities, but he's good about looking out for me."

"I'm sorry. About your mom, I mean." What could she say? His life sounded like the polar opposite of her stable, familiar, intact family life. She tried to think of something encouraging. "Well, it's quiet here—except for the fracking. So as long as you don't mind that, I think you'll like it."

An awkward silence followed, and the sounds of brittle leaves crunching under their feet filled the vacuum. The driveway sloped downhill and then up, where it crested as it met the road and the bus stop.

"Is there anything I should know about school?"

"Well..." School was school. Mostly boring. "Gallitzin Academy is pretty cool. The principal doesn't tolerate bullying and goofing off, so it's safe and comfortable. We've got the usual jerks and jocks and stuff, but pretty much everyone gets along." She sidestepped a hardened, muddy rut in the driveway. "I guess since everyone's parents pay so much to send kids there, most people are pretty serious about their grades and getting into college. It's not all nerds or anything like that though. There's a lot of fun stuff too."

He nodded, his reaction unreadable. "Okay."

"So, um, have you gone to Catholic school before?"

"Yep. Since kindergarten. Mom made Dad promise. Catholic schools all the way through."

His expression hadn't changed, so Rachel didn't know if he thought that was good or bad.

The bus lurched around the bend and the brakes squealed and hissed before it came to a stop. The bus driver, Merrill, had retired from a corporate desk job and seemed to relish being out of the office and behind the wheel all day. Granted, the wheel belonged to a big yellow school bus, but he drove it as if it were a sports car. Kids in the back seats knew to brace themselves. If Merrill came over a double-dip in the road, they were likely to be airborne. Should she warn Paul? No time now.

The accordion-style door opened, and Merrill's round, smiling face greeted them. With his greased comb-over and horn-rimmed glasses, you'd never suspect he harbored such a need for speed.

Paul chose a seat three rows in front of Rachel. She wouldn't have minded if he sat nearer, but maybe he didn't want to intrude. How would she introduce him anyhow? *This is Paul. He's living at my house for a few months.*

She didn't see him again until they boarded the bus at the end of the day, and they didn't speak until they walked back through the now-soggy leaves to the house.

Sean and her mom spent most of the evening at the guesthouse getting Paul settled. Rachel wanted to help, but she also wanted to give Paul some space. As it was, her mom had sent James back to the house when he had gotten in their way.

After a few days, they fell into a familiar routine. After school, Paul remained at the guesthouse while Rachel retreated to her bedroom. Closer to dinnertime, he came over to the main house and hung out until after dinner. Sean worked long hours, but at least four nights a week, he spent the evening with Paul. Sean seemed like a decent guy, but Rachel struggled to pay attention to what he said since his good looks distracted her.

Apparently, whatever he did with that gas drilling equipment toned his upper arm muscles. Between that and the sun-kissed complexion that brought out his bright eyes and tousled hair, Rachel was captivated.

One of the nights Sean didn't come over, Paul hung around and helped James build a LEGO kit while Rachel sat on the couch and finished her homework.

From his seat on the floor, Paul bumped her leg with his elbow. "Sorry to disappoint you, but Sean has other plans tonight."

Her cheeks heated. "What are you talking about?" Maybe she could play it off like she didn't know what Paul meant.

"Just that you probably miss seeing my brother stop by, that's all." Paul's lips turned up in a half-grin. Was he teasing her?

"Why would I care if Sean stopped by or not?" She hoped she sounded nonchalant, but a crack in her voice threatened to give her away.

He sorted through the pile of tiny LEGO pieces as James assembled some long flat ones. "Oh, I don't know. You seem to like checking him out, all dirty and sweaty after a hard day's work."

Rachel knew her cheeks and ears flamed beet red. "Sorry, I don't check guys out, and I hardly notice when Sean's here."

Paul laughed. For the first time, he let out an-honest-to-goodness full, hearty laugh.

She liked it.

Rachel couldn't help but smile as she gathered her book, notebook, and pen, and marched to her bedroom. Even from there, Paul's laughter rose above the LEGO sorting. Had she been that obvious? No female over the age of twelve would be able to keep her eyes off Sean—he was that gorgeous. From then on, she tried to avert her eyes when Sean was around, but she felt Paul watching her. His expression didn't betray him, but she swore he smirked at her.

Chapter 2
Solve For X and Other Unknowns

Rachel sat at the kitchen table, staring at the numbers and letters until her eyes crossed. She had always excelled at math. What was it about algebra that tangled her thought processes to the point she couldn't comprehend the equation in front of her? She let her head fall to the textbook with a thud.

The kitchen door swung open. Dad must have finished work early.

"Stuck on something?"

That wasn't her dad's voice. She lifted her head.

Paul stood in the doorway. He'd changed from his school uniform to sweatpants and a tee shirt—white with a green sports logo—beneath a leather jacket.

She groaned. "Stuck on *everything* is more like it. Math is supposed to be about numbers, not letters. Mixing the two just isn't right."

He smiled, came to the table, and peered over her shoulder at her open book. "Algebra, huh? Want some help?"

"Are you good at this stuff?"

He shrugged a shoulder. "I passed it."

"Passed it? That's not inspiring my confidence. A 'D' is a passing grade."

Smiling again, he removed his jacket and pulled out the chair on her left. "Didn't want to brag, but since you lack confidence in my abilities, I aced it."

"Then please show me how to do this. My parents have been useless since I got to fractions in fourth grade."

The wooden chair scraped against the floor as he

moved closer to her and pulled the math book towards himself. She caught a whiff of his leather jacket and the crisp November air.

"Okay. Let's look at number one. You're solving for x. What do you think you should do?"

Rachel slid her notebook into place, scratched the problem onto her paper, and pushed it towards him.

He took a few seconds to look it over. "Not exactly. See, all of these are divisible by three." He slid his finger along the line of numbers and letters.

"Okay. Fine. That will get me x, but what about y?"

"Here, let me show you."

She offered him the pencil, which he took with his left hand. Paul was left-handed? How hadn't she noticed that before? He nearly had to turn sideways to work the problem while keeping the paper between them. After jotting down the first line of the solution, he shifted in his chair and stretched his right arm around her seat back.

She scooted forward so that his arm didn't graze her shoulder.

After completing the problem, he leaned back. "See?"

She studied it and nodded. "Okay. Let me try the next one."

Rachel twisted in order to reach her right hand across the notebook while still allowing him to see her work. She finished it and sat back in satisfaction, careful not to bump his arm. "There."

Paul leaned forward again and looked over her work. "Close." He took the pencil, twirled it upside down in his fingers and used the eraser to correct her work.

She sighed. "I'm stupid. I'll never get this."

"I've seen stupid. You're not stupid. Not by a long shot. You'll get it. Try the next one."

Taking the pencil, she complied, and when finished, she squared her shoulders, lifted her chin, and smiled. She'd nailed this one. She held the pencil out to Paul.

He took it, sighed, and shook his head as if discouraged.

Rachel's heart sunk. She really *was* stupid.

Then he leaned in and drew a smiley face next to her answer.

"I got it right?"

He laughed. "Yes, you did." He drew a little stick body onto the smiley face and made another happy stick person.

The rumble of a truck grew louder as the kitchen door swung open again, and Paul laid down the pencil.

"Hey, sweetie. How's it going?"

Rachel's gaze flicked up as her dad set his empty lunch sack on the counter and turned to face her. His eyes darted to Paul and then back to her. "Paul. I didn't realize you'd be here."

Paul slid his arm from Rachel's seatback and scooted his leg away from her knee. "Mrs. Mueller picked some stuff up for me at the drugstore."

Her dad looked from her to Paul again, and Dad's hard stare made her think he was sending Paul a message.

"I stopped by to get it, and Rachel needed help with her algebra." Paul turned his attention back to Rachel and the book between them. "You want to try one more?"

"Sure." Rachel picked up the pencil and worked the problem under the pressure of Dad's gaze. Then she handed the pencil to Paul.

He drew a star next to her answer. "Good."

She smiled and held her hand out for the pencil again.

"You're a southpaw, I see." Dad's gaze fixed on Paul.

"Yes, sir."

"Might make more sense if the two of you were to switch places. Then you wouldn't have to be practically sitting in each other's laps." His tone was terse. "I'm surprised one of you didn't think of that." He didn't sound surprised at all.

Paul cleared his throat and tapped the pencil on the table at a rapid clip. "I think Rachel's got the hang of it now anyway." He pushed his chair back and stood. "I've got some homework to do myself. I'll see you at dinner." He grabbed a small pharmacy bag from the kitchen counter and bolted for the door.

"Thanks, Paul," Rachel called after him. She glanced at Dad, whose gaze remained locked on her. "What?"

He shook his head. "Nothing. You're just growing up too fast, baby girl. That's all."

***

Geez. Her legs may be short, but they could move fast. Paul jogged a few paces to catch up with Rachel as they headed for the bus stop. He needed a few more seconds to catch his breath before he could speak without sounding winded. "So, tell me about this Snowball Dance."

Rachel glanced at him and shrugged a shoulder. "What's to tell? It's a winter dance, but it's a Sadie Hawkins dance. Girls ask guys."

"Are you going?" He couldn't imagine any underclassmen boys turning her down, and he personally knew of at least one sophomore who would jump at the chance.

"Me? Uh, no. I'm not allowed to date. Not until I'm eighteen."

"Eighteen? For real?" He'd known some girls that couldn't date until they were sixteen, but eighteen seemed kind of extreme.

"Unfortunately, yes. I can go to dances though, go out in groups. Just no exclusive dating."

"So, you *can* go to the dance, but you've chosen not to." He slung his backpack higher up over his shoulder. Every time he turned toward her, it slid down his elbow. *Darn heavy history book.*

"Correct."

"Why not?"

"Nosy, aren't you?"

He smiled. "I guess I am."

She spared him a glance, focusing her emerald eyes on his before she spoke. "No one I want to ask, and even if there were, I can't see myself doing it."

"Why not?"

"I don't like rejection."

"No one does. Be glad you're not a guy." Seriously. She had no idea. Maybe it came easy to some guys, but for him, taking that risk was a heart-pounding, panic-inducing nightmare.

A dog bayed in the distance, the only sound other than their footfalls on the frosty ground. She pulled her gloves from her pockets and tugged them on, one at a time. "Have you been asked?"

"Maybe."

She smiled and glanced at him again. "I'll take that as a yes. So, who asked you?"

"Sophia Renault."

"Oh." Her voice came out flat. Being asked by Sophia was obviously not a good thing. "What did you tell her?"

"I told her I'd let her know today."

"Why didn't you say yes?"

"Now who's nosy?"

"Touché. So, why didn't you?"

"I don't really know her. I mean, she's pretty enough, but we've never spoken—I can't figure why she would even ask me."

She hesitated a few seconds—a few too long for his liking. "Maybe she thinks you're cute."

Paul stopped in his tracks. "Don't mess with me."

Rachel stopped a pace ahead of him and turned. "What do you mean?"

"You know something. What am I missing here?"

"Nothing."

"C'mon, Rachel. I've been at your school all of about three weeks. You know this girl. I get the feeling there's something you're not saying."

"I don't want to talk badly about her."

Commendable, but he needed the truth. "You want me to find out the hard way why saying 'yes' would be a bad idea?"

She sighed. "No, I guess not."

"Well, then spill it."

Rachel twisted her lips and puffed out a breath. "She's a leech. If you go with her, you'll never get rid of her. Not short of placing a giant notice in the school newspaper that you are not a couple and you don't want her to have your babies."

"My babies?" His voice came out so high it almost squeaked.

"Yeah. She's a little clingy."

"A little? Well, okay, thanks for the heads up. That'll be a definite 'no.'" Thank God he hadn't said yes.

"Anyone else ask you?"

"No." He paused again. "You reconsidering not going?" Teasing her was fun. Her cheeks flushed, and if he got her flustered enough, she'd start to trip on her words before making an escape.

"No." She picked up the pace again, and he tried to match her stride.

***

Rachel stared blankly out the dirty bus window.

A girl snagged Paul's arm on the way to the bus. He turned, said a few words, and then kept moving. Glancing up, he caught Rachel watching.

She snapped her gaze to the back of the green vinyl seatback in front of her.

Seconds later, he squeezed up the aisle to her row. He

lifted Rachel's backpack, dropped it into her lap, and slid into the seat next to her.

She hated to admit it, but she had wondered all day how he was going to turn down the dance invitation. "So, how'd it go with Sophia?"

He tilted his head from side-to-side a couple times and raised his palms as if to say, "so-so." "She seemed a little disappointed."

"What did you tell her?"

"No." He grinned, letting her know he was messing with her again.

She elbowed him in the side. "I mean, what explanation did you give?"

He shifted his backpack between his feet on the floor in front of him. "Same explanation I gave the other girl who asked me."

Rachel's eyes widened. "Someone else asked you?" He'd been at school less than a month, the dance was announced two days ago, and already two girls had asked him?

"Yeah. You don't have to sound so surprised."

"It's not that I can't imagine girls wanting to go out with you, but you've only been here a few weeks. Had *this* girl ever spoken to you before?"

"Yeah. She's my partner for chemistry lab."

"Who is it?"

He smiled. "Why do you want to know?"

She swiveled in her seat and faced forward. He was not going to turn this back on her. She couldn't care less whether he went or not. "Just curious. You don't have to say." Why *did* she want to know? "So, what did you tell them?"

"The truth." He lowered his voice to barely above a whisper. "I'm not into girls."

She spun around to face him and tried to keep her chin

from dropping. Was he saying he was—?

"I'm kidding." He laughed. "Gotcha."

She gave him a disgusted look and glanced out the window as another group of students poured out of the school doors and into the bus parking area.

"I told them I was only going to be here a couple months. Don't want to start something I can't finish."

"I bet Sophia ate that up."

He grinned. "Maybe. It made Eileen blush."

"Eileen?"

"Flaherty."

"She's pretty. And nice too. Not at all a psycho." She wanted to tell him he should have said yes, but her mouth wouldn't form the words. "Why didn't you say yes?"

"Well, for one thing, it would contradict what I had told Sophia, and I don't want to hurt her. And for another, I'm not into her. It would make things weird during lab anyway."

He was considerate of their feelings. She wouldn't have expected that. She didn't think most guys thought of stuff like that.

The bus lurched out of the parking lot and onto the road, and Rachel steadied herself with a hand to the seatback in front of them.

"There must be some girl you'd like to ask you."

He shrugged. "Doesn't matter. She hasn't asked me."

Merrill took the bus around a hairpin turn and everyone leaned to the left. Paul slammed into her, crushing her against the side of the bus.

"Sorry."

She righted herself in her seat and bit her tongue to keep from snapping at him. "No problem. Not your fault." What was with her? Why was she suddenly so irritated, and why did the name Eileen Flaherty bring a knot to her throat?

***

Something about Thanksgiving seemed...off. Despite the delicious dinner Rachel's mother made and the presence of the Rivera family from church, the weekend felt lonely somehow.

By Sunday evening, intense boredom had set in. Once the dishes had been cleared, Rachel sat at the table and picked at a bowl of mixed nuts. She cracked a hazelnut, discarded the shell fragments, and licked the nut before dragging it through the little pile of salt on her dish. Her dad raised his arms and whooped at the television screen as she popped the salty nugget into her mouth. If she had to watch one more stupid football game, she would scream.

A knock sounded on the door, and she leaped to her feet, eager for something to break the monotony. She peeked out the kitchen window. Paul and Sean stood on the porch. Thank God. A diversion from the doldrums.

Dad welcomed them in and motioned for them to take a seat on the couch. For the first time, Rachel's gaze traveled to Paul before Sean. He was already looking at her, and he smiled. She returned the smile, slid her hands in the back pockets of her jeans, and averted her gaze. Every time she glanced back, Paul's eyes were still fixed on her. Something seemed more confident, more contented, about him.

In time, he made his way across the room to her while Sean spoke to Dad about all the road construction on Route 15 between Williamsport and the Maryland border.

After a couple minutes of awkward small talk, Paul stuffed his hands in his jeans pockets. "Hey, I was wondering if you'd mind some company on your morning walks."

Her morning walk had become a ritual. No matter what else was going on, it always lifted her spirits. Getting outside of her home and outside of her head, which tended to buzz nonstop, into the big world around her gave her the perspective she needed. Things were never so bad that the sun stopped rising or the birds stopped singing. The world kept turning, and life was worth living. That walk was *her* time. Time to think or not think. Time to daydream or to pray. Time to check out Sean and the other guys at the drilling site with no one watching her. Despite her selfish reservations, she heard herself say, "No, I don't mind. Company would be okay."

The next morning, Rachel rolled out of bed, dressed, and marched to the door. As her hand touched the cool metal, something in her stomach fluttered. *What was that for?* She shook her head and opened the door to Paul.

Hands jammed into the pockets of his jacket, he stepped from one foot to the other, trying to keep warm. "Hey. You ready?"

"Yep. Let me get my jacket."

Paul held the door open for her as she stepped outside. The frosty air hit her like a slap to the face. She shivered and zipped her jacket as high as it would go. She glanced at Paul. He still had that happy, confident air about him. What had changed? "So, we didn't get much of a chance to talk last night." *Stupid football games.* "How was your weekend?"

He broke into a wide smile. "Outstanding. We did a Skype call with my dad on Thanksgiving from my aunt's house. He's been in a remote location, so we haven't been able to connect with him much this tour."

Heavy frost bent the field grasses, making them sparkle and spring to life wherever the rays of the morning sun struck them. *Beautiful.*

"You must really miss him." Rachel's dad never traveled for work. She had no idea what it was like to have a parent halfway around the world in harm's way. Meanwhile, Paul and so many other kids were missing their moms and dads who were defending her freedom. She couldn't help but feel a little guilty.

"I don't think I even realized how much I missed him until I saw him. It hit me when I heard his voice. I hope he stays stateside after this."

"So when do you get to see him again?" The path narrowed as it descended the bend that led to the drilling site.

Paul fell in behind her. "That's the best part. Things are moving ahead of schedule on this project he's working on, and he thinks he'll be able to get leave for Christmas."

Joy resounded in his voice, and he flashed her the biggest, broadest smile she had ever seen on him. It transformed his face, making him almost irresistible.

She couldn't help but smile too. "That's awesome. When he comes home, where is home exactly? I know it's Maryland, but I have no idea what part."

"Northern Maryland. We live in Thurmont, south of Gettysburg and Emmitsburg."

They came up on the house. *Done already? How did that happen?*

"Hey, thanks for letting me come with you this morning. I've been pretty lazy lately, I guess. With the move, I didn't sign up for fall baseball or basketball or anything like that."

"Well, you're welcome any time. It's good to have some company for a change." Despite her hesitancy to allow Paul to join her, she meant what she said; she'd enjoyed talking to him while they walked. It was a good thing too, since every weekday morning after, Paul waited for her. After a couple of weeks, Rachel began to relish their easy conversation as much as she did the fresh morning air.

***

Midway through their third week of walking together, Rachel's mom took notice. Like most evenings, Rachel spent the few hours between dinner and bed completing homework and studying. Typically Mom busied herself with something too—usually two things at once, like watching TV and reading the newspaper or having a cup of tea and working on the computer, so when she put down everything to talk to Rachel, Rachel knew something was up.

"You and Paul have been spending a lot of time together."

Rachel closed the book in her lap and scooted her feet back so Mom could sit on the couch with her. "Uh-huh. We just click, y'know? It's so easy to hang out with him and talk. Not to mention my algebra grade has gone from a C to an A."

"I'm glad—about the grade—and that you've found a friend. You need that. Just do me a favor, Rachel. Keep in mind that he's a sixteen-year-old boy, and you're a fourteen-year-old girl."

"I'm aware of that, Mom." Irritation burned in Rachel's chest. Why was her mom trying to make their friendship into something it wasn't?

"It's just that at your ages . . ."

Rachel's calf muscles tightened, and she curled her toes. "Mom, there's nothing like that going on with me and Paul. We're friends. He's like another brother to me." The rising pitch of her voice embarrassed her, and she gritted her teeth.

"If you say so, Rachel." She took hold of Rachel's hand.

Rachel felt like a little girl who had been falsely accused of misbehaving. Her eyes welled with tears.

"I wouldn't be much of a mom if I didn't caution you. Sometimes these things start innocently enough, and then they turn into something more. Paul's a very nice, bright young man, and I'm not saying there's anything wrong with you developing feelings for him—"

"I told you it's not like that." Every word Mom uttered perturbed her more.

"That's fine, Rachel, I'm just saying, *if* it changes, I want you to be smart about things. Your dad and I don't want to see you hurt. First of all, there's an age difference, and second, you know you're not allowed to date. I know this is an unusual situation with Paul living here, and, we'll see, but we might have to set some ground rules."

Tears rolled down Rachel's cheeks. Why? She felt like a fool. She hadn't done anything wrong. She didn't even like Paul that way, and her mom wasn't being mean or unreasonable or preventing her from doing anything.

Relieved that her mom didn't start questioning or lecturing her, Rachel leaned into her outstretched arms. She buried her face in her mom's shoulder, sniffling. The smell of her shirt comforted her. Not flowery or bleached. Just familiar and soothing and, well, Mom.

Mom gripped her gently by the shoulders and sat her up, peering into her tear-stained eyes. She smiled, and the love in her eyes made Rachel's heart swell. Did Paul even know what he missed having lost his mother so young?

"It's all better after a good cry, isn't it?"

Rachel laughed a little. "Yeah, I guess so."

She sniffed, grabbed a tissue from the end table, and wiped her runny nose. She gave her mom another quick hug, and anxious to be alone, scooted to her bedroom.

Rachel grabbed her favorite, pink chenille pillow and hugged it to her chest as she flopped onto her bed. *What the heck just happened there?* She was relieved that her mom hadn't made things worse by saying something guaranteed to irritate her like, "Oh, it's probably your hormones," or "If you don't like Paul in that way, what are all these tears for?"

It probably *was* her hormones, and she honestly didn't have a crush on Paul. She knew what that was like, and this was no crush. When she had a crush on Kyle Waldron, she could hardly contain herself around him. She wanted to wear this big ol' crazy smile, and she thought she would burst at the seams when he spoke to her. She hung on every word—remembered it, replayed it, analyzed it. She knew his every move: where he got on the bus, with whom he sat, which lunch table he used, and even the route he took from the cafeteria to the courtyard.

None of that was true for Paul. She liked him. She enjoyed spending time with him. She wasn't obsessed with his every move.

Rachel lay on her bed, her eyes tired and puffy from the tears, and stared into the ceiling fan. Her vision blurred as the blades spun. Dad claimed the fan helped circulate the heat in winter, but she didn't buy it.

She focused on a single blade and followed it around with her eyes before closing them and listening to the fan's soft electrical hum. Voices from the TV drifted in from the living room while James's old, wooden bed frame creaked as he turned over. She soon fell into a deep sleep.

In the morning, it all seemed like a hazy dream. Having fallen asleep so early, she awoke refreshed and well rested. As she and Paul made their usual morning round of the property, she recalled the conversation with Mom. What had been the point? Her mom hadn't suggested any changes. She just wanted her to be careful. Of what, she didn't know. Getting her heart broken? How could that happen when she wasn't even in love? She wasn't even in *like*. Wait—maybe it wasn't *her* behavior that tipped her mom off. Maybe it was something Paul said or did.

Did Paul have a crush on *her*? How could that be possible? No one ever had a crush on her. At least not as far as she knew. Paul was sixteen. Why would he even care about a fourteen-year-old? The whole idea caught Rachel off guard, and she studied Paul with a new care and intensity, waiting for him to say or do something that would prove his feelings for her were more than platonic. She looked for a glance that hung on a little too long, a certain look in his eyes, the way that he touched her— something, anything, that said, "I like you more than a sister or a friend."

Nothing. Nada. Not until four days before Christmas, when Sean and Paul were ready to leave for home and the visit with their dad. It was only a few careless words, but it was *something*. She knew it.

They'd had the day off from school, and Paul hadn't shown up for their walk, so Rachel went to the guesthouse. Her mom and dad hadn't set any rules about it, but she didn't think they'd be thrilled to find them hanging out there together alone. It'd just be a quick visit to say goodbye.

Rachel knocked, smiling at the corner of the concrete step where Dad had let her make a handprint. She had always liked the guesthouse and imagined living there herself someday. A few antique utensils hung on the kitchen wall, giving it a country feel. Her great-grandparents' round, wooden table and chairs sat in the center of the room, which connected to a larger living area. An overstuffed loveseat and stiff-backed chair provided the only seats, accented by an ornate floor lamp and a two-tiered end table. A small bedroom with an adjoining bath came off a short hallway. It was a great guesthouse, but not spacious living quarters.

She had been in there once or twice over the last couple of months with her mom, and had been surprised at how neat Paul kept things. She expected clothes and dishes scattered around, but the countertops were clean and the table bare. In fact, it seemed as if he hadn't really unpacked.

The door swung open, and Paul stood in the entrance,

his eyes wide. "Oh. Hey. Uh, c'mon in. I'm gettin' my stuff together." Paul welcomed her in, and she followed him to the bedroom where his suitcase lay open on the bed. As usual, things were neat as a pin.

"So, do you like living out of a suitcase or something?"

He glanced up from the clothes he piled on the bed. "Habit, I guess. Too many moves in too little time."

"Maybe you're lazy."

His gaze met hers.

She grinned. Got him.

"Yeah, well, that too."

"You don't think of this place as home."

"I think home is less about where you're at than who you're with."

"Hmm...Pretty philosophical coming from an Army brat." She plopped on his bed next to his piles of clothes.

"Yeah, well, even a stopped clock is right twice a day." He glanced at her sitting there and froze for a moment before he resumed his packing, an unreadable look on his face.

"This is the only place I've ever lived," she said, "so it sure feels like home to me, but I guess if you took my family and moved them somewhere else, it would feel pretty much the same. I mean, I'd miss this place—the actual hills and trees and stuff—but it couldn't compare to the way I'd feel if I left my family."

Paul shoved jeans and sweatshirts into his suitcase, intent on his task. He returned to the dresser to grab a pile of tee shirts, and his reflection shone in the mirror.

He smiled at her. "Actually, I feel more at home here with you than I have most anyplace else." After a few beats of silence, he added, "I can't wait to see my dad, but to tell you the truth, I'm also a little disappointed."

"About what?" Rachel grabbed some of his balled socks and tossed them into his suitcase as if they were miniature basketballs. One rolled over the packed clothes and onto the floor. She hopped off the bed and retrieved it.

"That I won't be here Christmas morning. Y'know, to see if you've been naughty or nice."

She pursed her lips and tasted the watermelon lip gloss she wore. *Is he flirting with me?* She didn't know what to say, so she didn't say anything at all. After a few minutes, she wished him a Merry Christmas with his family and told him she'd see him when he got back.

Rachel thought about Paul's remark over and over during the next several days. And even though she didn't have a crush on Paul, she was falling in love with the idea of him crushing on her. That warm, happy feeling spilled over into everything she did in the last few days before Christmas. She laughed and smiled while she baked and decorated cookies with her mom. She remained cheerful when holding onto the Christmas tree for what seemed like hours as her dad adjusted it in the tree stand. She was magnanimous in helping James wrap his presents. *This might be the best Christmas ever.*

Then the phone call came that changed it all. It left a dark and bitter cloud clinging to everything. Suddenly the cookies were fattening, the tree was a nuisance, and her brother was inappropriately jolly.

Chapter 3
Dashed Christmas Dreams

Rachel slid the hot pan of cookies onto the stove top, closed the oven door, and removed the snowman mitt from her hand. Eight-dozen shapes filled with buttery goodness—done and ready for decorating. She crossed the kitchen to get the metal spatula as the phone rang. Mom's gloved hands were sunk wrist-deep in a sink filled with mixing bowls and measuring spoons.

"I got it," Dad called as he cut across the living room to where the phone rested on the dining room table. "Yeah, what's up, Sean?"

Rachel's ears perked.

Her dad paced around the kitchen, saying things like, "Oh, my gosh," and "I'm so sorry," and "What can we do?"

Whatever happened, it wasn't good.

Mom tore off her gloves and blocked his path, whispering, "What's going on?"

Dad shushed her with his hand and turned to pace in the other direction. With all of his rapid back and forth movement, the butter cookies on the counter would be cool in no time.

"We'll keep you in our prayers." He hung up. It seemed like an eternity before he said anything else. "That was Sean."

Yeah, we know that much.

"His father was killed by a roadside bomb near Kabul."

Rachel's mom sank into a chair at the kitchen table and clapped her hand over her mouth. "Oh, my God."

Using the Lord's name in vain was grounds for a stern correction in the Mueller household. Rachel's mom hadn't broken a commandment. She meant what she said—she was calling on God, stunned and confused.

"He was scheduled to board a plane home for Christmas. Instead, he'll come home to be buried...A chaplain and an officer came to the door this morning and told them."

"Those poor boys. They must be heartbroken. I can't even imagine..." Her voice trailed off.

Dad paced the room again and ran his hand through his hair. "Sean said they don't need anything, but they won't be back for a couple of weeks." He rubbed his palm over the stubble on his jaw and stared blankly at the golden brown reindeer-shaped cookies, but made no move to snatch one like he normally would.

Rachel surveyed the cooling cookies and the Christmas cards taped around the doorway. She'd asked Paul how they decorated for the holidays at his house, and he had gone on and on about their traditions—the way his dad always wrapped each tiny present in a big box because he loved to watch his boys unwrap them. Since their mom died, they would get Chinese food on Christmas day, like in *A Christmas Story*. His dad would read to them from the family Bible, tell them about their first Christmases, and share stories of how their mom hung fresh evergreen boughs and mistletoe throughout the house, made twenty pounds of melt-in-your-mouth chocolate fudge, and hid their presents in shoe boxes and garment bags in the back of her closet.

Now all that was gone. His home was gone.

"Are we going to the funeral?" Rachel needed to go. How could she explain that to her parents? Her heart ached imagining what Paul must be going through.

Her dad studied her for a moment. "They haven't made arrangements yet, but I think we should go if we can."

"Yes." Mom wiped her eyes with a tissue. "Christmas

isn't going to be the same this year. Not for us, and not for those boys. Ever."

Mom brewed tea and filled an oversized mug with it. She returned to her seat at the kitchen table in silence while Dad headed outside to check the Christmas lights. He was fond of Paul and Sean, but he had also lost friends in Iraq—close friends whose deaths had left him sullen for months. Maybe this felt too familiar.

The rich buttery smell of the cookies that had moments ago made Rachel's belly rumble now turned her stomach. Her heart ached for Paul. How could he keep going now that he'd lost both his mom and his dad? What would she say when she saw him?

***

Rachel's family went about the holidays as planned. Christmas Eve culminated in a lasagna dinner, presents under the tree, and Midnight Mass. On Christmas morning, the frenzy of unwrapping and celebrating led into a quiet afternoon of relaxing and trying out new presents. Rachel's mom made a delicious dinner with ham, sweet potatoes, green bean casserole, homemade rolls, and a birthday cake for baby Jesus. From the outside it looked normal, but from the inside every sweet moment was tinged with gloom.

Rachel slid the last piece of chocolate birthday cake from her fork into her mouth before dragging the utensil across the plate and scraping up every crumb of chocolate. She licked the fork and held it between her teeth.

Feeling full, she set her fork and napkin on her plate. "I wonder what Paul and Sean are doing."

Her dad wiped the chocolate crumbs from his face with a napkin. "Why don't we call and see? It might help to know someone's thinking of them."

He punched in Sean's cell phone number while Rachel stacked the dessert plates and James played with his pirate set in the living room. Her dad cleared his throat then left a message.

"Sean, it's Ron Mueller. We wanted to wish you and Paul a blessed Christmas, such that it is, and let you know we're thinking of you and praying for you." Her dad gave Rachel an encouraging smile and squeezed her shoulder as he moved to return the phone to its base.

Sean didn't call back that night or all week.

***

Finally, on New Year's Day, Sean called to let them know the burial arrangements.

"Sean says they're doing okay," her dad reported. "They spent Christmas with their aunt and uncle and the rest of the week going through their dad's things. They scheduled the funeral for Thursday." Three days away.

Rachel's family made the two-and-a-half hour drive to northern Maryland the evening before the funeral. Still wide awake when they arrived at the hotel, she nevertheless tried to sleep since her three traveling companions doused the lights and pulled up the covers. At least she had a double bed to herself. Her parents took the other double bed, and James got the pull-out sofa bed.

Unfortunately, she couldn't slow her brain, so she lay motionless on her side. A sliver of light showed between the curtains, coming from the parking lot. Her gaze drifted to a fire alarm in the corner of the ceiling. A little red light flashed. One, two, three...Eight seconds passed between flashes. She rolled onto her back and studied the geometric patterns of holes in the ceiling tiles. She shifted to her opposite side, and one ankle itched and then the other. What if the place had bedbugs? She spent a half hour itching and scratching before she drifted asleep.

It seemed as if she dreamt all night. She couldn't remember most of the dreams—a fragment here or there— maybe a person, a conversation, a place—but she couldn't shake the last dream as they got ready for the funeral in the morning.

She and Paul lived on the third or fourth floor of a big-city brownstone apartment building like the ones on *Sesame Street*. They were older, maybe in their twenties?

A blast outside their window shot debris up from street level. Rachel screamed, and they ducked their heads. As bits of concrete and litter descended, they stepped tentatively toward the shattered window. Paul proceeded to climb out on the rusty fire escape that hung from the brick building. He jumped up and down a couple times, testing his weight. Then he held his hand out to Rachel, and she took it. Ill at ease, they stared down into a gaping hole on the cobblestone street below.

Ash and small pieces of what looked like paper continued to waft down into the hole. A glittering object caught Rachel's attention. Without thinking, she lunged for it. It gleamed just out of her reach, and she straddled the rusty metal railing, wrenching her leg in the process. Pain shot through her knee. As she grabbed at her throbbing knee, she lost her balance and wobbled precariously.

Rachel opened her mouth to scream, but nothing came out. Instead, she inhaled a chalky cloud of concrete dust and dirt. She coughed, and her grip on the railing loosened.

Paul swung a leg over the rail and climbed out alongside her. He inched toward her and then behind her, his arms on either side of her anchoring them to the bars.

The metal groaned heavily and snapped, pulling away from the side of the building and falling toward the big hole in the street. Paul's arms tightened at her sides as they fell backward. She seemed to melt into Paul. It made no sense once she awoke, but she was sure they had fallen together as if they were one person.

She braced for impact, but instead of the backbreaking thud of flesh on hard ground, she felt her body sink into softness until it almost buried her. She and Paul—were they separate entities now?—landed side by side on a white, downy bed.

She rolled from her back to her side as she tried to sit up, but sunk further into the mattress as she came face to face with Paul, who was trying to do the same thing from the opposite side of the bed. His body weight forced him closer to her as she changed position on the soft mattress, and she thought—no felt—that he was leaning in to kiss her.

She stared into his deep blue eyes before her own eyelids fluttered closed. She leaned into him, closer... closer—

The bedsprings bounced. And bounced. By the third bounce, Rachel was fully roused and spied the source—James: awake, alert, and annoying.

"Get off my bed, you little creep! Now." Once he bounced off, she lay back down and pulled the covers over her head trying to reassemble the dream in bits and pieces. Already the images blurred and faded, and as her parents woke and James turned on the television, the noise in the room ruined her concentration. Still, she couldn't shake the lingering feeling that the dream had left her with—a woozy romantic feeling filled with the anticipation of a kiss.

It rattled Rachel. She didn't like Paul that way. He was like a brother, right? The conversation she had with her mom before Christmas must have gotten all muddled up in her subconscious. She couldn't be feeling this...whatever it was she felt for Paul as she got dressed for his father's funeral. She snatched her clothes from the garment bag and headed for the bathroom.

James banged on the bathroom door as Rachel

smoothed out the crushed black velvet of her skirt. She hoped her Christmas dress was sedate enough. Stitched red and green flowers ran along the cuffs and hemline of the simple black dress. She didn't have anyone to impress, did she? She shook her head and let out a breath. It was a funeral, for Pete's sake.

She pulled a comb through her hair and fastened small silver clips on either side of her head then stared into the mirror and recalled what she could of her dream. Again, the warm, tingling feeling of anticipation filled her chest. What would have happened if James hadn't woken her?

"C'mon, Rachel. I have to go!" James flinging his wiry frame against the door jarred Rachel to her senses. She set down her brush, twisted the knob then jerked it open. James fell through the door onto the cold tile floor.

"Ow." He rocked back and forth, clutching his knee. "Mom, Rachel knocked me onto the floor."

"I did no such thing. He was being obnoxious and throwing himself on the door when I opened it."

Her dad scowled at them as he knotted his necktie. "James, dial it down a notch." His voice was stern. "We're going to a funeral."

The church façade consisted of gray stone accented by immense concrete pillars. It matched the gathering clouds, heavy with snow. The carved archway above the center door depicted a chorus of angels. Maybe the dreary weather contributed to the feeling, but despite its beauty, the building seemed cold and dead, a contrast to the warmth and comfort Rachel usually experienced as she entered church.

Her family took seats about halfway back between the sanctuary and the rear of the church. They sat in the company of about a dozen people, all of them waiting for Paul's family to arrive. Rachel stared up at the fresco of the

Last Judgment on the domed ceiling. Jesus didn't look like a hippie at a love-in like so many paintings she had seen as a little kid. Here, he appeared stern but not mean. He looked more like the just judge he was supposed to be, not an ogre. Even so, it intimidated her. She ought to go to confession again soon.

Paul's family arrived in the vestibule, and everyone stood as the pallbearers carried the casket, draped with the American flag, to the front of the church. The tall, white-haired priest said a blessing and sprinkled it with holy water. The spicy smell of incense filled her nose as it swirled from the altar out into the rest of the church.

The Mass proceeded much like any other Mass. Then the priest spoke about Paul's dad and how he had served his family and his country. The rest of the homily focused on Mr. Porter's hope in the resurrection, where he would be reunited with his wife, and Rachel's eyes welled with tears.

At the conclusion of the Mass, they sang the "Song of Farewell." The choir comprised elderly parishioners who sounded ready to greet the angels themselves. They wouldn't take any awards in a choral competition, but the fragility of their aging voices lent poignancy to the song.

The gulf between this world and the next seemed so vast to Rachel. Paul would never see or touch his father or hear his voice again. She imagined the angels carrying his dad off, up through the domed ceiling, past the stern Jesus; and instead of peaceful, she felt empty and sad. She also felt James elbow her in the ribs.

"Rachel." He nudged her again. "Rachel."

"What?" she breathed, wiping tears from her face.

"Do you think guardian angels can hang out together? Like, couldn't Paul's mom and dad hang out with Paul's angel or something? And then it could go back to Paul."

His theology was a little sloppy, but Rachel could see

his point. Paul wouldn't see, hear, or touch his dad again, but he wasn't lost to him forever. They were still somehow all connected, and, someday, they would all be reunited.

"I guess so." Rachel didn't want to encourage further conversation.

The pallbearers carried the casket out of church, and Paul's family followed. Some middle-aged adults, probably Paul's aunts and uncles, led the group. The women looked somber as they wiped stray tears and held onto their children's hands. A few teenagers straggled alongside them.

Sean and Paul followed. Even in grief, Sean looked exceedingly handsome. The lines of his suit were tailored perfectly to his muscular physique. His expression stoic, he clenched his jaw, every muscle in his face rigid. She guessed he was trying not to cry, but no one would fault a guy for crying at his own father's funeral.

Paul didn't cry either, but his eyes were red and puffy, his face splotchy. His sadness created an ache in Rachel that ran from the base of her throat, tight with restrained emotion, straight through her chest. It wasn't fair that he had lost not one, but now both parents.

With hands planted deep in his pockets, Paul stared beyond the open doors at the rear of the church, never turning to see who sat in the pews. Sean put an arm around his shoulder, and Paul bit his lower lip.

Rachel glanced away, trying to forestall her tears. It didn't work. She grabbed a pack of tissues from her purse and wiped the wetness from her cheeks.

In turn, her family left the pew and returned to their car for the ride to the cemetery.

The funeral procession must have been thirty cars long. Rachel hadn't realized how crowded the church had become. The drive to the cemetery was short, but hours away from where she—and, for now, Paul—lived. She wondered how often he'd be able to visit the gravesite.

The cars climbed the narrow, steep cemetery lane to the burial site. Paul's dad would be laid to rest near the crest of the hill. A mound of dirt sat alongside the grave. It hadn't been so cold yet that they couldn't dig, but already it grew colder and flurries fell from the heavy, gray clouds hanging low in the sky. A bitter wind kicked up the snowflakes, making them whirl.

As Rachel exited the car, the wind sent a blast of cold air up her dress, causing her to shiver. She smoothed the skirt down and plodded to where Paul's family gathered with the priest.

The mourners pressed close to the gravesite so they could hear, and at least in Rachel's case, in hope that the huddle of bodies would shield her from the elements.

The scenes that followed became etched in Rachel's mind. The snippets of the service made an immense impact. The hollow echo of the rifle fire, the bugles mournfully calling out "Taps," and a uniformed soldier presenting the regimentally-folded flag. Not a bit of red showed as he handed it to Sean in its neat, triangular formation.

A luncheon followed the funeral, but because of the snow, Rachel's parents decided they should get on the road. Rachel had only a brief moment to offer her condolences.

She stepped toward Paul.

His gaze skimmed over her and rested on her parents. When finally he looked at her, his blue eyes filled with tears. He stared, almost pleading with her.

What should she say? Nothing she said would make anything better. So, she did the only thing she could think of, and she hugged him.

A sob shook Paul as her arms encircled him. His breath warmed her neck, and he smelled faintly of a fresh, menthol-scented soap. He leaned into her until she felt as if she were holding him up.

She squeezed tighter.

He pulled away and attempted a smile, not quite succeeding. "Thank you for coming."

Rachel nodded. "I wanted to be here."

"I guess I'll see you next week. We've got a few things to take care of here, but Sean needs to get back to work."

Paul was coming back, but for how long? "Well, drive safely."

What a dumb thing to say. Everything was off—the cold feeling she'd had in church, the stern image of Jesus, the brewing storm. Everything right down to her weird dream. Nothing seemed normal anymore, and for Paul, she wondered if it ever would be.

Chapter 4
Grief Spiral

A cold blast of air hit Rachel, and she shivered. A dusting of snow capped the distant mountains overnight, and the bare tree branches now coated in white stood out against the still-dark sky. She pushed up her sleeve and glanced at her wristwatch. Was Paul coming with her or not? She glanced back at the darkened windows of the guesthouse and stepped off the porch, digging her gloved hands into her pockets for warmth.

Soon after she'd switched off her light and climbed into bed last night, Sean's truck rumbled up the driveway. The engine idled and two truck doors slammed shut. A minute later, the door to the guesthouse closed. After ten minutes, the guesthouse door shut again followed by the truck door. Paul was home. Alone.

She rounded the bend at the southernmost tip of her parents' property, and a pair of cardinals flitted about in the trees. While she missed Paul more than she cared to admit, she dreaded the awkwardness that was sure to accompany him. Still, as difficult as it would be, she was determined to get past the discomfort and be a friend to him.

Stomping the snow from her boots, she tromped over the familiar path toward home. The lights in the guesthouse flicked on, and she sucked in a breath. Paul was up and, she guessed, getting ready for school. *Lord, what do I say to him?*

Rachel traipsed up the steps to her house and sighed. She'd better think of something. She spooned shredded wheat into her mouth as she thought about Paul and what he needed to hear. As she dressed for school, she decided a hug would be best since she couldn't mess that up too badly. She hoped after that the words would come.

She ran a brush through her hair one last time and snagged on a knot. The kitchen door clicked shut, and Mom's voice carried down the hall. Rachel's hand stilled, and she listened as her parents asked Paul how he was doing. She dragged the brush through the rest of her hair and rushed into the hall, careful to slow her pace as she reached the kitchen, shrugging into her coat as she walked.

Paul stood in the entranceway with his leather jacket zipped past his navy necktie and his khaki pants neatly creased. His eyes, still puffy, now had dark circles underneath them too. His expression registered nothing as he spoke to her parents, but his gaze shifted to her, and he gave her a sad smile.

For a moment, she second-guessed the hug, but still not knowing what to say, she walked to Paul and slid her arms around him. Her cheek brushed the leather at his collar as his arms squeezed her, pushing some of the air out of her puffy winter coat. She said the only thing she knew to be true: "I missed you."

Paul didn't say anything, but he released her and said goodbye to her parents. He held the door, and she stepped onto the porch ahead of him. He reached into his jacket pocket, pulled white ear buds from his coat, and placed them in his ears.

"Did you get an iPod for Christmas?" The cloud her breath made dissipated in the air, and she stepped into the frosted grass so that they could walk side-by-side.

"Sort of. It was Dad's. Sean said I could have it. I thought it would be cool to see what he listened to."

"Neat." Of course he'd want to listen to his dad's music, but maybe he also wanted to eliminate the possibility of conversation. Her mom had told her that everyone grieved differently, and she shouldn't take it personally if Paul was less inclined to talk than usual. If he didn't want to talk about his dad or anything at all, that was okay.

The music from the iPod blasted so loudly she could hear the bass thumping, but Paul adjusted it down, and they walked all the way to the bus stop without speaking.

That's the way it went for the rest of the week. Rachel tried to be patient, but by Friday she missed Paul more as he walked beside her than she had when he was more than a hundred miles away.

"Do you want to start walking with me again on Monday?"

Paul shrugged. "I think I'd rather sleep. I'm exhausted all the time."

"Come on. The exercise might give you some energy."

"Maybe, but I don't fall asleep until after midnight, and I can't get up in the morning as it is."

"Please. Will you try it?" She turned her best puppy dog eyes on him and batted her lashes a few times until he smiled. "I got used to having a walking buddy, and now I'm bored. Plus, there's nobody to block the wind."

Paul's smile broadened. "Okay. I'll try it for a few days and see how it goes."

"Awesome." Should she press her luck and try to coax him out of hibernation a bit more? "We got some new board games at Christmas, and my mom started a family game night. It's every Friday, so if you hang out after dinner tonight, I can whoop your ass at a game of Risk."

Paul's eyebrows shot up.

That was the great thing about never using foul language: when you did, people paid attention.

"Whoop my ass? What did you get for Christmas, a potty mouth? And what makes you think you can whoop my ass anyway?"

He teased her for the first time since he'd come home,

and a warm beam of light burst through the darkness in her heart. His blue eyes glowed, and they crinkled at the corners. She hadn't seen him smile like that since before Christmas.

Paul stayed for game night, and while James played Sorry! with her mom, Rachel's dad whooped both their asses at Risk. Rachel packed up the game pieces and board and returned them to their box. She placed the game on its shelf and slid her cold feet under the baseboard heater beneath the window. The snow fell in thick, wet flakes as her icy toes thawed and warmed in her snowman socks. In the next room, she overheard her parents speculating how much snow they'd get. She sensed someone behind her and turned.

Paul shuffled a step closer to her with his hands tucked in the pouch of his hooded sweatshirt.

She gazed out the window again. "It's beautiful, isn't it?" She never tired of watching snow fall, so delicate and fragile.

"It is. Rachel..." He waited until she turned to him again. "Thank you for inviting me tonight. I feel..." His gaze wandered to the snowfall. "I don't wish I were dead. I know how that must sound, but, well, the bar's been set pretty low lately, and not feeling that way is actually a big improvement."

A lump formed in Rachel's throat. "Paul, you wouldn't ...please tell me you'd never hurt yourself."

"No." He shook his head. "No. You don't need to worry about that. It's just that I've felt hopeless since we buried him, and tonight, well, tonight I don't. It's not much, but it's like the smallest, most distant star in the night sky. Right now, that's enough. So, thank you for pestering me to come."

Rachel smiled though tears blurred her vision. "That wasn't pestering. It was persistence."

"Whatever. I'm grateful." Something shone in his eyes—warmth? affection? gratitude? He smiled and touched her elbow. "Good night."

She padded to her bedroom, her snowman socks gliding on the bare floor, while Paul said goodnight to her parents. She had been praying for him every morning and night, but not with any specific intention. Now she knew what to pray for: hope.

She left her bedroom door partway open and tiptoed to her dresser. Silencing her bangles, she slid them from her wrist and into her jewelry box.

Paul's voice drifted from the living room. "Thank you, sir. I'll let you know, but what I need is my dad, and no one can bring him back."

A few seconds of quiet...then Dad. "Rachel makes you happy."

Paul cleared his throat. "Yes, she does."

"I'm glad. I mean that. Let her be your friend. She wants that. Wants to be there for you."

"Okay." Paul sounded unsure. Was he unsure of her friendship or her father's unsolicited advice?

"How old are you, Paul?"

Rachel's eyes widened. Her dad knew Paul's age. She'd heard him talking to Sean before Christmas about getting Paul a Pennsylvania learner's permit. She sat on the edge of her bed and listened.

"Sixteen."

"My daughter's fourteen."

"I know, sir." Those words could have come off smart, but Paul said them with sincerity.

Rachel rolled her eyes. Dad was warning Paul to keep their friendship just that—friendly. She pulled her plush throw pillow to her chest and hugged it. Thank God she wasn't present for that embarrassing exchange. Why did her parents keep trying to make like there was something going on between her and Paul when there wasn't?

A full minute passed, but she hadn't heard Paul leave. She set aside the pillow and tiptoed to the doorway, craning her neck to see into the living room.

Her dad held Paul's hand in a firm grip then pulled him into a hug. From a distance, she witnessed Paul crumble, his shoulders shaking.

Dad's voice was barely audible. "It will get better. I promise. Take one day at a time. If that seems like too much, then one hour. Talk to Sean. Talk to Rachel. If it's something you feel you can't share with either of them, I'm a pretty good listener."

If they said more, Rachel didn't hear. She closed her door, careful not to make any noise, and slipped over to her window. She pulled the quilt from her bed and draped it over her shoulders. The front door clicked shut, and she spotted Paul plodding back to the guesthouse. A funny tingling stirred in her belly, and she wrapped an arm across it. Butterflies.

Once Paul had gone inside, she dressed for bed and brushed her teeth. She lay in bed and stared at the moonlight as it lit her dresser. How long would Paul lie awake tonight? She relaxed and turned onto her side, facing the wall. Her gaze fixed on the small wooden crucifix that hung there, and she prayed for Paul until she drifted to sleep.

Monday morning, two inches of snow covered the ground, but according to Rachel's dad, the school had not called a snow day yet. Rachel got up and dressed, figuring she'd take her morning walk anyway and enjoy the peace and beauty of the fresh snow. Paul should've been at the house by now if he wanted to go with her. She pulled on her earmuffs and gloves and decided to hold Paul to his word and make him go.

She walked to the guesthouse, kicking the white powder

out of her way as she went, and knocked on the door.

No answer.

She knocked again.

Paul opened the door.

Her eyebrows shot up.

He was fully dressed and ready to go. "Is school canceled?"

"Nope."

Paul groaned. "So much for a day off." He fished his ear buds from his pocket and positioned them in his ears.

They walked in silence.

Rachel gritted her teeth. It had only been a week, but she wanted to grind those darn ear buds under her boot. She liked music too, but walking with a deaf mute got old fast. After ten minutes of biting the inside of her cheek and glaring at the dangling wires hanging from Paul's ears, she couldn't hold back any longer.

"If you're going to ignore me every morning, maybe we ought to walk separately."

"Huh? Wait a second, I gotta turn this down."

She huffed an angry breath. Of course he had to turn it down.

"I said, if you're going to ignore me, maybe we ought to walk alone."

"Whatever." Paul shrugged. "Fine by me."

His indifference stung Rachel. Paul had never spoken to her with anything but kindness and good humor.

Her response came loud and harsh. "I'm sorry that your mom died. I'm sorry that your dad died. I know it sucks. For some reason, God saw fit to let it happen. You're alive. Maybe you should try living."

***

She strode ahead, moving faster than before. How dare she—Rachel with her perfect life. How could she know what he'd gone through growing up without a mother?

How could she know the agony of watching as your father's body was lowered into the ground? It hadn't even been a month.

"Do you really think you know what I'm going through, 'Little Miss Perfect Life'?" He made air quotes around the name he'd called her. "You don't *have* to spend time with me, you know. I get along fine all by myself. Been doing it my whole life." He ripped the ear buds from his ears and threw them toward the ground, only they were connected to the iPod, so they dangled from his pocket.

She stopped and faced him, her jaw clenching.

"Why don't you run along home where your mommy can bake you cookies and your daddy can tuck you in at night? Where you can sleep knowing he's in the next room, not thousands of miles away waiting to be blown to bits or gunned down."

The fire in her green eyes burned. "What do you want, Paul? Do you want me to be sorry my parents are alive? Because I'm not. I can't help the way I've been raised any more than you can. You want to stick your head in the sand and play pity-party-for-one, then go for it. Excuse me for thinking I could be your friend."

She huffed and crossed her arms over her chest. Her eyes glistened. "You act like I suggested we dance on your parents' graves. Is sparing me a few words too much to ask?" Her voice grew louder and more shrill with every word. "I'm sorry if I'm no good at this. I was trying. I thought maybe you'd like to talk about it. About him. That I could listen." A lone tear escaped her left eye. "Screw you," she hissed, and turned on her heel back toward the house.

He lunged forward and grabbed her wrist, turning her back towards him, but couldn't think of a thing to say to stop her.

She glared at him, her eyes a mixture of pain and

animosity. "Do you have something else you want to say to me?"

What had he done? Her eyes were all watery, and she bit her lower lip as if to stop it from trembling. He'd made her cry, and he needed to apologize. He was angry, but not with her. Not really. He was mad at the doctors who failed to keep his mother alive. Mad at his dad for staying on active duty. Mad at the terrorists who killed his dad. Mad at God for allowing it all to happen. The truth was, he needed her. If it weren't for her, he wouldn't have the will to get out of bed in the morning.

Out of nowhere the need to kiss her hit him with full force. He stared at her, his heart pounding. Was it from anger or something else? She wrenched her arm from him, and the impulse died.

"I didn't think so," she spat and ran back toward her house, leaving him standing there like an idiot.

He gave up on the walk too, and went straight to the guesthouse. After he dressed for school, he returned to the house to meet her, but she was gone, already at least a third of the way up the driveway. He reached the bus stop, and she turned her back to him. He needed to make things right with her. He had no right to lash out at her the way he had. He couldn't explain that or the crazy urge he had to kiss her.

"Rachel—"

"Sorry. Busy living my perfect life. No time to talk."

When the bus doors opened at the end of the day, he had to shove his way out from the back of the bus, and she bolted ahead of him toward the house.

He caught up to her. "Rachel, c'mon."

"I'm sorry I can't relate to the depth of your suffering. Hey, maybe someone I love will die, and then we can be friends, huh? My dad has high blood pressure, you know. Maybe he'll have a massive heart attack or something."

Before he could reply, she took off in a run. Tears stung the backs of his eyes. Really? Hadn't he blubbered enough over the past few weeks? Darn, stubborn girl.

***

She'd been too hard on him. She was hurt, and she had wanted to hurt him back, but for goodness sake, hadn't the boy suffered enough? What was she thinking? She recalled yelling "screw you" at him and cringed. Where had *that* come from? If he'd rather listen to music than talk to her, so what? Why couldn't she have been more patient? Now she'd alienated him.

Rachel stood at her bedroom window, watching as Paul climbed into Sean's truck. He couldn't get away from her fast enough.

If was after ten o'clock when the truck tires crunched over the gravel again, and she refused to look out the window.

Five minutes later, a knock sounded at the door. She tensed, but didn't move.

The television turned off, and her dad answered the door. She scooted to the edge of the bed and inclined her ear to the hall but could still barely hear him.

"Paul, is something wrong?"

Rachel crept closer to her door, opening it a little wider in hope that the sound would travel better.

"No, sir. I know it's late, but I saw the lights on. May I speak to Rachel if she's still up?"

A long pause. "She's up. I don't know if she's still dressed."

"Please, sir. I owe her an apology."

Dad sighed. "Come in. I'll get her."

Rachel leaped onto her bed and landed on her belly with her book open in front of her. He wanted to apologize to *her*? She's the one who owed him an apology, but she didn't think she could face him. Not yet. She needed to think about what she'd say.

Two seconds later, Dad knocked on her door and stuck his head in. "Good. You're still dressed. Paul's here. He wants to talk to you."

"I heard. Tell him I'm in bed. I'll talk to him tomorrow."

Her dad stepped into the room, and the door clicked shut behind him. "Rachel, he's going through a lot. Cut the boy some slack, will you? Whatever happened, he's sorry, and he wants to tell you so. The least you can do is go out there and listen to him."

Rachel twisted around into a sitting position and faced her dad. "It's not that. I'm the one who should be apologizing. I got miffed that he wasn't talking to me, I pushed him too hard, and I said some awful things."

"All the more reason to go out there and speak to him." He stared, waiting for her decision.

Dad was right.

He held the door open, and she walked into the hallway. Dad trailed her to the living room.

Paul sat on the edge of the couch, his face buried in his hands. As she entered the room, he straightened and stood.

"I'm going to bed." Dad lingered at the edge of the room. "Don't be long, and lock up when he goes, okay, Rachel?"

"Sure, Dad."

Once her parents' door closed, she walked around the couch to where Paul stood. "Want to sit?"

"Okay." He sat angled toward her, their knees touching. His gaze fixed on his hands. He rubbed them together a few times then rested them on his knees and looked her in the eye.

"Rachel, please forgive me. I'm ashamed of the things I said to you. I'm angry, but not with you. You were a convenient target. I know you meant well." He lifted his hand, and she thought he might take hold of hers, but instead he rubbed his palm back and forth over his jeans. "If anything, I'm jealous of you."

"This," he said as he grabbed the iPod from his jeans pocket, "feels like the only connection I have left to my dad, and it's not very strong. I feel like...I feel like it speaks to me."

"What do you mean?" Her heart broke at the thought that something as tenuous as a playlist was the sole connection he had left to his parents.

"I know this sounds weird, and I know it's probably my imagination, but if I put the music on random play, the song is about something I'm feeling or something that's happening."

"That *is* weird." Strange, but if it brought him comfort ..."Paul—"

"Rachel, before you say anything, can you forgive me? I'd like to hear you say it."

"Yes. Of course I forgive you." She took a breath and prayed God would give her the right words. "What I wanted to say is that I should apologize to you. You're right that I don't know anything about what you're going through. It was selfish and inconsiderate of me to badger you into talking to me. I just...well, you're like a brother to me, and I care about you. I want to see you happy."

He winced. What had she said wrong? Couldn't she even get an apology right? He seemed to recover from whatever bothered him and offered her a smile.

"Apology accepted. Everyone keeps telling me that it will get better, so I'm taking their word for it." He stood, and she followed him to the door. He put his hand on the knob and turned to her. "Walk with me tomorrow? No ear buds?"

She smiled. "Sure. Good night."

"See ya."

She closed the door behind him and locked the deadbolt. "Sleep well, Paul."

***

Paul locked the door of the guesthouse behind him. Loneliness descended like a thick fog, blanketing him. Smothering the glimmer of hope his conversation with Rachel had ignited. His world remained cloaked in darkness like it had every day since his dad died. Why did it hurt so much when he was around Rachel? Maybe he felt *everything* more when he was with her. Maybe because all he wanted was for her to hug him again like she had at the funeral, to comfort him. Or maybe it was because she thought of him like a brother, and that wasn't at all the way he felt about her.

After going through the motions of dressing for bed, brushing and flossing his teeth, he yanked down the covers on his mattress and lay down. He should pray. Hadn't their dad gotten on his knees and prayed with them every night when he and Sean were boys? A stab of bitterness pierced him. What good had prayers done any of them? God seemed bent on taking away everyone Paul loved. Maybe tomorrow night he'd rattle off some rote prayers. Tonight he laid the iPod on his nightstand, put the ear buds in his ears, and pressed play.

Wipe the tears from your eyes
Boy, don't you cry
Hang on, stay strong

Chapter 5
Swiss Miss Hit or Miss

Paul silenced his alarm for the second time and sat up, breathing deeply. He pushed aside the curtain and squinted into the morning sun reflecting off the snow. Yesterday, a mid-March storm dumped another eight inches onto the foot and a half already piled on the ground. An oversized snow mound buried the Mueller's picnic table on the porch, and snow reached nearly halfway up the birdfeeder between the guesthouse and their home.

Had it *already* been three months since Dad died? Had it *only* been three months since Dad died? Though he knew it'd been eight months, it seemed like yesterday they'd hugged goodbye. And yet it felt like a lifetime ago.

He pushed down his covers and forced himself out of bed each morning thinking of the only thing that made waking up worthwhile—Rachel.

Was he confusing his grief and loneliness with his feelings for her? No, he'd been attracted to her even before his dad died. No need to over-analyze the situation. She was a great listener. He could tell her things he couldn't say to Sean.

Sean, grieving in his own way, hadn't been around much lately. He insisted nothing was wrong, but he always had an excuse for why he couldn't hang out. Even when they were together, Sean's mind wandered somewhere else.

A squirrel skittered atop the snow. Easy for him. Paul's morning walk with Rachel would be nearly impossible. They had worn down a good path, but each snowfall made the trudging more difficult.

The snow crunched under his boots as he slogged to the Muellers' door. He stomped the excess powder off his feet and stepped inside.

Rachel stood at the stove stirring a steaming pot that filled the kitchen with the aroma of chocolate. She wore navy sweatpants and a long-sleeve gray tee. A French braid hung from either side of her head. She looked older. And good. *Very* good.

"Something smells delicious."

She smiled, and warmth spread all the way to his cold toes. "Homemade hot chocolate. There's no way we can walk through that." She jutted her chin toward the outside. "Want some?"

"Sure. I'll get us some mugs."

Warming at the thought, Paul hung up his coat and set his boots on the door mat. He strode to the cabinet and pulled out two large ceramic mugs with cartoonish cats and witty sayings on them. He handed them one at a time to Rachel.

With a playful glint in her eye, she ladled the hot cocoa into them and sat at the kitchen table. Paul took a seat across from her.

"Be careful. It's hot."

"Thanks for the warning." He cupped his hands around the mug and blew. "So, it looks like I'm going to be here long enough to watch the snow melt."

She furrowed her brow. "What do you mean?"

"Sean's decided to keep working here—with the gas drilling company. If Dad had finished his tour, he'd be home by now, and I'd be moving home with him." His throat tightened and tears stung the back of his eyes. He cleared his throat and kept silent for a moment, irritated that talking about his dad still choked him up. "Sean's going to stay. He talked to your dad about it, and it's okay."

Her brows raised, her eyes lit up, and her lips turned up

into a smile. "That's great." Suddenly the smile vanished from her face. "I mean, as long as you're okay with that."

Paul took a tentative sip of his hot chocolate. The one thing that could make his life worse was leaving Rachel.

He shrugged. "I like it here, and there's nothing to go home to now. It seems like forever ago that I lived anywhere but here."

"Well, if you're good with it, then so am I. I like our routine here." She smiled again and sampled her hot chocolate.

"Me too. I really…" He shut his mouth for fear he'd say too much.

Her green eyes glowed as her small hands wrapped around her hot mug, and she waited expectantly for him to finish his thought. What he wouldn't give to reach across the table and hold her hand. Time for a change in subject.

"You have any marshmallows?" He lifted his mug toward her.

"I don't think so, but we've got whipped cream." She pushed away from the table and retrieved a large aerosol can of Reddi-wip from the inside of the refrigerator door. She shook it and pointed the nozzle straight into Paul's mug. The whipped cream spattered out of the mug, spewing dollops of white fluff on the table, Paul's face, and his hand.

"Oh, my gosh. I'm so sorry." Her eyes were wide, and she covered her mouth with her hand in a failed attempt to hide her laughter. "The nozzle must be clogged."

"Yeah, the way you're laughing, you sound really sorry." Paul wiped his face with the back of his hand, gave her a devilish smile, and wrenched the whipped cream from her.

Rachel darted around the other side of the table.

"Here, Rachel, let me give you some."

She shrieked and dashed to the opposite end of the table.

Paul chased her but then stopped and changed direction, snagging her by the wrist. He shook the can and squirted at her nose. It sprayed in every direction, getting her hair and her chest, but not her face.

He froze, stunned. "Oh man, I didn't mean to get it all over you." He really was sorry.

Rachel used his momentary remorse to her advantage, snatched the whipped cream back, and pointed it at Paul as if it were a loaded weapon. She pressed on the nozzle, releasing a thick stream.

He flung his arm in front of his face, but he was too slow. Whatever had been clogging the can must have dislodged, and the whipped topping hit Paul smack in the face.

Rachel laughed so hard she choked.

He tried to grab her, caught her sleeve in his hand, and then slipped. He hit the floor laughing and took Rachel down with him.

They were disentangling their sticky arms and legs when Paul glimpsed her dad shuffling toward the kitchen, adjusting his sports jacket at the cuffs. Not sure which would bother him more, the mess or the two of them tangled up on the floor, Paul scooted away from Rachel.

"What the heck, Rachel! Look at this place." Her dad's pinched brow and stern voice communicated his displeasure, but his lips twitched in amusement. Would he yell or laugh?

Rachel couldn't stop laughing, and after glancing between her and her dad, Paul couldn't hold back his laughter either. He let out a snort.

Rachel laughed even harder.

"Rachel?" Her dad gawked at the two of them as if they were crazy.

"The nozzle..." A fit of laugher overcame her. "... malfunctioned."

Paul picked himself up off the floor, quelling his laughter. "We'll clean it up, Mr. Mueller." He looked down at his whipped cream-covered clothes. Good thing they hadn't dressed for school yet.

"You'd better." Rachel's dad shook his head in disgust, but a smile played at the corner of his lips as Paul brushed past him to get rags and a mop.

***

The chains hanging beneath the school bus rattled as it pulled away from the Mueller's drive. Paul leaped across an icy patch to catch up with Rachel and to clear the imminent spray of slush from the bus's rear tires.

They batted around ideas for Rachel's English literature essay most of the way home. As they approached the house, Paul spotted the top of the picnic table on the porch—visible again. A few birds fluttered around the bird feeder.

"Rachel, can I ask you something?" He'd avoided this question for a while, afraid of hitting a nerve.

"Shoot."

He sidestepped a murky puddle and jerked his backpack higher onto his shoulder. "How come you never mention any friends?"

She narrowed one eye at him and then focused on the icy slop ahead of her. "I have friends."

"You don't talk about them."

"Not much to say."

He waited, hoping she'd elaborate.

"I don't talk about friends because I'm not close with anyone. My best friend Susan moved to Missouri with her family last summer. Since she left..." She shrugged her shoulders. "I have plenty of friends at school, but we're not so close that we do much outside of school. I guess I haven't found anyone I click with, you know?"

A block of wet snow slid from the roof of her house onto

the bushes below, taking several long icicles with it.

Should he ask the obvious? "What about..." His gut tingled in anticipation. "What about us?" There it was. Now he was going to look like a fool.

"What *about* us?" Was that a smile playing on her lips?

"We're friends, right?"

Rachel grinned. "You want to be my BFF?"

A flurry of responses flooded his mind, and his heart pounded in his chest. He gathered as much courage as he could muster. "Actually, I—"

"Paul." Rachel's mom stood on the front porch waving a manila envelope. "Something came for you today." Her eyes were solemn.

Curious, he jogged up the steps and took the envelope she offered.

"Thanks." He turned it over and back and then focused on the return address: Fort Detrick, Maryland. He recognized that handwriting, and his breath caught.

It was from Dad. Why would something be sent to him and not Sean? He stared at it for a few seconds, put it under his arm, and with a nod to Rachel, scurried to the guesthouse.

Chapter 6
Letters from Heaven

Paul dropped his backpack, grabbed a butter knife, and sat at the kitchen table with the envelope. He slid the knife under the flap and pried it open. A folded piece of white paper and a smaller, sealed envelope slid out. He unfolded the paper and recognized his dad's writing, same as on the outer envelope.

Dear Paul,

If you're reading this, it means I didn't make it home. I love you and Sean very much. I did everything I could to stay safe. Risk is part of this job, and I am proud to have served our country.

I had hoped to give you the enclosed letter in person. When your mom realized that something was wrong, she panicked. It's like she knew what was going to happen. She wrote letters to both you and Sean and asked me to give them to you on your eighteenth birthdays. You're getting yours a little early, but I know it will mean as much to you now as it would then.

Your mother was a wonderful woman, and it breaks my heart that you grew up without her. She would be so proud of the young man you have become.

Love,
Dad

Blinking back tears, Paul stared at the letter. Then he re-read it and lingered over the familiar curves of his dad's handwriting—part cursive, part printed. He marveled that his dad had touched the letter, and now he held it too.

He breathed deeply, opened the small envelope, and unfolded the other piece of paper: a note from his mom. He had so little that was hers. She had become like a fairytale figure to him—an ethereal, beautiful being who had given him life, and whose presence he sometimes swore he felt.

The note was written on lined, lavender stationery, the handwriting crisp and uniform. Every letter perfectly formed. Here and there an extra flourish or a descending letter with an extra curlicue stood out. He read it slowly, savoring each word.

My Dear, Sweet Paulie,

How do I write a letter to a young man I hardly got a chance to know? I have so many questions. Did you keep those big, beautiful blue eyes or have they turned to hazel like your dad's? What is your favorite sport? What kind of music do you like to listen to?

I'm sorry that I could not be there with you to teach you and most importantly, to love you. But I have been with you in spirit, always praying for you. The greatest gifts your dad and I could give you were our love and our faith. Stay close to Jesus, Paul. He loves you more than we ever could.

We will be apart for a short while, but someday we will be together again—you, Sean, the baby we lost, your dad, and me. Spend your life loving and living so that we can spend eternity together.

All my love,
Mom

Paulie. His dad called him that when he was little. A tear rolled down one cheek and then the other. He read for the first time what he had always been told—"She loved you, Paul." Somehow it was different to read it on paper, written with her own hand, in her own words.

The urge to find Sean overwhelmed him, but his brother was still at work. Paul folded his arms in front of him on the table and laid his head over them. Sadness, joy, despair, and hope all mingled together in his heart and mind. For ten or fifteen minutes he didn't move; he just cried. After the tears subsided, he stared at the letters, letting his fingers run over them, feeling the indentations the pens had made in the paper.

Somebody knocked on the door. He jumped and then leaned sideways to see out the window.

"Not now, Rachel," he muttered. He got up anyway, wiped his eyes with the back of his hand, and opened the door.

"Hi." She had changed out of her uniform and pulled her hair up in a ponytail. "My mom said the letter was from an Army base. Is everything okay?"

Paul reconsidered; the sweet balm of her voice soothed him.

"Yeah. Thanks. You can come in." He closed the door and followed Rachel into his cramped living area. He scooped a damp towel and his pajamas off the couch and pitched them toward the hall.

"It was a letter from Dad with an old letter from my mom. He was supposed to give it to me when I turned eighteen, but I guess he had this ready to send in case...in case he didn't come back."

"Who mailed it?" She twisted the rings on her fingers and bit her lower lip.

He didn't want to prolong her visit; otherwise he would offer her a seat instead of leaving her standing uncomfortably between the living area and kitchen.

"I don't know. I guess one of his Army buddies. It's his handwriting on the envelope, so he must have had it all prepared."

Her eyes filled with compassion as she took a hard look at him. "Are you okay?"

She must've realized he'd been crying. Was there no end to the times he would embarrass himself in front of her?

He walked behind the couch, brushed away a few crumbs, and pressed his palms into its cushioned back. "Yeah, it's just weird. I hardly have anything from my mother. I can't even remember her voice, so it's good to have something she wrote."

He had thought over the years about how he felt growing up without her and even how his dad felt having to raise him and Sean alone. He hadn't thought about how hard it must have been for his mom to leave them all behind. He felt sorry for her.

"I can't imagine my life without my mom." Rachel glanced at the letters on the table.

Paul shrugged. "It's all I ever knew."

He returned to the table and picked up the letters, rubbing them between his fingers. "Even though my dad was in the Army, I didn't think he'd die. I guess I figured since my mom was already dead, God wouldn't take my dad too." He let out a humorless laugh.

Rachel stepped closer and gingerly placed her hand atop the papers. "It's hard to understand. My mom says sometimes you can only see God's plan in hindsight, if you can figure it out at all. There must be some reason it happened and that you and Sean are here." She lifted her hand and resumed twisting her rings.

He gripped the papers, holding onto them as if his life depended on it. Fighting back the tears, he glanced at the door, then back at Rachel. "I guess so. Thanks for stopping by. I appreciate it."

Although he liked having her here, right now he wanted to be alone. He wouldn't be able to keep the tears at bay much longer.

Taking the hint, Rachel headed for the door, and Paul stepped around her to hold it open. She smiled her thanks, an awkward second or two passed, and then she flung her arms around him.

Paul's eyes closed, and he squeezed them tight. *Don't cry.* Savoring the feeling of her arms around him and the sweet strawberry fragrance of her, he felt a little less alone.

She unwound her arms and pressed her lips to his cheek. "Bye."

When Paul remembered to breathe again, he looked at the letters still in his hand. Should he put them somewhere for safekeeping or leave them out so he could read them again and again? He decided to tuck them in his nightstand drawer and make a habit of reading them each night before bed.

***

After Sean read and re-read Paul's letters, he re-arranged his schedule and spent nearly the entire weekend with Paul. To his credit, Sean didn't blather on about the letters or Dad or Mom, whom he remembered in great detail. He didn't go on about his own letters from Mom or Dad. He was simply there, and it was good.

Sean hadn't been gone from the guesthouse five minutes Sunday evening when Paul's cell phone rang. The Mueller's number showed on the screen. *Rachel?*

"Hello."

"Paul, it's Mr. Mueller. I saw Sean leave. If you're not busy, come on over. It's Rachel's birthday. Join us for cake and ice cream?"

Rachel's birthday? Why hadn't she said anything?

"I'd like to, but I, uh, I didn't realize it was her birthday. I don't have anything for her. He scanned the room, searching for something that would make an appropriate gift."

"She doesn't expect anything. We'd just like you to join

Carolyn Astfalk

us. I'm sure your being here will be present enough."

Maybe so, but he wanted to give her something special anyway. His gaze landed on the small box of his dad's belongings that sat on the floor beside his bed. "Okay, sir. I'll be over in ten minutes."

Rachel was radiant. Her skin glowed, her eyes shone, and her hair was pulled up haphazardly in some kind of clip, leaving wavy tendrils hanging on her neck. Ordinarily he reminded himself not to stare at her, but seeing as how she was the center of attention this evening, he gave his eyes free rein.

Once they devoured the chocolate cake and ice cream and cleared the crumbs from the table, it was time for presents. Rachel unwrapped a peach-colored cardigan sweater and matching skirt from her parents. James gave her a blank, bound journal and a fish head pen. His own small gift, which he had hurriedly wrapped in white tissue paper, was the only package remaining.

Her pretty green eyes turned to his little present. "Who's this one from?" She looked right at him. "You, Paul? You didn't even know it was my birthday, did you?"

He shrugged.

She picked it up and turned it over in her hands. "I wasn't expecting anything."

Paul could tell by the way her eyes shined she was both surprised and pleased.

"I know. I wanted to give you something."

Was that a blush on her cheeks as she held the small box in her hands and tore at the wrapping paper? She opened the box and pulled out a roughly-hewn, cobalt blue glass, just a little larger than a votive cup. A starburst design was etched into the side.

"It's beautiful." She turned it in the light and ran her fingers over it.

"It *is* beautiful," her mom said. "Where did you get it, Paul?"

"My dad bought it in Afghanistan. We don't know what he intended to do with it, but I thought Rachel would appreciate it."

Her eyes darted from the glass to him, and the smile left her face. "Oh, Paul, I do, but I can't accept this. You should keep it." She held it out to him.

He shook his head and withdrew his hands from the table. "It's yours. I want you to have it."

She hesitated and glanced at her mother. Then she looked back at him and gave him a smile that turned his insides to jelly.

"Okay, then, thank you. It's perfect for small wildflowers. I usually put them in a shot glass, but it's like this was made just for them. I can't wait for the violets to bloom."

Paul grinned at her pleasure. She liked it and had already found a use for it. The little blue glass had puzzled him and Sean. They couldn't imagine what it was for or why Dad wanted it. Thank God he hadn't let Sean chuck it into the recycling bin. Like the music on the iPod, if it meant something, anything, to his dad, Paul wanted a part of it. Somehow entrusting it to Rachel didn't feel like letting it go.

Chapter 7
Change of Seasons

Rachel rubbed away a patch of condensation on the kitchen window. Despite the hunks of crusty snow alongside the driveway, all but a few dirty mounds in the shaded parts of the yard had melted, leaving behind patches of mud and determined shoots sprouting from the ground. Spring had sprung.

The morning walks got easier, but messier. Ankle-deep muck filled low spots, but in other places, fresh leaves and buds peeked out of the earth. Paul had stepped in a deceptively-large mud puddle the day before, coating his black leather oxfords in brown sludge. Served him right. If he had been watching where he was going instead of yanking her backpack, it wouldn't have happened.

She loved this time of year second only to autumn. Something about new life and the whole romance of springtime made her want to squeeze every last drop of living out of the day. Maybe it was spring fever that had caused her parents to cave in and allow James to get a pet rabbit.

After another swipe at the fogged window, she peeked through the smeared glass and smiled.

Dad and Paul worked side by side, constructing a rabbit hutch. James sat cross-legged nearby on a piece of plywood, cradling the little albino bunny in his lap, petting Charlie's soft, white fur.

Paul steadied a two-by-four on the saw horse while Dad lined up the circular saw. The blade met the wood with a whining ring, and the bunny flinched. The board split in two, the saw's buzz subsided, and Dad lifted his goggles.

He said something to Paul, and they both laughed.

She jumped at the sound of her mother's voice and whirled around.

"I'm sorry, Mom. What did you say?"

Her mom breezed into the kitchen tying an apron around her waist. "I asked how they're coming out there."

"Good, I guess. They have most of the frame up."

Rachel's mom pulled the heavy stand mixer out from a bottom cabinet and hoisted it onto the counter with a thud. "I have to make cookies for the concession stand for James's baseball opening day. Want to help?"

"Sure." Rachel walked to where her mom plugged in the mixer. "Chocolate chips?"

"You got it." They had made the recipe a hundred times. Mom pulled the bag of brown sugar from the freezer and retrieved the granulated sugar from a canister on the counter, humming as she worked.

Rachel grabbed the butter and eggs from the refrigerator. How many afternoons had they shared making this same recipe?

Dad stuck his head in the door. "Hey, can you get the wire clippers? I think they're in the basement on the workbench."

"I'll get them, Dad." Rachel bounded downstairs and grabbed the wire cutters, which were right where he had said. She headed outside and handed them to her dad, who watched as Paul measured out another length of chicken wire.

"Thanks, Rachel." He clipped the wire in three places, and Paul tossed the cut length off to the side before rolling out some more.

"Paul tells me we're not going to be seeing much of him this summer." Dad glanced at the measurements on the pencil sketch he'd made of the rabbit hutch.

Rachel's eyes darted to Paul. His eyes widened, as if

Dad had just blindsided him.

"Why not?" She directed the question to her dad, who just nodded in Paul's direction.

"I got a job." Paul held out the length of chicken wire for her dad to snip, but his gaze stayed on her. "I—I didn't get a chance to tell you. I just got the call last night...I was going to tell you...this morning."

Paul lowered his head and threw her a glance, as if he'd done something wrong.

Good.

Her heart sank, and she swallowed, hoping the disappointment didn't show on her face She had figured they'd spend the summer together. Going swimming, taking walks, lying around watching reruns and Netflix.

She plastered on a smile. "Well, good for you." It had come out smarmy and bitter, not sincere as she had hoped.

"I need to earn money, Rachel." His tone was defensive.

"Of course you do. Summer's boring here anyway."

Dad's head moved back and forth between them as if he were watching a tennis match.

"And I'll probably be too busy to hang out anyway." To prevent either of them from calling her on that contradiction, she pivoted on her heel and stalked back to the house. Just before the screen door slammed, her dad's voice carried to the house.

"What's she all in a snit about?"

Rachel peered over her shoulder in time to see Paul shrug. He really didn't know what was the matter? Her whole summer was ruined, that's what.

Rachel washed her hands then measured the flour into a mixing bowl. A cloud of white dust billowed in her face, and she waved it away. "Mom, did Paul tell you he got a job?" Why did her voice sound so shrill?

"Yes, he did. Over at Shalamon's Orchard. Seems perfect." The whir of the mixer combining the butter, sugar, and eggs made it hard to hear. "He can walk there and back. It'll start slow in the spring, go to full time in the summer and then ease up again come fall when the apples are in."

So, he had found time to tell both her parents, but not her. Despite her disappointment, Rachel wanted to be excited for Paul, but she couldn't stop thinking of how little they'd see of each other. Her parents weren't forcing her to work this summer since she wasn't sixteen, but she had planned on doing as much babysitting as she could. She'd need something else to keep her busy now. Her gaze fell on the blue glass Paul had given her, two daffodil blooms hanging over its rim. She had an idea, if she could get her mom to go for it.

Rachel combined baking soda and salt with the flour and handed the bowl of dry ingredients to her mom. She spared another glance out the window where James still sat with his bunny. Dad held the chicken wire in place while Paul stapled it to the hutch.

"Mom, I want to make a big flower garden this summer." She grabbed a rubber spatula from the drawer and handed it to her mom.

"Where would you put it?" Mom scraped down the sides of the bowl, dumped a bag of milk chocolate chips into the mixer, and turned it on.

"Well, when we're walking every day, I notice this little clearing. You have to duck under some trees to get to it, but it's a nice level patch below the driveway as you walk down to the gas well."

Her mom sighed and wiped her hands on her apron. "You're going to do this yourself?"

"If I can use your tools, and you buy the bulbs and seeds." Rachel gave her mom a sweet smile, then pulled baking sheets from a cupboard. The remaining pans and racks clattered as she withdrew each one. "Maybe I could collect bouquets and sell them at a stand by the road. Just something simple using the honor system."

Her mom stopped what she was doing, leaned against the countertop, and thought about it for a minute. "Okay. We'll come up with a budget, and you can do your thing."

"Great. Thanks, Mom." Rachel kissed her mom's cheek, her own cheeks flushing with excitement.

Mom spooned the cookie dough onto a baking sheet. "You're welcome."

***

The following week, Rachel and her mom made a trip to Meyer's Nursery for seeds and bulbs. Rachel looked at the list she'd made and then at the rack of seeds. She hoped this flower thing wasn't a mistake. She'd been so irritated that Paul would be working all summer that she had just blurted out the garden idea. Why did his being gone all day even matter to her?

"Mom, you like Paul, don't you?"

Her mom pulled a pack of morning glory seeds from the rack and grinned. "What's not to like? He's easy to get along with, and he's never once complained about my cooking."

Rachel grabbed two packs of sunflower seeds and gave the rotary rack a little push. "Last year when I had a crush on Kyle Waldron, I was obsessed with him. I knew his every move. I studied the way he held his pencil and parted his hair. I talked to my friends about him all the time, and I felt butterflies in my stomach every time I heard him speak."

Her mom glanced up as if she was waiting for her to continue.

"And then Paul moved here." She swallowed. "I didn't think much of him. I mean, I liked him, but I always kind of thought of him as a brother. But lately, I don't know, I really want to be with him, like, all the time, but I don't feel weird about it like I did with Kyle. It feels normal and relaxed."

"Is there a question for me in there?"

Rachel shifted her weight to the other foot and fingered the seed packets in her hand. She hoped Mom couldn't see how fidgety this subject made her.

"Well, how did you feel about Dad when you met him?"

"We were much older than you and Paul..." She emphasized "much" and gave Rachel a pointed look. "But I guess I felt sort of the same way. And there were a few butterflies too."

Yeah, there were butterflies with Paul lately. Like when he had held her hand last week so she wouldn't lose her balance stretching her legs over another large puddle.

"I think the feelings you had for Kyle were more infatuation. You liked him in a superficial kind of way without really knowing him. With Paul, I think you have a genuine affection. Those are much deeper, lasting feelings." Her mom chose a couple more seed packets and handed them to her.

"I guess that sounds about right."

She didn't know how to broach this next part. She didn't want to, but it wasn't something she could ask her friends at school. Because of their schedules, they never saw her and Paul together.

"Do you, uh..." This had been a bad idea, but there was no going back now. "Do you think maybe Paul likes me?"

"Well..." Her mom seemed to weigh her words carefully. "He hasn't said anything, but if I had to bet on it, I'd say he does." They ambled further down the row toward the spring bulbs. "He's considerate of you, and sometimes I catch him staring at you during dinner."

"Really?" She hoped she didn't sound too ridiculously excited.

"Really."

***

The summer days seemed long without Paul around, but Rachel still felt as if summer were whizzing by. She looked with satisfaction at her flower garden as butterflies flitted from blossom to blossom. Last night's thunderstorm had dumped a couple of inches of rain in under an hour. She'd swear the sunflowers had grown at least four inches overnight. At this rate they would bloom in a couple of weeks.

Rachel hiked back to the house and tossed her gloves on the gardening bench. She dragged herself up to the porch, flumped down, and propped her feet on an overturned crate. Her wristwatch read six o'clock. Paul would be harvesting peaches for at least another hour.

The pipes below the sink creaked as her mom drained the boiling water off the spaghetti noodles. Her dad's voice carried out through the screen.

"I don't know, Linda. I don't think it'll get resolved until I pay a visit to the Department of Conservation. If the state wants to put in a gas line, they can use their own land."

Rachel's mother responded with something she couldn't quite make out. Dad must have been closer to the window because she could hear him loud and clear.

"Oh, Sean said to let you know he's taking Paul out to dinner on Friday night. It's a surprise for his birthday."

Water ran from the kitchen faucet. "Okay. I'll just plan for one less. Do you think we ought to get a cake for him for Saturday?"

"Okay by me. You might want to run it by Sean to see if he has anything else planned. Do I have time to get changed before dinner?"

"You've got about five minutes."

Rachel jumped up and brushed the dirt from her knees. The screen door slammed behind her as she raced into the kitchen.

"Hey, Mom."

Mom glanced up from where she stood shaking excess water from the colander full of spaghetti. "Hey, sweetie. How's the garden going?"

"Good. The sunflowers shot up." She sat on the stool behind the counter and inhaled the scent of her mother's spaghetti sauce—lots of oregano. "I heard you and Dad talking about Paul's birthday. I think we should get a cake for him."

Her mom smiled. "I thought you would."

Rachel's cheeks burned. On more than one summer evening, she and Mom had sat on the porch cooling off and talking about boys—or one boy in particular.

"I'd like to get him something. He gave me his dad's beautiful glass."

"I'm sure he'd appreciate it. Do you have something in mind?"

Rachel washed her hands at the sink, grabbed the small stack of dishes on the counter, and set them out on the table. "Well, I have one idea."

"You've been thinking about it, huh?" Her mom smiled at her as she removed a large bowl of salad greens from the refrigerator.

Rachel shrugged. "I have a lot of time to think while I'm pulling weeds and dead blooms."

"Well, maybe we can run to the store after dinner and take a look."

Rachel thought Paul's birthday was in the summer, but she hadn't known when. Had she known sooner, she could've ordered something online. But with only a couple of days until his birthday, she had few options. She appreciated Mom taking her to Smells and Bells, but the shop gave her the willies.

The owner had converted his double garage into a small, cramped store. Rachel drifted by the displays, orderly but dusty, as if no one had touched a product in the last fifteen years. A musty odor accompanied the dust. Thankfully, the jewelry was protected from the dust and mustiness by a Plexiglas case.

"How about that one?" Rachel tapped the glass, pointing to the highest quality chain she could afford. Nice, but still inexpensive.

Mom looked over her shoulder as the owner placed it in Rachel's hand. "Is that the one you want?"

"Yeah. What do you think?" She held it in her palm and let the chain dangle over her fingers.

Her mom rubbed Rachel's shoulder. "I think it's a very thoughtful gift."

Rachel spun the display case and selected another gift. "What about this? Will he think I'm a religious dweeb?"

Her mom lifted her hand and smiled. "I'm not sure what a 'religious dweeb' is, but I think he'll like it. It's masculine enough, and if you want the best for someone, you want to help them be good and virtuous, right?"

"Yeah, I guess, but I don't want him to think I'm weird."

"He's not going to think you're weird, honey. You're both Catholic, and you go to a Catholic school. This isn't weird to him. If he were a Hindu or Buddhist or some other religion, I'd tell you to forget it."

Rachel laughed and placed one of the items back in the case. She held up her first choice for her mom to see. "Okay. I'm sold. This is the one."

Rachel paid for her gift, and the owner of the creepy store, who looked like a walking relic himself, thanked her. He put the item in a small box, which she hoped didn't smell musty.

Chapter 8
Birthday Redux

For his birthday celebration, Sean took Paul to a sports bar where you could have a beer—well, if you were of legal age—eat pizza, bowl, shoot pool, or play arcade games. Several of Sean's friends came and none of Paul's, but they were decent guys.

"Hey, Paul, right?"

Paul knew he'd met the lanky, long-haired guy at least once, but he couldn't for the life of him remember his name.

"Yeah. How's it going?"

The lanky dude stuck out his hand, and Paul shook it. Daniel? Darryl? It started with a D.

"Happy birthday, man."

"Yeah, thanks." Damien? Davin?

Lanky dude planted himself on the barstool next to him. "What are you drinking?"

Paul lifted his frosted mug. "Uh, root beer." Darren? Dennis?

"Oh, yeah. Underage. Let me get you another."

Lanky dude motioned for the waitress and asked her to refill his drink.

Sean leaned over the pool table, racking the balls. "Hey, Dom, you in?"

Dominic. That was it.

"Sure, but what about the birthday boy, here?" Dominic slapped him on the back just as he swallowed a mouthful of root beer.

Paul sputtered, coughed, and struggled to pull a brown paper napkin from the dispenser.

"You okay, man?"

Paul nodded as he coughed.

"I'm playing to win," Sean called from the table. "Paul sucks at pool. He can sit this one out."

Paul bit his lip to keep from bringing up the last time they had played pool, and Sean had scratched, costing them the game and twenty-five dollars. They had lost to a couple of girls, and not even hot-looking older girls. They were probably Rachel's age.

As birthday celebrations went, it couldn't have been less about the guest of honor.

Paul blew a paper wrapper across the bar with his straw. Besides the guys, Sean brought along someone else too. Amanda. She was cute—shoulder-length reddish blond hair, blue eyes, and petite. Quiet, but from the few minutes he'd spent with her, he sensed it wasn't because she didn't have anything to say, only that she chose her words carefully—and most of her words were for Sean's ears only.

Sean played darts with Amanda as his partner. They sipped from each other's drinks. He ordered nachos, and they ate from the same plate.

As Paul watched Sean with Amanda and his buddies, he realized how meager his friendships were. He had plenty of friends at school, but like Rachel's, they stayed at school. That was partly because he lacked transportation and partly because he kept them at arm's length. Since Dad died, Paul guarded his privacy. He had Sean and Rachel and that was enough.

Sean moved to a racing game in the arcade, and Amanda sat in his lap and helped steer the wheel. *Cozy.* Watching them made him uncomfortable. Even halfway across the room, he felt like an intruder at his own birthday party.

Paul scowled and turned back to his root beer. The foam on top of his fresh mug fizzled, popped, and disappeared. How had Sean managed to keep Amanda a secret from him? And why?

If Rachel wanted to sit in his lap, he'd be broadcasting it to the whole world. Paul couldn't resist letting Rachel get close. Talking to her was like breathing; it was so easy, so normal, and so right. If things were different, he would've asked her out by now, but he was living next door. Heck, her mom did his laundry half the time. No wonder she thought of him as a brother.

Sean's laughter carried across the room. He encircled Amanda's waist, lifting her off the ground. She feigned a struggle, and Paul thought he was going to be sick. They were connected at the hip all night. Of course, this explained why he had seen less of Sean since about a month after Dad's funeral.

What would it be like to be that free with Rachel? Heaven. But getting there scared him to death. If he let on how he felt, and she didn't feel the same way, it would ruin their friendship. He decided over his third root beer that unless she gave him a sign she was interested, he'd keep his feelings to himself.

***

Paul wanted to talk to Sean about Amanda, but since she accompanied them back to the guesthouse, he made sure Sean planned to come back in the morning, alone. He wanted to know why Sean had kept him in the dark.

Sean rolled in before lunch the next day, bringing Chinese take-out. He set the brown bag on the counter, and the smell of General Tso's Chicken teased Paul's senses.

"So what did you think?"

"About what?" He was asking about Amanda, but after being left out of the loop all these months, Paul wasn't going to make it easy for Sean.

"Amanda."

"I think it's pretty rotten of you—an older brother who happens to have sole custody of his younger brother—to sneak around seeing some chick and never tell me what's going on."

Sean removed several containers and a handful of sauce packets from the bag along with a couple of fortune cookies. "Yeah, well, what did you think of *Amanda*?"

"I liked her. She seems nice. She's cute. And if she can tolerate your sorry ass, you'd better hang onto her."

Paul poured two glasses of cold water and set them on the table.

Sean smiled—so big, the little dimple in his right cheek showed. "Good. I'm glad you liked her." He spooned out rice and chicken onto two paper plates.

"Listen, I wasn't trying to hide her from you or anything. We met right after Dad died, and I didn't want you to think I was ditching you for some girl."

"So you ditched me without telling me about the girl."

Sean shook his spoon at him. "Hey, I've been here. Is there any time you needed me and I wasn't here? I stop by every day after work. I'm here half the weekend with you. Or almost half."

In truth, he *had* been there. At least in body if not in spirit.

"I wish you'd told me. I would've been okay with it. All this time I thought something was wrong or you were really upset about Dad or something."

Sean pushed the takeout containers aside and picked up his fork. "Maybe I should've told you sooner, but I thought it would be better this way. I'm sorry."

Paul's stomach grumbled. "Let's pray so we can eat."

They said their traditional grace and tucked into their lunch.

"It's okay, I guess. About Amanda." They'd had a chance to talk on the ride home from his party. She'd grown up nearby as the oldest of four girls, ran the office for her dad's contracting business, and while she and Sean seemed identical in temperament, their interests were polar opposite. Both were focused and responsible, but where Sean was laid back and outdoorsy, Amanda was prim and bookish. Paul waited until Sean caught his eye. "You really like her, don't you?"

Sean gave him another one of his dimpled smiles, and Paul realized it had been a long time since he'd seen one.

Had he taken Sean for granted? Barely older than a teenager himself, he had shouldered some big responsibilities in Dad's absence. It didn't seem fair, but he had never heard Sean complain or seem bitter or resentful. Rather, he'd been generous and responsible, all the while robbed of his freedom.

"I think she might be the one. She reminds me of Mom somehow too, the way she laughs. That's not why I'm into her, I mean, that would be creepy, but it sort of makes me like her even more. It's like Mom's saying, 'This is the girl, Sean.'"

Paul's tongue almost blistered from the unusually spicy chicken, and he gulped his water. "I'm happy for you. I mean that."

"Thanks." Sean spooned out more rice and General Tso's chicken. "Eat up. Life is good."

Sean left by mid-afternoon since he had a date with Amanda that evening, and Paul worked on his homework before walking over to Rachel's house. Her mom had told him to come over at six o'clock sharp. He knocked on the door. No answer. No light shined between the curtains and it seemed kind of dark, but both cars were in the driveway. Did he get the time wrong? He knocked once more, and since the door was unlocked, he let himself in.

"Hello?" No answer. He called a little louder. "Rachel? Mrs. Mueller?"

Carolyn Astfalk

The lights came on, and James's enthusiastic scream drowned out everyone else, yelling, "Surprise!"

Rachel popped up from behind the couch. She smiled at Paul, her shiny, chocolate-brown hair falling over her shoulders onto her soft white summer sweater.

Paul's cheeks warmed. "How did you know?"

"Sean mentioned to Mr. Mueller that he was taking you out last night," Mrs. Mueller said. "Did you have a good time?"

"Yeah." He nodded. "I met his girlfriend, Amanda."

Rachel rounded the table and stood behind her seat. "Sean has a girlfriend?"

"Yeah, news to me too." Paul sat at the dining room table.

Mrs. Mueller uncovered the large baking dish in the center of the table, and set out a basket of rolls.

Paul didn't like a big fuss about his birthday, but Rachel seemed happy that they'd pulled off their surprise. If this party meant he got to spend the evening hanging out with her, it was all worth it.

They said grace, and Mrs. Mueller spooned hearty servings of chicken casserole onto everyone's plates.

"This is delicious, Mrs. Mueller."

"Thank you, Paul. You've never told us—who did the cooking in your house?"

Paul swallowed a mouthful of casserole. "Well, let's see. We had a variety of cooks: Mrs. T, Sara Lee, Mrs. Butterworth, Chef Boyardee, Marie Callender, Jimmy Dean."

James laughed loud and hard, a smattering of chewed-up chicken spraying his plate. Rachel's dad glowered. "James, enough." He shook his head and sipped his water.

"I guess that means your dad wasn't much of a cook." Rachel dug her fork into the casserole on her plate.

"No. Great father, lousy cook. Let's just say our smoke

detectors were tested regularly. He used to tease that he married my mom for her culinary skills. Everyone says she was an excellent cook." Paul realized with some relief he had spoken about Dad without tearing up.

After dinner, they sang "Happy Birthday."

Paul blew out the seventeen candles on his cake—chocolate batter with chocolate frosting, just how he liked it. His eyes met Rachel's as he made his wish, and his heart hammered in his chest. An irrational fear struck him. *Could she read his mind?*

Paul thought the cake would be the end of it, and then Rachel, her mom, and James brought out gifts.

"You didn't need to do this." He wasn't just saying it; he meant it. It was enough that they went to all this trouble.

"We wanted to, didn't we, Rachel?" Mrs. Mueller shot a glance at Rachel.

"Yes, we did." Her cheeks reddened, and her gaze dropped to the table.

James pushed a clumsily wrapped package toward Paul.

Paul tore off the wrapping paper and held up a pen with a glow-in-the-dark eyeball on the end.

"Cool. Thanks, James. I'll use this when I'm up late doing homework, and it's dark."

Mrs. Mueller handed him a card.

Paul opened it, and an iTunes gift card slid out.

"Thanks. There's still some space on my dad's iPod. Now I can load it up."

Finally, he accepted a small box in plain white wrapping paper from Rachel. She straightened in her chair and smiled, waiting.

"You didn't need to get me anything." He turned the small box over in his hands.

"Are you kidding? You had five minutes' notice on my birthday, and you brought a beautiful vase that belonged to

Carolyn Astfalk

your dad. I had three whole days; I had to come up with something."

Paul smiled, ripped off the wrapping paper, and removed the lid on the small box. He lifted out a sterling silver chain and medal. The silver medal depicted St. Paul standing, holding a staff. Along the circumference it read, "St. Paul, Pray for us." He let the chain swing and laid the medal over his hand, looking at the front and then the back. How could she have known?

He must've been quiet too long.

"It's a medal." Her voice sounded uncertain. "A St. Paul medal."

He slid it between his fingers. "I know, I know. Did Sean tell you?"

"Tell me what?" She looked worried. Did she think he didn't like it?

He smiled to reassure her. "I bugged my dad for a medal. He wore a St. Michael the Archangel one. When I was little, I used to ask him if I could wear it. He said someday he'd get me my own, but he never did."

He hung the chain around his neck, tucking the medal under his shirt. "I love it, Rachel, thank you."

Her face lit up like a Christmas tree, all bright and warm. He wanted to take her face in his hands and kiss her. His palms quivered, and he fisted his hands under the table.

"Paul, you're welcome to stay and watch a movie with us." Rachel's dad shuffled several movie cases between his hands. "Which is it, Linda?"

"Uh . . . the Leonardo DiCaprio one." Rachel's mom lifted the DVD case off the counter. "*Inception*."

"Sure. I'll stay."

He enjoyed the movie, but sitting next to Rachel after she'd given him such a thoughtful, personal gift drove him to distraction. He couldn't follow the intricate plot line.

Had they been alone, he would've tried to kiss her; there was no way he'd be able to resist.

The urge to kiss her had become almost relentless over the summer. Sometimes when he got done at the orchard, she'd be on the porch waiting for him. He'd sit at the picnic table, and she'd bring him leftovers her mom had kept warm. Once they'd sat and talked until midnight. Her dad came out and reminded him he had to be at work at 7:30 in the morning. He'd said goodnight and gone back to the guesthouse where he'd showered and tried to rid his mind of her before he fell into bed exhausted. He was pretty sure a shower wasn't going to cut it tonight.

When the movie ended, he thanked everyone again and walked back to the guesthouse. After a shower, he climbed into bed. Just as he had expected, he couldn't sleep, so he grabbed the iPod and put the ear buds in.

He closed his eyes and listened, remembering every detail of the night. The sweetness of the cake frosting. The sound of Rachel singing his name. The smell of the candles when he'd blown them out. The feel of the cool medal against his chest for the first time. The smile on Rachel's face when she realized how much he appreciated her present. Best...birthday...ever.

Chapter 9
Verdant Retreat

Rachel scrunched her shoulders as sweat beaded and trickled down her back. September shouldn't be this hot. Even the sunflowers in her garden showed signs of distress.

She pressed a cool glass of mint iced tea to her forehead before gulping half of it. She kicked off her shoes and sat on the porch in the shade of the house, wriggling her sweaty toes. The box fan whirred in the kitchen, creating a soothing white noise that, paired with the heat, left her struggling to keep her eyes open. Her dad's loud, anxious tone startled her to attention.

"Linda, come look at this letter."

Mom's voice came from somewhere inside the house. "Just a minute." Seconds later her voice came louder, clearer. "What's up?"

"It says, 'The Pennsylvania Department of Conservation is in the preliminary phases of acquiring land for the installation of a natural gas pipeline to serve the communities of northern Pennsylvania. The Department has determined that the natural gas pipeline pathway that will cause the least environmental impact includes a small portion of your property.

"An attorney for the Department will be contacting you in the coming months to arrange for equitable compensation for your land in accordance with applicable Pennsylvania statutes. We anticipate your cooperation and look forward to working with you.'"

"They want to buy our property?" Mom asked.

"A portion of it, anyway. And they can't even send a real

human being to talk to us about it. I'll be damned if they're going to get one square foot of this land."

They rehashed the issue for weeks. Dad's irritation mounted daily. Time and again he launched into a diatribe about lawyers and the state using its *own* land for a pipeline. The official-sounding letter added more fuel to the fire.

Bored of the conversation by the fourth go-round, Rachel pushed open the screen door, crossed the porch, and stepped into the yard. She peered down the driveway at the path that ran through the woods beyond. Any minute now, Paul would emerge through the trees from the orchard.

He still worked after school three or four days a week plus Saturdays. They were harvesting apples, and now that some of the workers had gone back to college, Paul had even more to do.

She strolled around the side of the house and puttered with the flowers along the window well. Then she spotted him.

Paul's head hung low, and his shoulders slumped as he dragged his feet toward the house. He drooped more than her sunflowers that had dried and turned to seed.

She stooped to pull a few more weeds before he reached the house. She hoped it wasn't too obvious that she had been waiting for him. Then again, maybe that wouldn't be such a bad thing. Maybe if he knew how she really felt about him, things would be different. She sighed. Who was she kidding? If he felt anything more than friendship, he would have done or said something by now; he'd been living with them more than ten months.

Paul cut across the yard toward her.

Rachel stood and shaded her eyes with her hand. "Hey."

"Hey, yourself."

Sweat and dirt covered his blue cotton tee shirt and stains marked his faded jeans in spots. His damp hair clung to the nape of his neck, and she guessed he had emptied the water bottle in his hand over his head somewhere on the way home.

"You look beat."

"I *am* beat. If I never see another apple again it will be too soon."

"Uh-oh."

His gaze locked on her face, and his eyebrows rose in alarm. "What?"

"I think Mom made apple dumplings for dessert."

He smiled and ran his hand through his hair. "Don't tell her what I said. I'm sure it'll be delicious. I'm starving."

The smile left his face, and he looked out over the hillside to where the last of the drilling crew headed out.

Rachel followed his gaze. "Plans with Sean?"

"No. He has a date." His eyes didn't meet hers, and his shoulders hung defeated.

"Is everything okay?"

He turned back to her. "Yeah. Why?"

"You seem a little sad is all."

He hesitated a second and blew out a breath. "Geez, am I that easy to read?"

Rachel smiled. "To me you are." It was true. How didn't he feel this connection that she did? Like they were two perfectly-tuned instruments meant to be played together.

Paul stared at her for a couple of seconds. His blue eyes matched the hydrangeas she'd clipped for a bouquet that morning.

"Can't hide much from you, can I?"

Did that fact bother him? She hadn't realized there was anything he *wanted* to hide from her.

"Today's my dad's birthday. Or it would've been."

She laid her hand on his arm, feeling the grit and sweat.

"I'm sorry, Paul."

"Just another day, but we had talked about this birthday. Last year, he was already deployed, and he said this year he'd be back and settled in at home, and he and I were going to go on a trip together. Just a weekend thing because I'd have school, maybe backpack a couple nights or something like that."

"That would've been great." She let her hand drop. "Now you're stuck here."

"There are worse places for a guy to be stuck." He tossed his empty bottle up, caught it, and plodded toward the guesthouse.

Rachel's mind buzzed. There had to be something she could do—something to cheer him up. "Wait!" There was one thing. She hadn't planned on it, but she could swing it, and it might give him a little solace.

"Are you busy after dinner?"

He faced her. "I've got to study for an English test. Chaucer. Why?"

"I want to show you something." He would try to weasel the details out of her, but he wouldn't succeed.

"Okay. Are we going somewhere?"

"No. It's a short walk from here."

Paul squinted at her. "Can I have a clue?"

"Nope."

"All right then, after dinner. I'm going to get a shower, and I'll see you in a little bit." He smiled then walked to the guesthouse.

His hair had lightened into a streaked dirty blond in the summer sun. It hadn't been cut in almost two months, and the ends curled where it hung below his ears. Working in the orchard had left his arms muscular and tan. Even so, she would be glad when he was done working for the season, and they could spend more time together.

***

Paul shoveled a final forkful of grilled tilapia into his mouth. The sun sank lower in the sky, and Rachel asked if she and Paul could be excused. Then she whispered something in her mom's ear.

"Go ahead." Mrs. Mueller piled dirty silverware on her empty plate. "I'll clean up here, and you can have your apple dumplings when you get back."

"Mmmm." Rachel pushed in her chair. "Paul was hoping you'd make an apple dessert." She winked at him.

He bit the inside of his cheek to keep from laughing.

"Great dinner, Mrs. Mueller." He got up from the table and followed Rachel to the door. He closed it behind him, wondering for the hundredth time what she was up to. The sun had begun its nightly descent; not much daylight remained.

"Lead the way, Rachel."

"I intend to, but first you have to close your eyes."

"Seriously?"

She folded her arms across her chest, making her snug tee shirt even more appealing. "Only if you want to see my surprise."

"Okay." What could she be hiding outside that he wouldn't have already seen? He peeked at her just to see what she would do.

"Are you going to keep them closed or do I have to blindfold you?"

He smiled. She was feisty today. "I'll keep them closed."

A little whoosh of warm air hit his face, and he guessed she was waving her hands in front of him to make sure his eyes were indeed closed. Her slim, soft hand took hold of his, and his pulse quickened. He reminded himself that she wasn't really holding his hand. His eyes were closed, and she was leading him; it was the natural thing to do. The reminder did nothing to slow his racing heart.

They walked for a few minutes in the general direction

of the drilling site.

"How can I be sure you're not going to club me and leave me in a ditch?"

She squeezed his hand. "Don't worry. I won't hurt you. Promise."

They continued walking for a few more minutes. It seemed like the regular path they traveled each morning during the school year, but he couldn't be sure. Rachel stopped suddenly, but she didn't release his hand.

"We've got to duck under some trees and around some bushes, but it's not too bad. Follow my directions."

"I don't have much of a choice." Leaves brushed his ankle, and a branch scraped his forehead. "Ouch!"

"Sorry. I forgot you're taller than me."

"Yeah, well, it's all fun and games until someone loses an eye."

A pine fragrance tickled his senses as they crouched beneath a needled limb.

Rachel yelped and dropped his hand.

"What happened?" Should he open his eyes?

"Ugh. Just a spider web."

She took his hand again, and the farther they went, the more a honeysuckle scent filled his nostrils.

"Okay. You can open your eyes now." She sounded triumphant.

A sea of flowers cascaded over a gentle slope. Most of them looked like wildflowers, but they weren't growing wild here. Every corner teemed with bright oranges, yellows, and reds. Small blue flowers, leafy greens, and vines twisted around stepping stones beneath his feet. A small bench hewn from a fallen log lay to his right. The hillside and rows of trees framed the garden on every side, making it feel like a room.

"Whoa. Where are we?" He turned back the way they came, but couldn't see beyond the brush they had come through.

"The house is back that way." Rachel pointed up the hill. "This was my summer project. My secret garden."

"You did this?" He was incredulous.

"Yep. Do you like it?"

"It's beautiful. If I didn't know better, I'd never believe we were still on your parents' property. And not far from the drilling site."

A huge smile spread across her face, and her eyes danced. She was obviously proud and pleased that he was impressed.

"I wondered what you'd been doing all summer."

She tilted her head, and her smile transformed into a coy grin. "You think about me when we're not together?"

Lord, help me, she's flirting.

"I think about a lot of different things when I'm not with you, Rachel Mueller." *Your hair, your eyes, the softness of your skin, how your jeans fit, what it would be like to kiss you . . .*

He swore she blushed, but it was hard to tell because she was backing away from him into the garden, her arms outstretched.

"This is my retreat." She lowered her arms. "I come here for quiet or just to think or pray or daydream."

"What do you daydream about?" If he wasn't careful, he was going to get answers he didn't want to hear. There had to be *somebody*, some guy she had her eye on.

She shrugged. "This and that. The future. . .having a boyfriend."

Bullseye. He wasn't going to touch that one with a ten-foot pole.

She dusted a few leaves from the bench but didn't sit.

"I thought maybe you'd like to come down here some time too, when you want to be alone or you're thinking about your dad. I'm going to put a little American flag over there."

She pointed to an area in the far corner with a patch of red, white, and blue flowers. "We could add a marker or something too."

Rachel was offering to share her "retreat" with him? The place was so pretty she could charge admission. A pair of Monarch butterflies flitted from flower to flower, the only sound the constant chorus of crickets, cicadas, and katydids.

She beamed. Again, that urge to kiss her overcame him. How long before he gave in? That would be one way to find out how much she liked him. She'd either shrink away in revulsion or slap him or something. But maybe she'd kiss him back.

"Anyway, I'll give you the place to yourself for a while. Tell your dad I said 'happy birthday'." She started to turn, then faced him again. "You get back to the main path by going through here." She pointed over her shoulder and stepped under a low branch.

"Rachel?"

She stopped.

"Thank you. This is amazing." *You* are amazing is what he wanted to say, but he chickened out.

She smiled, then sidestepped a bush and ducked beneath a branch.

Once she disappeared from view, Paul gazed at the flowers. A bumblebee darted from blossom to blossom. He sat on the log bench and stretched his legs in front of him. A black and yellow garden spider awaited its prey from the center of its web spun among the tall grasses.

The beauty of the flowers moved him. They'd had nothing like them at home. Dad grew only grape tomatoes. He liked to snap them off the vine and pop them into his mouth. In the fall, he bought a potted mum from a roadside stand and plunked it outside the door until either frost or neglect killed it. The only flowers they'd ever planted were on Mom's grave.

White petunias and red geraniums. Aunt Ginnie had planted them this year. Sean said they'd get back this summer to visit the graves and see the headstone with Dad's name added to it, but they hadn't. Sean was too busy with Amanda, and Paul worked at the orchard nearly every weekend.

Every year on Mom's birthday, Dad took them to the cemetery. A Subway was along the route, and they picked up sandwiches for a makeshift picnic. Dad would talk to Mom as if she were there, telling her everything that had happened over the past year. Paul thought it a little morbid at the time, but he'd give his right arm to be doing the same thing right now at Dad's grave—to feel the cool marble beneath his hand and trace the engraving with his fingertips.

He'd thought her birthday was the only time Dad visited the gravesite until Sean clued him in.

"Don't you know where Dad goes every Saturday morning?"

Of course he did. "He does ten miles on his bike."

"Yeah, and do you know where he rides?"

Paul named the neighborhoods Dad rode through, only realizing as he spoke that it would take him by the cemetery.

Every week. All those years. *That* was love.

This was as close as he was going to get to Dad's grave for the foreseeable future. He glanced around, paranoid that someone might hear him. There was no one.

"Hey, Dad." His voice cracked. "God, I miss you." He clenched his hands and then opened them, rubbing them on his shorts. "The notes and the Mass cards have stopped. Sometimes I think Sean and I are the only ones who remember." His throat closed around his words. This was harder than he expected.

"We never really talked about girls. Never had a reason to." He chuckled. "I listened to you talk to Sean about girls a dozen times. 'Stay away from this one.' 'Don't get mixed up with that one.' 'Treat her like a lady.'"

The one thing he wanted to tell Dad, he couldn't. "This is different." The one thing he wanted to say to Rachel but didn't dare. "*She's* different."

Paul's thoughts dissolved into a sense of peace, and he sat in the garden another half hour enjoying the beauty and the fragrance and then the myriad stars twinkling overhead. *Thank you, Lord, for bringing me here.*

Chapter 10
Bared Souls

Brilliant red, orange, and yellow leaves transformed the landscape, blanketing the ground and forcing the squirrels to forage for their meals. Rachel's dad assigned raking duty to Rachel, Paul, and James.

Rachel leaned her rake against a large oak tree and examined her sore palms. "I'm getting blisters on my hands. Time for a break."

James dropped his rake into the grass and bounded towards her. "Bury me in the leaves, Rachel."

Paul and Rachel obliged and buried him five times. He continued to cover himself even when she and Paul wearied of the game.

Rachel dropped into the heap of leaves and lay back. The sun filtered through the foliage still clinging to the branches and warmed her. She inhaled the musty smell of leaves—the smell of fall. "You know what I feel like doing? A leaf rubbing."

Paul brushed broken leaf fragments from his jeans. "A what?"

She raised her brows. "You've never done a leaf rubbing?"

"I don't even know what you're talking about."

"Really?" How could he have gone seventeen years and never done a leaf rubbing?

"Rachel, I grew up without a mom."

True. *How many other things had he missed out on?*

"Wait here." She jumped up and ran into the house.

Rachel returned with plain white paper and crayons. "Get some leaves, different kinds, different sizes. Ones that aren't totally dried-up. It won't work if they're too brittle."

Paul skimmed a few leaves from the top of his pile and brought them to her. He knelt beside her as she used the flat surface of a large boulder for her demonstration.

"Now watch." She slid an oak leaf underneath her paper and, laying an unwrapped purple crayon on its side, rubbed over the leaf, revealing its veins and edges. "You've really never done this?"

"Uh-uh. Let me try."

She handed Paul a piece of paper and a crayon.

He rubbed the crayon over his leaf.

James had gone off on his own, using his rake as an imaginary lightsaber.

A question nagged Rachel's thoughts. Something she'd wanted to ask for a long time. She sucked in her bottom lip then cleared her throat. She spoke gently. "Paul, how did your mom die?"

He didn't look up from his leaf rubbing. He added another leaf under the other end of the paper.

"An ectopic pregnancy."

Rachel stopped coloring, trying to remember what the term meant.

"It's when the baby starts growing in the fallopian tube instead of the uterus. The pregnancy ruptured the tube, she had a lot of internal bleeding, went into shock, and died. I think it's rare, but even if a fraction of a percent of women die from it..." He shrugged. "Well, if it's your mom, it's a hundred percent."

"I'm so sorry. It must've been hard on your dad. He lost his wife and his baby."

"Yeah. I was pretty little, and I don't have many memories of it, but Sean says Dad didn't think he could handle us. Like he didn't have enough patience. He didn't know how to take care of us like Mom did. We spent a lot of time with my Aunt Ginnie and Uncle Joe for a while, but then I guess Dad got over it and adjusted." He turned his solemn blue eyes to her and shrugged. "I don't know why he worried. He was a great dad."

Rachel's chest tightened and a lump grew in her throat. Her voice came out weak. "My mom says we don't know what we're capable of until we do it."

"I guess so."

Moisture glistened in his eyes, and she realized they hadn't spoken of his dad this much since he'd died.

He turned an unfocused gaze at James, who still battled imaginary bad guys. "It's weird though..." He cleared his throat and his voice grew stronger. "Because he was this big Army guy, responsible for all these men and equipment and stuff, and he didn't think he could handle his little boys. But he did."

"Do you still think of him all the time?"

He turned his attention back to Rachel and shrugged. "Yeah, pretty much, unless I'm preoccupied with something else, but it doesn't hurt as much as it used to." He rubbed the crayon across the paper again. "Want to know something crazy? I don't want the hurt to go away."

"Why not?"

"I'm afraid if I stop hurting, I'll forget."

"You forget your cell phone or your keys. Maybe a homework assignment." She laid her crayon aside and clenched and released a fist. She held her breath, willing herself to be brave, for Paul's sake. Stilling her shaky hand, she placed it over his heart. She doubted he could feel her hand through his thick, soft, flannel jacket, so she rubbed it back and forth a couple of times. "The heart doesn't forget."

He swallowed hard and his Adam's apple bobbed up and down. "My heart will never forget you, Rachel Mueller." He swallowed again and blinked. "The kindness you and your family have shown me is something I'll carry with me the rest of my life."

She sat back on her knees and laid her hand in her lap. Touched by his sweet sentiment, she smiled.

His blue eyes never wavered from hers. What was he trying to say—or avoid saying—with that burning look?

She grew uncomfortable under his scrutiny and searched for a change of topic. "Well, let's see your masterpiece."

Paul held up his leaf rubbing. Two delicate, heart-shaped leaves in red crayon.

"Beautiful."

***

Late Sunday morning, Paul leaned against the cool stone exterior of the guesthouse and waited. Large gray clouds gathered and billowed overhead. The sun's rays pierced the gaps between the voluminous puffs and lit the meadow and drilling site.

Sean had called and said he'd be right over. Paul hoped they'd go on a hike. They used to hike with Dad, and here they had access to several state parks and game lands but seldom took advantage of it. Sean said they needed to talk first.

What was so important it couldn't wait? And why couldn't they talk while they drove or hiked? Paul's grades were fine—better than fine. He had all A's. He hadn't been in any trouble. He was dealing with Dad's death as best he could. If it was money, he could get a job for the holidays as long as he found transportation.

The truck rumbled up the drive and Sean hopped out and bounded for the door.

"Hey," Paul said. His brother's gaze seldom seemed so focused and intense.

"Yeah," Sean mumbled as he yanked Paul's arm and pulled him inside.

"What the heck is going on?"

Sean paced to the window and back, his hand clamped over his mouth. They hadn't been inside more than five seconds when Sean blurted, "Last night, I asked Amanda to marry me, and she said 'yes'."

Paul still stood in the doorway. A lead weight plunged to the pit of his stomach. He knew he was supposed to respond with enthusiastic congratulations, but he needed a minute to process the news.

Sean sat on the loveseat and immediately bounced his knee. He bit his lower lip and then his thumbnail. His eyes widened as he anticipated Paul's response.

Paul sunk his hands into his jeans pockets and shuffled toward Sean, trying to think of what to say. "Wow. I'm happy for you. Congratulations. I just didn't expect it so soon."

Now that it was in the open, Paul recognized the relief—and the almost giddy energy about Sean.

"It's not that soon. I mean, it feels like we've known each other forever. We both know what we want, and we're sure. If there's one thing Dad's death taught me, it's that we don't always have all the time we think we do."

Paul sat in the chair opposite Sean. "I know what you mean. I feel that way too, sometimes." It was true. Paul felt an urgency to get on with his life, with school, for fear that something—or someone—would slip through his fingers and be gone. It was the one thing propelling him toward confessing his feelings for Rachel.

"I know some people will think I'm doing this to get over Dad, but that's not it. I want to have my own family. We never had that kind of normal life. Amanda and I love each other, and we want that. We're doing this for the right reasons."

A little defensive maybe? What kind of reaction had he expected?

"You don't have to justify it to me. I understand."

Sean leaned forward and rested his elbows on his knees. His eyes homed in on Paul's and fixed there— intense. "Paul, this doesn't affect us. I'm not abandoning you. I'm always your brother, and until you're eighteen, I'm responsible for you. I'll always be here for you."

"You're a pain sometimes, but I couldn't ask for a better brother. Really."

"Thanks." He stood and paced behind the loveseat. "I hope I haven't screwed you up too bad." He broke into a grin. "I need a best man. Are you in?"

Paul smiled. "Are you kidding? If you even asked one of your loser friends, I'd—"

Sean grabbed Paul's arm and yanked him up. He locked his arm around Paul's neck, forcing him under his arm.

"You'd what?"

Paul snaked his foot around Sean's ankle and tried to trip him. Sean's leg didn't budge, and before Paul could wriggle out of the headlock, Sean pulled him into a hug. Other than forced apologies during their childhood, Paul couldn't remember Sean ever hugging him. It was good.

Sean released him and gave him a slap to the back. "The wedding's going to come up fast. Christmastime."

Paul didn't know a thing about wedding planning, but that seemed quick even to him. Was Amanda pregnant?

"There's no way you can do it that fast. Doesn't the Church make you wait so many months anyway?"

Sean waved his hand. "Dispensations. Amanda's uncle is a priest. He'll be around for the holiday and do the wedding."

Paul was skeptical, but he nodded.

Sean clapped his hands together and rubbed them. "Oh, and you can bring a date."

Could he? The only girl he wanted to ask wasn't allowed to date. It was a one-time thing though, like a school dance. Maybe her parents would allow it.

"Are the Muellers invited?"

Sean gave him a cocky grin. "Yes. Hmm...are those two things related? Let me see: Muellers...date." He made a big display of weighing one against the other with his hands. "You want to bring Rachel?"

"If you invite her family, she doesn't have to come as my date."

Sean chuckled. "I should've known. How long's this been going?"

"Hey, we were thrown together, and we like hanging out. That's all."

Sean still smiled. "If that's all, why is your face getting red?"

Paul's cheeks grew warm. Darn traitorous fair skin. "My face isn't getting red."

Sean punched him in the arm. "Yeah. How long's this been going on?"

Paul rubbed his arm where it stung from Sean's fist. "There's no 'this.'"

"I'll rephrase the question. How long have you been hot for her?"

Geez. He made it sound dirty. "When did we move here?"

"November last year."

"Yeah, November last year."

Sean rolled his eyes. "Does she know?"

"What is this, the Inquisition?"

"You just admitted you're hot for her." He started speaking loud and slow, as if Paul were addlebrained. "Does ... she... know...how...you...feel?"

Paul sighed. It was no use. "I don't know. Her dad's mentioned his badass triple-barrel shotgun at least three times, so I think *he* knows."

Sean laughed and clapped his hands. "So you haven't told her, and you haven't kissed her?"

"No." Sean had probably never feared rejection in his life. Girls fell at his feet like hail during a thunderstorm—hard and fast.

"Don't be a wuss. Between now and the wedding, let her know you're interested. Then at the wedding, kiss her. Girls get all sappy about weddings."

"Well, maybe she'd have noticed me sooner if she weren't always looking at your ugly mug."

"Yeah, it sucks having a brother as handsome as me." Sean rubbed his hand over his stubbly beard. "So, how does she feel about you?"

"I don't know. She used to say I was like a brother to her, but—" He shrugged. "Not lately." He remembered her flirting with him the evening she had shown him her secret garden. He could hope, couldn't he?

"There's an easy way to find out." He gave Paul a few seconds to mull it over then said, "Listen, let's take that hike, and then we'll meet Amanda for dinner. We're going to celebrate. Your mission between now and the wedding is …" He motioned with his hand, trying to coax the rest out of Paul.

"To let her know I'm interested," Paul droned.

"Don't screw it up." Sean slapped him on the back again, pushing him headlong towards the door.

***

Rachel released the branch she'd sidestepped and came to a halt. Paul sat on the log bench in her garden, his head buried in his hands. She'd thought he was in the guesthouse, studying.

Should she sneak back out to the trail and give him some privacy? Her garden really needed some TLC...and the days were getting shorter. She'd just stay out of his way and be quick.

She didn't want to frighten him by sneaking up, so she rustled the remaining leaves on the nearest branch. "Hey."

Paul jerked his head up and swiveled around to face her. "Rachel. I didn't know you were coming down here." His voice quavered, making him seem anxious about something.

"Just deadheading blooms before the sun goes down."

He stood and wiped his hands on his jeans. His irises were so dark they appeared indigo, and she loved seeing him in his standard fall attire—jeans and a hooded sweatshirt.

What did *she* look like? Now that the weather had cooled, she typically wore long tees with leggings. Her corduroy jacket kept her neck and shoulders warm. She had pulled her hair up into a ponytail on the walk from the house without even brushing it first. Had she known Paul was down here, she would've taken a little care.

"You don't have to go. Just ignore me." She turned to wade through the overgrown flowers, but Paul snagged her sleeve.

"I can't do that." He spoke faster than usual and still sounded anxious. Something was definitely up.

"I'm sorry. I'll be quick." For some reason she made him uncomfortable this evening.

"That's not what I meant. I'm glad you're here." He let go of her sleeve and ran his hand through his hair. "Please be patient with me. I'm just...I'm nervous."

"It's me, Paul. Since when do I make you nervous?"

"You don't. It's not you. It's...it's what I want to say to you." Why was he stammering? "What I *need* to say to you."

Rachel's mouth went dry, and her heart raced. Was he moving? Was there something at school, or had she done something?

He bit his lip. "Becoming your friend is one of the best things that has ever happened to me."

She smiled, but she also sensed a "but" coming.

"But the truth is..."

There it was. He had asked her to be patient, so she waited for him to continue. The seconds were excruciating. She wished he'd spit it out, whatever it was.

"The truth is I don't want to be *just* your friend."

He stepped closer, close enough for her to smell the subtle spiciness of his cologne. When did he start wearing cologne?

He took her hand and interlocked his fingers with hers.

Her heart pounded against her chest. She knew what he was about to confess before the words left his mouth.

"Rachel, I'm crazy about you. Majorly crazy."

His declaration emboldened her, and she took his other hand in hers. "You can't see it, but my heart is smiling." Her words were barely more than a whisper, but she hoped he felt their significance. Her smile felt impossibly bigger than her cheeks.

Relief and pleasure spread across his face, and he tightened his grip on her hands.

"I'm crazy about you too, Paul."

His giddy smile matched hers, and he took a final step toward her. Was he going to kiss her?

She stilled her nerves and waited, her head tilted up at just the right angle. . .

The next thing she knew Paul's hands were gone, and he hunched over his left leg.

"Shoot. I twisted my ankle. Something sharp jabbed my foot. I felt it through my shoe."

She put a hand to his elbow and helped him stand. "Are you okay?"

"Yeah, it just threw me off balance."

They crouched to see what he'd stepped on. A blunt object stuck out of the ground near his left foot.

Rachel kicked at it with her shoe. "I found a lot of big rocks up here when I cleared and planted."

Paul examined what looked like a piece of rock. After running his fingers along its edges, he got down on his knees and pushed the dirt away with his hands.

"What do you think it is?"

"It's not a rock. It's an old piece of wood. Painted gray." He scraped at the hard dirt and clay caked around the object but still couldn't dislodge it. "Do you have a small shovel or spade here?"

"Yeah, right beside the bench. Hold on."

Rachel retrieved the garden shovel and handed it to Paul. He poked carefully around the wood, alternating between digging and twisting it loose from the hard ground. Finally, it came free.

He held a weathered piece of painted wood about eight inches long. It looked gray, but that might not have been its original color.

Paul handed it to her, and she turned it over in her hands. Fancy script covered the back, the writing a shade darker gray than the paint beneath it.

"Something's written on here." She angled the wood so Paul could see. "It looks like a 'U' at the beginning. U.S., I think."

"Let me see." Paul pulled it closer. "U.S. Army."

Rachel ran her finger along the bottom. "Look, there's a date scratched down there too."

"It's 1863. That would've been during the Civil War, right?"

"Yeah, um," Rachel sifted through the American history dates stored in the recesses of her brain. "1861 to 1865, I think." The significance of their find dawned on her and she gasped.

"This could be some kind of Civil War artifact," Paul blurted.

"You think so?"

"I wish we knew what it was from. Maybe there are

more pieces around here."

Paul glanced at a horizon streaked with wisps of orange and pink. "The sun's starting to go down. Maybe tomorrow we could do some digging."

He took her hand again, and she mourned the fact that their moment had been ruined. He wasn't going to kiss her now.

"I know you didn't get a chance to take care of your flowers, but could I walk you back to the house? Maybe we could have some hot cider."

"That sounds good. As soon as the sun sets, it gets cold." Only Rachel didn't feel cold. Her new knowledge of Paul's affection warmed her from the inside out. As he led her toward the path and her home, she couldn't fathom ever feeling cold again.

Chapter 11
Christmas and Advent

Paul jumped on the shovel, one booted foot on each shoulder of the blade, in an effort to drive the cutting edge through the layer of clay. After four jumps and little progress, he rested an arm over the handle and wiped his brow on his flannel sleeve. He pined for boots with thicker soles.

Rachel dragged a garden rake through the dirt, loosening the clods of soil he'd already overturned. Her sweatpants sagged at the knees where they were coated in dirt, but they did little to hide the shape of her legs. Unfortunately for him, layers of cotton and fleece on her upper body concealed every hint of the curves he knew lay below. She brushed back the long bangs that fell into her eyes.

He had said it. Out loud. To her face. "I'm crazy about you."

Rachel hadn't laughed, told him to get lost, or given him the "let's be friends" line. Instead, she admitted she was crazy about him too. He'd been about to kiss her, and then he made a fool of himself snagging his foot on that piece of wood jutting out of the ground.

It had been weeks now, and he hadn't had another good opportunity to kiss her. He figured at this point he could wait until Sean and Amanda's wedding.

He and Rachel had gotten some raised eyebrows from her dad when he noticed them holding hands, but so far no warnings or threats had been issued, nor had her dad mentioned that darned shotgun.

"You want to switch off?"

She'd caught him loafing. And staring.

He took one look at the cheap tennis shoes she wore and shook his head. "No. I got it." Cold wind buffeted them from the west, and he shivered. "We ought to call it quits soon anyway."

Rachel's hair blew into her face, and she tried to push it behind her ears. "Okay. Five more minutes."

Still curious about the piece of Civil War-era wood they'd found, they dug in the garden room, as Paul called it, whenever they had a chance. The days grew shorter and shorter, leaving less and less time to work, but they hoped to stumble on other artifacts or clues that would tell them more about the piece of wood they'd found.

Paul's shovel made a loud thunk as metal hit metal. "I've got something."

Rachel dropped to her knees and pushed aside the dirt with her gloved hands.

Paul scooped out the earth with his hands too. After a few minutes, he extracted a jagged piece of metal. Rachel leaned in as he brushed the last of the clumped dirt from the object.

"It looks like part of a metal jaw," Rachel said.

"I think it is. Maybe part of an animal trap."

They continued to search, but found only a jagged piece of amber-colored glass.

Paul looked at the darkening cumulus clouds amassing over the tree line. "I think we should call it quits."

They gathered their tools and made their way out to the trail.

"We should probably suspend our operations until spring." He waited a beat for Rachel to catch up with him. He swapped the rake for the shovel so that he carried the heavier of the two implements.

Rachel grinned. "Thanks. I like how you put that— suspend our operations. You make it sound like a top secret assignment instead of aimlessly digging for who-knows-what."

Paul shot a smile at her. "Seriously, though. We should probably give it a rest. The weather's turning, the days are short, and the ground's going to freeze."

"I guess you're right. Christmas is coming anyway. It's not like we have nothing to do. And then the wedding."

Rachel switched the rake to her opposite hand. "You never said what you thought of the timing. With Christmas and your dad and all."

Two days after Christmas, Sean and Amanda would be married. When Sean had told him the date, Paul couldn't understand why they would want to get married so close to the anniversary of Dad's death. After Sean explained all the practical reasons it would be the perfect time for him and Amanda, he told Paul he wanted to reclaim the Christmas season. It would never be what it was, but if they could fill it with happy memories to crowd out the sad ones, why not do it?

Paul shrugged. "I didn't like it at first." He paused and blew out a breath, the warm vapor creating a white puff that dissipated in the cold air. "Scratch that. I hated it."

"And now?" Rachel peered at him through the windblown hair streaking across her cheek.

Paul resisted the urge to sweep it off of her face. "Now I like it. It's good."

"Are you excited about it? The wedding, I mean."

"Yeah. Sure." He was. Less so about the wedding and more so about kissing her, but she didn't need to know that.

***

Rachel lifted the candy cane to her mouth and twirled it between her lips. The cool peppermint lingered in her mouth as she slid the sweet stick over her tongue. No color remained on the straight end of the stick, which she had skillfully licked into a point as sharp and delicate as the icicles that hung from the gutters.

The minty freshness tantalized her nose, but only for a second. The dominant fragrance in the room remained the sweet and savory aroma of the ham Mom had served for Christmas dinner. When the heat kicked on, a gust of fresh pine momentarily wafted beyond the Christmas tree's limbs, causing Rachel to inhale deeply and savor its woodsy scent.

Paul sat next to her, his hand interlocked with hers, and if he shifted in his seat or leaned in to whisper something to her, his cologne would join the panoply of fragrances that from now on would be uniquely "Christmas" to her.

The mini multi-colored lights from the Christmas tree cast a soft glow on the otherwise dark room. Here and there a red or yellow bulb lit a hidden alcove in the tree where an ornament hung. An eclectic mishmash of ornaments bedecked the large, fine-needled evergreen Dad and Paul had hand-cut for their celebration. Garish ornaments fashioned by little hands hung next to antique balls, ceramic snowflakes, vacation mementos and pop culture touchstones. As Paul had joked while he fastened hooks to the ornaments, "Nothing says 'let's celebrate the Savior's birth' like an eerie, talking Death Star."

As Christmas drew near, Paul had seemed reserved and sullen at times, but he also enjoyed simple things, like helping her dad string lights and assembling the track for James's model train. Thinking of Paul as part of their family gave her a warm rush. He'd spent Christmas Eve with Sean at Amanda's parents' house, but Christmas Day, while Sean visited Amanda's great-grandmother in Wilkes-Barre, Paul was all hers. She hadn't felt so contented and happy at Christmas since she'd been a little girl waiting to see what Santa Claus left for her.

"Do you remember the year we brought the baby brown bats in with the tree?" Rachel asked.

"Bats?" Paul echoed.

"Yes. I try to forget, and every year Rachel reminds me," Mom said.

"They came in on the tree, which Mom beat with the broom. She toppled the tree and sent the bats flapping wildly around the room. One was dragging tinsel on its wing."

Paul laughed, and Rachel nudged him with her elbow.

"Shhh...James." She nodded to where James slept on the floor beneath them wrapped in his Teenage Mutant Ninja Turtle Snuggie.

Paul quieted, but she couldn't stop her own giggles.

"Why don't you tell him about that innocent pup you killed with your outdoor display?" Dad grinned over his mug of coffee.

"You killed a dog at Christmas?" Paul tried to act incredulous, but he laughed again.

"A stray. And I didn't kill it. It just bled—a little," Rachel protested. "It was its own stupid fault for trying to eat the bulbs."

Peaceful silence filled a lull in the conversation, the only sounds a ticking clock and the intermittent hum of the furnace.

"You have any funny Christmas stories, Paul?" Dad crossed his legs at the ankles and reclined onto the couch.

"Hmm..." Paul sipped hot cocoa and rested the mug on his thigh. "Well, one year I whined for so long about wanting to make a gingerbread house that in frustration Dad took us out to the garage and helped us build one out of sheet metal and shell casings."

"That sounds really festive. Not," Rachel said.

He squeezed her hand and smiled. "Okay. How about this one? When Sean was seven, he wolfed a whole box of chocolate-covered cherries and then puked all over the nativity set."

Rachel clapped a hand over her mouth, her candy cane

dangling between her fingers like a cigarette. "Eww."

"Yeah. I don't think he's eaten one since. I don't care for them either."

Rachel couldn't blame him.

Despite the fact that Paul and Rachel sat side by side on the couch all evening with their hands intertwined, her parents hadn't noticed—or didn't care. Neither of them had acknowledged the change in their relationship although mistletoe was notably absent from their Christmas decorations this year. She thought it odd, since Dad usually tacked it above every doorway.

Rachel had been waiting for Mom to broach the subject of Paul ever since her dad had first seen them holding hands. She had nothing to hide; she'd shared her attraction to Paul with her mom. Rachel treasured keeping their newfound status as a couple to themselves. They hadn't even kissed yet—a fact that drove her crazy.

She hated to see Paul head back to the guesthouse alone that night and considered asking her parents if he could sleep on the couch. Paul hadn't complained though, and they would find lots of time to spend together for the remainder of the holidays, including the wedding in a couple of days.

***

Rachel propped her bare feet on the coffee table and applied wine-berry polish to the toenails on her right foot. She gritted her teeth as James plopped onto the couch beside her, jolting her arm.

"Whatcha doin'?"

"What does it look like? Painting my toenails." She switched the polish to the other hand and began work on her left foot. James quickly bored and trotted off. *Thank goodness.*

Dad's legs, ending in his ratty loafers, moved into her frame of vision but didn't distract her from her task.

"I hope you're not wearing open-toed shoes to the wedding. There's a dusting of snow out there, you know."

Rachel capped the polish and huffed out a breath. "No, Dad."

He plucked green grapes from the stem and popped them into his mouth, one at a time. "So, why paint your nails when no one's going to see them?"

Sweet stars above, he's clueless.

"*I* see them, Dad. *I* know they're painted."

"Oh."

He obviously didn't understand. If he'd been married nearly twenty years and didn't get it yet, Rachel doubted he'd ever get it.

Once the polish dried, she heated the curling iron in the bathroom and proceeded to clip her hair in strips, which she unleashed individually, curled—counting carefully to thirty—and then fluffed.

Mom's reflection appeared in the mirror behind her. "It looks so pretty, Rachel. You should do that more often."

A smile creased her face. "Thanks, Mom."

"You've been primping all morning."

"I want to look my best." She let a final curl fall and pulled it free with her fingertips. "Do you think Paul will notice?"

The corner of Mom's mouth raised in a grin. "I have no doubt he'll notice. He'd have to be blind not to."

Rachel bit her bottom lip, but couldn't suppress the smile. She couldn't wait for Paul to see her. She hoped his duties as best man wouldn't keep them from sharing a few dances together.

The usher sat Rachel's family near the back of the church. They were running late—thanks to James and an ill-timed trip to the bathroom—and those were the only seats left. She had a hard time getting a look at Sean, but she did have a clear view of the best man. She could practically feel her pupils dilating as she gazed at him. Didn't that mean she was attracted to him?

His hair looked perfect, as short as she'd ever seen it, thanks to a cut the day before. He wore a black tuxedo, and his bowtie matched the bridesmaids' dresses—a holly berry red. Her mom had pinned a red rose to his lapel before he'd left for the church.

Could fifteen be too young to be in love? It couldn't, because her heart overflowed with love of a decidedly non-fraternal nature.

Rachel's mom dabbed tears from her eyes when Amanda and Sean kissed at the end of Mass. Rachel rolled her eyes. Her mom cried at fake weddings on thirty-second Hallmark commercials.

Everyone funneled out the back of church and into their cars to head to the reception at a nearby hotel.

"I found it," James called as he located their table in the ballroom. He circled the table, looking for his name card. "Here's mine. Chicken. What did you get, Rachel?"

Rachel walked around the table toward James. When she didn't see her place card, she turned and walked in the opposite direction. She spotted cards for James, each of her parents and two other couples, but she couldn't find a card with her name on it.

"Mine's not here." She bit her lip and tried to hide her disappointment. Where would she sit? Wouldn't Paul have made sure Amanda had her on the list? Her parents obviously sent in the response card.

"We'll ask Paul," Mom said, rubbing Rachel's shoulder. "Maybe he can figure out where it got to."

Rachel nodded. "Sure." Where was Paul, anyway?

***

Paul leaned against the bar and ordered a ginger ale. At every idle moment his thoughts turned to the mission Sean had given him for the evening—kissing Rachel. This would be her first kiss, and he wanted everything about it to be special. God knew he wanted to do much more than kiss her, things he knew he shouldn't think but felt almost helpless to stop. He half-feared this kiss would be like the little Dutch boy pulling his finger from the dike, and all his restraint would drain away. He turned from the bar with his drink and scanned the room. He spotted Rachel and her family and headed towards them.

Paul had been so preoccupied at the wedding that he hadn't gotten a good look at Rachel, but now he couldn't take his eyes off her. Her long brown hair hung over her shoulders, but he had never seen it so curly. She wore a shiny green dress with a red rose print. The sleeveless, scoop-necked top showed off her slender arms and neck, and the cinched waist and full, knee-length skirt only accentuated her natural beauty—a beauty that emanated from her eyes and spilled over into her whole countenance. He didn't pay much attention to girls' clothes, but he loved that Rachel always looked feminine and attractive—even alluring—without looking as if she were on her way to a gig at the strip club south of town.

He approached the table, thoughts of kissing her crowded everything else out. He'd need to clear his mind long enough to make the toast, but after that he belonged to Rachel.

"Hi, Mr. and Mrs. Mueller." His gaze slid back at Rachel and he smiled. "You look beautiful."

She blushed. "Thank you. You too. I mean, you look good. Not beautiful."

James came over and tugged at his sleeve. "Dad says he feels sorry for you because you have to wear a monkey suit. When are you going to put it on?"

Paul laughed and tugged at his vest. "This *is* the monkey suit."

Rachel rested her hand on his arm. "Paul, my place

card is missing. I don't know where I'm supposed to sit."

He looked first to her parents and then to her. "I thought, um, if it was okay with your parents, you could sit with me and some of the bridal party." He shifted his focus to her dad and waited for an answer.

Rachel's dad tilted his lips in a one-sided grin. That half-grin and the knowing look in her dad's eyes told Paul he hadn't put anything past her dad. He was aware of every look, every touch that passed between Paul and Rachel. Paul thanked God he seemed to have his approval. Or did he?

"Is that okay?" Rachel turned toward her dad, wide-eyed with a hint of pleading.

Paul hadn't considered the importance of the seating chart Amanda had spent hours poring over until now. The next words Rachel's dad spoke would affect more than where Rachel hung her purse for the evening. With a yes came tacit approval for their relationship. Paul held his breath, but the response his life hinged upon didn't come from her dad. Rachel's mom answered for them.

Chapter 12
Operation S.W.A.K.

Rachel found her place card at Paul's table with the bridal party. Paul had planned for them to sit together, if it was okay with her parents. *Sweet.*

Sweat had beaded at the nape of Rachel's neck as she waited on Dad's answer. His lips had twisted into a scowl, and his mouth opened, but the words came from Mom: "Sure, honey."

Paul sighed with relief then a smile creased his face. He murmured his thanks and led Rachel to their table before Dad had a chance to add his two cents.

Once everyone found their places, servers filled their glasses for a champagne toast.

Rachel slipped her arm through Paul's. "Are you making the toast?"

"Yep. One of my best man duties I was told not to screw up."

Rachel smiled. She could almost hear the derisive tone Sean sometimes used with Paul. "Nervous?"

"Nah, I got it all up here." He tapped his head twice and grinned.

And he did. He gave a perfect toast—humorous but touching, a testament to the love between him and Sean. Following the toast, everyone raised their glasses. The servers had set them at each place indiscriminately; only the bartender carded people. Rachel felt a bit self-conscious about taking a drink, but no one noticed or cared. She raised her champagne flute and sipped along with everyone else. The sweet liquid bubbled and fizzed as it crossed her tongue.

Paul slid into the seat beside her.

Rachel swallowed another mouthful of champagne. "You did great."

"Thanks. I'm glad it's over." He held his own drink out to her before he set it on the table. "What do you think of the bubbly?"

"Mmmm. Much better than I expected. Dad always complains it's too dry, but I like it."

Paul finished off his glass and pushed it aside. "Looks like they've got plenty."

The other members of the bridal party had done their toasts at the bar and left their glasses at the table untouched. Paul leaned forward, grabbed two of the full glasses, and placed one in front of each of them.

Rachel finished her first glass and set it aside. By the time the servers handed out cake and the dancing began, Paul had consumed three glasses of champagne and Rachel, two.

After the bridal party dances, Sean and Amanda strolled around to each of the tables, greeting their guests. Paul and Rachel sat and watched the dancing get underway while they talked. Paul's remarks about some of the dancers struck Rachel as particularly funny, and twice she dissolved into a fit of unstoppable laughter that forced her to both grip her sides and cross her legs so she didn't pee her pants. That, in turn, made Paul laugh harder.

When they'd both gotten a grip on themselves, Rachel rested her hand on Paul's sleeve. "Sean looks amazing. Amanda is one lucky woman."

She clamped her mouth shut. What was wrong with her? She hadn't thought before she'd said it. She hated when girls were careless with guys' feelings, and here she'd been wholly insensitive to Paul.

"He's a good guy."

Her heart felt near to bursting with affection for Paul.

She expected him to chastise her or make a snarky remark in protest, but he didn't. She wanted to gush about how she thought she might be falling in love with him, but she had already learned champagne made her prone to rambling, so she bit her lips together.

As she rubbed her hand up and down Paul's arm, she realized the champagne also made her less self-conscious about such displays of affection. "Whoever marries his younger brother is pretty lucky too."

She pulled her hand back, suddenly aware that she was potentially embarrassing herself in front of her parents as well as a room full of strangers.

Paul turned to her, his unsteady gaze roaming her face. "You think so?"

"I know so." She beamed at him.

His eyes crinkled at the corners as he unleashed a killer smile on her—one that sent her heart racing. "Would you like to dance?"

She nodded and let Paul lead her by the hand to the dance floor. Feeling a little off balance, she made a conscious effort not to sway as they passed her parents' table. The high heels she rarely wore weren't helping matters. She avoided eye contact with her dad who, her peripheral vision told her, tracked her every movement. Paul nearly tripped as they made their way around dancing couples whose arms and legs darted out in every direction.

The disc jockey played standard wedding fare and had everyone dancing at a breakneck pace for the next half hour. The coordination required for keeping time with the music proved tricky, and Rachel longed for a slow dance with Paul. The rhythm never slowed though, and she did her best to keep up without unceremoniously whapping innocent bystanders.

Finally, Paul shouted to be heard over the music. "Are you hot?"

She waved her hand in front of her face a few times and pulled the front of her dress away from her body to allow the air to circulate over her skin. "Yes."

"C'mon." Paul led her over the parquet dance floor and out the double doors into the hallway.

***

The hall smelled of stale cigarette smoke, but the air was a good ten degrees cooler. A couple of cushioned seats and bland, abstract artwork lined the corridor, which faced one of the parking lots. Paul leaned against the wall to catch his breath. The absurdity of his assigned challenge from Sean struck him. He couldn't kiss Rachel for the first time in front of all these people—especially family. Maybe out here would be better.

He tugged her hand.

She swung around to face him, the doors shutting behind her. "It feels so good out here, nice and cool."

"Yeah, it does." He placed his arms gently but clumsily around her waist and pulled her closer. He hadn't felt this happy and carefree since before his dad had died.

Rachel smiled up at him.

His knees grew weak. Good thing the wall held him up.

She slid both palms up his shirt beneath the tuxedo lapels and toward his shoulders.

He shivered and considered that what people said about alcohol diminishing your inhibitions must be true, at least in Rachel's case.

This is it. Tightening his grip on her waist, he pushed off the wall and bent his head towards hers. Her lips were a hair's breadth away...

The glass doors opposite them opened with a whoosh.

Paul jerked back and turned to see who had invaded their space. His heart, already pounding at a steady clip, ratcheted up a notch as the thought of Rachel's dad barging in on them crossed his mind.

Rachel giggled as an elderly but ample lady toddled out the door beneath the exit sign. The blast of cold air mixed with the old lady's pungent, floral perfume carried the moment and the mood away.

Paul released Rachel from his grip, and he patted the hotel key card in his interior jacket pocket. It offered access to the room he and Sean had shared last night. *His* room tonight, since Sean would stay in the honeymoon suite with Amanda.

What am I thinking? He couldn't take Rachel to a hotel room. He wanted to share a first kiss, not take her to bed— although that idea held its own appeal more and more every day.

He leaned forward and grabbed hold of her waist again. She tilted her head, and he stared into her eyes, a deeper green than he'd ever seen them. Forest green if he were to compare them with a pack of crayons. The golden flecks near her pupils shimmered, even in the dull light of the hall. He brushed aside a stray curl then whispered in her ear, "I want to take you..." The word upstairs came to his mind, but not out of his mouth. "...back inside for another dance. I think if I ditch this jacket, it won't be so friggin' hot."

She gave him a sidelong glance as if she didn't quite buy it. "Okay."

Paul took her hand and led her back amidst the couples jostling for room on the dance floor. Only two songs played before the mellow chords of a slow dance finally filled the room. He and Rachel had sobered up, and what seemed so natural a half hour earlier felt awkward again.

Carefully, but not clumsily this time, Paul put his arms around her waist as she threaded her arms up and around his neck. She swayed back and forth to the music according to his lead.

Her gaze followed his across the room, and he leaned

down and whispered, "Every instinct I have is telling me to pull you closer, but I don't want your parents to get the wrong idea."

"It's okay." The shyness that had been noticeably absent since their champagne binge returned. "This is enough." Her eyes closed.

He admired the pink glow of her cheeks while he tuned into the melodic strains of the ballad.

That song faded into the next. The tempo picked up, and neither of them knew how to dance to it. To make matters worse, the lyrics were about making love and getting tangled up in bed sheets—clearly a song aimed at the bride and groom and not a couple of teenagers on their first date.

They left the dance floor and took the empty seats at a table with her parents and James. Most of the guests had left after the cake cutting, and only friends of the bride and groom still clustered in small groups, dancing and drinking.

No more than a half hour later, Rachel's mother gathered their things. Her dad hoisted James off the chairs where he'd fallen asleep.

"Time to go," Mrs. Mueller said. "Let's say goodbye to Sean and Amanda."

Paul's mouth went dry. They couldn't leave. Not yet. He had to kiss Rachel.

Amanda and Sean finished dancing, and when they spotted the Muellers readying to leave, they came over. Rachel's parents hugged them while Paul's mind whirred frantically through any possible way he could think to get Rachel alone. Coming up with none, he muttered a curse.

"We wouldn't have missed it for the world." Mrs. Mueller pulled a kink out of Amanda's long veil.

Amanda noticed the wedding favors Mrs. Mueller carried. "Oh, please take some cake home with you." Her forehead wrinkled. "Where did they put it?"

There it was—his opportunity, served up to him on a cake platter. Forget privacy. They had waited long enough for this kiss.

Paul's gaze darted around the room, and he spotted the remainder of wrapped cake on a corner table on the opposite side of the dance floor. Relief coursed through him, and he winked at Rachel.

"Rachel and I will grab a few pieces."

Paul led Rachel by the hand for the umpteenth time, determined that this time he had a destination and a purpose. He stopped alongside the cake table, picked up two wrapped pieces of cake in each hand, and placed them in Rachel's open palms. "Here you go."

He searched the dance floor and beyond. Enough dancers filled the room to block Paul's path of vision. Good. If he couldn't see Rachel's parents, they couldn't see him.

His gaze settled on Rachel.

He had ad-libbed a toast in front of more than a hundred people without a trace of nervousness, and now, about to do the one thing he'd been dying to do for months, he feared his knees might give out on him. Nervous or not, he wouldn't waste another second.

He rested his hand on her lower back, then leaned down and gently kissed her on the lips, slowly and with all the tenderness he felt for her.

Her spine stiffened, but in an instant she relaxed, and he savored the softness of her lips. She tasted like champagne and cake frosting.

Paul started to pull away, but after all this time, that little kiss wasn't enough. He kissed her again, more firmly this time as he wove his hand into the luxurious curls that spilled down her back.

He withdrew and smiled.

She returned the happy expression. No wonder she hadn't pressed against him or slipped her arms around his neck like he'd hoped—she still held four plates of cake.

He waited for a reaction.

"Wow."

As reactions went, that was a good one. He combed his hand through her hair and stroked her cheek with his thumb.

"A drop in the bucket, Rachel. That's a tiny fraction of what I feel for you, of all the kisses I want to share with you."

He leaned his forehead against hers and whispered. "Thank you. For this. For tonight. For being there for me this past year." Would she be able to see the emotion welling in his eyes? He blinked back the tears.

Her voice came out breathy and soft. "There's nowhere I'd rather be."

He could only drag this moment out so long with her parents waiting. He kissed her temple and, taking half of the cake from her, took her by the hand yet again and led her back to her family.

***

A lull settled over the remainder of Christmas vacation. Paul's phone beeped indicating an incoming text message. He shoved himself off the couch where he'd been watching TV. Watching didn't really describe what he'd been doing. That would imply some kind of attention or concentration. He'd been staring at the screen while his brain replayed kissing Rachel in a continuous loop.

He glanced at his phone and saw a picture of white sand and clear blue water framed by palm trees. The message from Sean, three days into his honeymoon, said "Greetings from the Caribbean."

Paul tapped back, "How's the honeymoon?" He turned off the television while he waited for Sean's response. In a few seconds the phone beeped again, and he read Sean's response, shouted in capital letters. "FANTASTIC! Might even leave the room tomorrow."

He smiled. Sean's bliss was contagious, but even for a honeymoon, that bordered on too much information. Before he had a chance to reply, another message came. "Did you kiss her?"

Geez, relentless. He wouldn't let up, even on his honeymoon.

"Yes." At least he'd have him off his back now and minding his own business.

"How was it?"

Seriously? He shook his head as he tapped back, "How old are you?"

Again the reply came, "How was it?"

Just plain none of Sean's business. "What are you, a girl?"

"How was it? Scale of one to ten."

Sean wouldn't let up, and Paul had to give him something. Might as well be the truth. "Twenty-nine."

Sean rewarded his honesty with a smiley emoji and, "See you next week."

Chapter 13
XOXO Marks the Spot

Paul poured a tall glass of milk, took a swig, then gulped the remainder. He wiped his mouth on the back of his hand and set the empty glass in the sink. What would it take to fall asleep tonight?

Time elapsed since he kissed Rachel: three weeks, six days and one hour. Not that Paul kept track. They spent time together nearly every day, but outside their morning walk and the trek to and from the bus stop, they never had a minute alone.

Paul loved their morning walks. They talked, flirted, and laughed, but they moved. First, they had a tight morning schedule with no room for dawdling, and second, even though their walk covered a lot of ground, they were continually within view of the house, the road, or the drilling site. Paul always felt like someone could be watching them.

This weekend he would find a way to be alone with Rachel, even if only for a few minutes. How hard could it be to find five minutes alone with her?

While he had trouble sleeping in the weeks following Dad's death, Paul had been sleeping well for months. Ordinarily, he climbed into bed and dozed off within minutes. Tonight he couldn't get his mind off Rachel.

He climbed back into bed. He'd read a book, counted sheep, drank a glass of milk, and tried every relaxation technique he could think of to no avail. When he rolled to his side, his iPod on the nightstand gave him an idea.

Music. Soothing music. *That'll do it.*

He put the ear buds in and selected random play. The

bass pounded in his ears, the rhythm throbbing.

"I toss and turn, awake all night.
Your kiss burning in my dreams."

Seriously? Not helping. He yanked the ear buds from his ears and tossed them on the nightstand with his iPod. This bout of insomnia called for desperate measures.

Paul broke out his American history textbook, guaranteed to kill your libido and put you to sleep. He hefted the 300-plus page book onto his bed. His teacher assigned chapters seventeen though twenty over the weekend. Reluctant to dig into the text, Paul started by flipping through the pictures.

Chapter three focused on the secession of the South, chapter four on the formation of the Union Army, and chapter five on communication and transportation during the Civil War. The mostly black and white pictures showed thriving cotton plantations, ragged soldiers, and an early printing press. He almost passed over a color photo—probably a museum photo—of a Civil War wagon. Something about the wagon caught his eye, and he turned back to it.

The wagon had two smaller wooden wheels in the front, where it would be attached to a team of horses, and two larger wheels in the back. The wood was painted a steel blue gray color. Written on the side was, "U.S. No. 101." The script of the "U" looked similar to what he and Rachel had found on the wood in the garden room.

The caption read: *Wagon used for transportation of supplies to the Union Army during the Civil War.*

Paul dog-eared the page and closed the book. Tomorrow, he'd tell Rachel what he'd found. The book had done its job; sleep came.

***

In the morning, Rachel's heart fluttered as she greeted Paul, who strode into the living room carting his thick history textbook under his arm. The flipping pages fanned their faces as he sought the correct one. Finally, he jabbed his finger at a black and white photo of a Civil War wagon. His bloodshot eyes indicated a lack of sleep, but his tone was alert and eager. "See, doesn't that look like the same writing that's on the wood we found?"

Rachel dragged the book onto her lap as she sat on the couch. "Hmmm...I guess it does. Do you think it's the same?"

"It could be."

"Wow. I mean, I never thought we'd find anything like this. Something from the Civil War."

Paul twisted his lips and took back the book as he sagged into the couch. "Yeah. I wish we could go down there and dig some more right now, but it'll be months until the snow stops."

"And longer until it melts." Rachel sighed. "But it's not so bad today. Just some crusty snow here and there." She held his gaze, a smile stretching across his face. There was no point in wasting an unseasonably warm, 55-degree Saturday in January.

"Want to at least walk down there and check things out? We can't dig, but—"

"Let's go." Rachel jumped off the couch and went for her boots by the door. She knew they couldn't dig in the mud. Paul may as well have said, "Let's sneak into the woods so I can kiss you again."

Dad had left with James, and Mom was engrossed in the details of a fundraiser she'd agreed to organize for James's school.

"Going for a walk, Mom," she called, excited about the idea.

Paul held the door for her like a gentleman and waited outside as she zipped her jacket. He wore an insulated gray sweatshirt jacket over jeans, and stood with one hand tucked into a pocket.

She smiled and took his free hand, and they set off for the garden room at a more leisurely pace than usual. In the shaded brush that bordered the garden room, the snow was still packed so deeply they couldn't get to where her flowers lay decomposing under a cover of icy snow.

"This way." Paul led her several yards beyond the far "wall" to the eastern side of the garden room.

He was a man on a mission this morning.

She understood. If he thought about their first kiss even half as many times as she did, he was desperate to get her alone.

Paul led her up a gentle slope where she'd noticed a lot of loose coal in the summer. No vegetation clung to it, and even now, patches of black earth and stone were visible. The bare patches and the moss-covered slope that ran up the hillside beside it led to a small plateau at the top of the hill. Rachel had never climbed up there, but that's where Paul headed.

They both slipped on the muddy crest, leaving their knees soaked and their boots muddy. Deep ruts, the tracks of heavy machinery, lined the muddy hilltop. The site offered a perfect view of the gas rigging towering above the tree line. One of the gas companies had probably brought equipment up there to survey the landscape below. Behind them the ruts continued in the distance where the trucks likely met up with a fire road on the neighboring state game lands.

Rachel gazed out over the landscape, trying to appreciate its barren beauty, but all she could think of was if and when Paul would kiss her.

His arms encircled her from behind, and she smiled. *Finally.*

The wind kicked up, and she pushed her hair behind her ears. She closed her eyes and concentrated on every sensation. The wind carried the scent of muddy earth. The sun warmed her face, but not as much as Paul's arms tightening around her. They stood like that for a minute or two before he used his hands at her waist to turn her around. She complied, feeling her pulse kick up a notch. Butterflies stirred in her stomach.

"Rachel."

One word that said a million. His hands slid through her hair, holding either side of her head as his lips descended on hers. While their first kiss had started feather light, this intense kiss set off a flurry of feelings that overwhelmed her—love, longing, and something else that had her gripping the front of Paul's sweatshirt as if it were her last weak tether to the world outside the two of them. She could get lost in this—in him—so easily, and for the life of her she couldn't think why that would be a bad thing.

***

Paul trudged through the packed snow between the guesthouse and the Mueller's house. Snow shouldn't still be falling this far into March. He'd hit his limit with winter after the last two storms that left them holed up inside for a day or more. Had he been alone with Rachel, he was certain they could find a pleasant way to pass the time. As it was, he could only take so many movies, video games, and even sled riding. He'd even drafted an outline for the Civil War paper due at the end of the school year.

He stomped the snow off his boots as he climbed the steps to the Mueller's porch. More dirty snow fell onto the door mat as he kicked the toes of his boots against the house.

Once the snow melted and the trees began to bud, he could return to work at the orchard. He needed both a change of pace and a chance to earn money. He'd saved almost every penny earned the previous summer in his car account. Sean had enough of chauffeuring him around, especially since he lived with Amanda in a house a little farther away and not a hotel room a couple miles down the road.

Paul slid his warm hand out of his pocket and knocked on the door. His stomach grumbled. Saturday mornings beat all. Instead of cold cereal or a Pop-tart, he got to enjoy baked-from-scratch pancakes or waffles with the Muellers.

Paul twisted the cold doorknob and stepped inside. He expected the aroma of pancakes and maple syrup to greet him. Only the faint fragrance of laundry softener drifted through the basement door.

He spotted James on the living room floor with his pirate play set. His pirate tangent never ended. As usual, he wore a sash, skullcap, and eye patch.

Rachel reclined on the sofa, her knees bent and a notebook propped against them. She was so engrossed in her writing that with the pirate cries she hadn't noticed him knock and enter.

Her parents weren't anywhere in sight.

He approached Rachel slowly from behind and gently massaged her shoulders.

She slammed her hand over the notebook, effectively covering whatever she'd written.

He leaned forward. "What're you working on?"

She peered over her shoulder at him and smiled, her lips tight. "Just procrastinating on my chemistry assignment."

"Let's see what you've got." He reached for the notebook.

She shifted it off her lap and closed the front cover.

"Top secret assignment, huh?" He sat next to her on the couch.

"Something like that." She moved to toss the notebook onto the coffee table, but James snatched it from her hand.

"It's mine now, you landlubber." He flipped the

notebook back open and tore off for the other side of the room.

Rachel exploded off the couch and lunged for James.

A black, paper X stretched across the seat of her sweatpants. A strategically-placed piece of duct tape appeared to be holding it on. Paul tried to stifle his laughter, but a short laugh, a cross between a spit and a snort, burst from him.

"What?" Rachel scowled.

James had maneuvered his wiry body beyond her reach behind the end table.

Paul looked to James, who frantically waved his hands to discourage Paul from ratting him out.

Sorry, James. My allegiance lies with your sister.

"I guess X really does mark the spot, huh?" He motioned her back with a curl of his index finger, then turned her around.

She looked over her shoulder. "What is it?"

Paul leaned into her, using a serious but quiet voice. "I think a pirate may have laid claim to your booty."

"What?" Rachel twisted her hips. She spotted James's work and growled at her brother. "I'm going to kill you."

James darted down the hallway towards his room with Rachel in pursuit.

"James, if I catch you with that tape, I'll bind your wrists and tape you to a chair."

In less than a minute, she loped back to the living room, slightly winded, crushing a wadded-up ball of paper and duct tape in her hand.

Paul laughed. "I'm just sorry I'm not the pirate that got there first."

"Yeah, laugh it up." She snapped as she pounded his arm with her fist, but her poorly suppressed smile gave her away. "You didn't have to remove X's from the garbage can, the air return, and the toilet seat this morning."

Paul chuckled and sat on the couch again. "The toilet seat? You want me to give him a hard time?"

"Please."

James had the nerve to creep back into the living room, and Paul captured him and slung him over his shoulder.

"Mercy, mercy," James cried. "I'll give you the notebook. She's not doing homework. She's doodling your—"

Rachel narrowed her eyes and bit out each word with a snarl. "Say another word, and I'll kill you!"

Paul dropped James on his feet with a thud.

James pushed the notebook into Paul's face before he fled again.

Rachel's eyes widened in horror as Paul glanced at the open notebook.

In Rachel's neat, even strokes, it read, "Paul + Rachel" inside a hand-drawn heart with an arrow through it. Smaller hearts dotted the page, shaded with pencil and surrounded by wavy lines and flourishes. She had gone over the letters several times so that their names stood out on the page.

Paul looked to Rachel, her eyes less terror-stricken now than stunned. In the natural light, her irises shined in several blended shades of green. The dark striations and gold flecks mesmerized him. She bent her head and her lids shuttered closed. Her long, dark lashes stood in stark contrast to her fair skin.

He lifted her chin with his index finger.

Her eyes opened, wide and innocent.

"Don't be embarrassed."

She blinked rapidly and averted her gaze.

"Hey. I would write it in the sky if I could." He gave her a lopsided grin.

Rachel's features relaxed, and she smiled.

Her parents were still nowhere to be seen. He moved

closer and bent his head to kiss her when he was walloped from behind. He nearly butted heads with Rachel as James's body weight toppled them onto the couch.

"That's it." Rachel scrambled to her feet and grabbed the red- and black-striped length of fabric James used as a pirate sash. "Tie him up."

"Aye, aye, Captain." Paul tied James's wrists behind his back, leaving a lot of slack.

"You're worse than a chaperone, you know that?" He lifted James onto the coffee table. "Walk the plank."

With a shove, he forced James forward into a sea of pillows and furniture cushions.

James's grin stretched from ear to ear as he called out, "Scurvy dog!" and fell into the upholstered ocean.

Rachel pushed her fists into her hips. "Paul, you're supposed to discourage him, not give him more ideas."

James writhed on the floor and struggled with his bound wrists.

"Just trying to keep him occupied."

Paul took Rachel's hand and walked her behind the couch. "The scallywag's been marooned, beautiful lass." He pressed her into the back of the couch and stepped closer until their bodies touched.

Rachel grinned at him. "You don't play fair."

"So sue me."

Still no sign of her parents.

He feathered his hand up under her hair until he held her cheek in his palm and then lowered his head and kissed her—not the reckless kind of kiss he longed to give her, but enough to remind her how much she rocked his world.

When he opened his eyes again, hers were already wide open, startled, and focused on something or someone behind him.

The authoritative bass of her dad's voice made him cringe.

"Rachel, I'd like to speak to you. Now."

Uh-oh. Paul's muscles tensed and a ball of dread knotted in his gut. It was just a kiss, but Mr. Mueller had probably not expected to see his teenage daughter backed up against the couch like that. He turned to face him. "I'm sorry, sir, I shouldn't have—"

"No, you shouldn't have, Paul. It's time for you to leave. We'll talk later. "

"Yes, sir." Properly chastened, he headed back to the guesthouse and waited for the repercussions.

***

Wetness from Paul's kiss lingered on Rachel's lips, and while Dad's head was turned, she raised her sleeve to her mouth with as little motion as possible. The last thing she wanted was to draw his attention to her lips.

"Rachel, take a seat on the couch. James, go play in your room."

James stood staring as if he had no intention of vacating the living room. Dad added a stern, "Now."

Dad sat in front of her, on the edge of the coffee table, and rested his arms on his thighs. His narrowed eyes and the downward twist of his lips conveyed his meaning even without the words that followed. "Do you want to tell me what I just saw here?"

"Just a kiss." Rachel tucked her legs up underneath her. She wished she could disappear into the upholstery.

"The kiss doesn't bother me as much as the fact that the two of you were pressed so tightly together Flat Stanley couldn't have fit between you."

Rachel snickered, but when her dad caught her with a glare, she stopped and dropped her gaze.

"Honey, you may not mean anything by letting him do that, but at the least there's a subconscious message being sent, and believe me, a seventeen-year-old boy's body gets that message loud and clear. Those ten or fifteen seconds just fueled his fantasies for days. I don't care how nice a boy he is."

What was she supposed to say to that? The idea that she had a starring role in Paul's fantasies flattered her.

Her dad stood and paced toward the kitchen and back as he rubbed his unshaven jaw with his hand. "This is why your mother and I didn't want you dating until you were older."

Rachel set her feet back on the floor and leaned forward over her knees. "*You* brought him here, Dad."

Her dad sighed and rubbed the stubble on his chin with his thumb and forefinger. "Yes, I did, and I would do it again. It was the right thing to do, and in many ways, Paul feels like family."

He turned his attention to Rachel. "You're both good kids, good students, well-grounded in your faith, but you're teenagers, and you're infatuated."

Infatuated? Rachel bristled at the suggestion that she and Paul shared merely a superficial attraction, but she kept her mouth shut.

"Your mom and I didn't feel the need to say anything about your...your relationship, but maybe we've been naïve. Have we, Rachel? Have we been naïve?"

"No, Dad. All we've done is hold hands and kiss, I swear."

Her dad studied her for a few seconds then seemed to accept her answer.

"Just keep a little more space between the two of you, okay? And keep the kisses G-rated, all right?"

"Okay, Dad."

"Do I need to have this conversation with Paul too?"

Rachel shook her head. She could think of myriad ways she'd rather die than by extreme embarrassment.

"Okay." Her dad clapped his hands together and rubbed them a couple of times. "Pancakes: banana or chocolate chip?"

"How about banana-chocolate chip?"

"Done. Text lover boy, and tell him fifteen minutes."

Rachel winced. Her dad hadn't punished her, but he would make her pay.

Chapter 14
Precipice

"Rachel, you sure you don't want to come with us?"

Standing around in the biting cold wind watching little boys throw baseballs around or lounging on a soft bed with a good book and a pint of Ben & Jerry's? "I'm good here, Mom."

"Okay. We'll be back in a couple of hours." Her mom smiled and shut the door behind her.

She shuffled to her bedroom, selected her favorite playlist from her laptop music app, and turned on her e-reader. She paged through her unread books, chose a romantic suspense novel, and leaned against her headboard.

A movement outside caught her attention.

She set the e-reader on the bed and strolled to the window.

Paul? Her heart pounded against her chest. He'd opened his door and flung something out. Probably another stupid stink bug.

He wasn't supposed to be there. He told her this morning he was going to Sean and Amanda's for the day. What was he still doing here?

She pulled her coral-colored hoodie over her white, scooped-neck, tunic-length tee shirt and navy leggings. She paused the music and headed next door to find out what was up.

***

The crunch of gravel drifted to Paul's ears as the car pulled out of the driveway. James had baseball practice, so everyone would be gone for a couple of hours. Good. With no distractions, he could make some headway on that Civil War paper. He kicked his tennis shoes off and sat at the kitchen table to pore over the books one last time before he went to the laptop to write.

A soft knock on the door caught his attention. He hadn't heard a car pull up, and none of the fracking guys were around on a Saturday. He thought he was the only one on the property, so he peeked out the window before heading to the door.

Rachel?

His hand tingled as he opened the door. A blast of cold wind made him shiver.

"Hi." Her hair was pulled up in the back, highlighting the beautiful lines of her neck. She was so pretty, even without makeup.

"Hey, I thought you went to James's practice."

"I got a reprieve. I thought you were going to Sean's."

"Amanda's got strep, so they canceled."

The wind whipped at her hair, and he ushered Rachel in out of the cold. She tugged her sweatshirt off over her head, and her tee shirt lifted in the process—not so much that he could see bare skin, but enough that he could see the top of her leggings or yoga pants or whatever it was that until a few seconds ago had been all covered up. He forced himself to turn away.

"So your parents said you could stay, thinking I was gone for the day."

When he turned around again her shirt was back in place although he couldn't get over how soft and curvy she looked today.

She shrugged. "I guess so."

He knew he was already on thin ice with her dad, although there hadn't been a lecture, as expected. He should send her home, but he wouldn't. He couldn't. Besides, what would be the harm in them hanging out together for a while?

Paul ambled to the table and closed his history book. "Well, the War of Northern Aggression can't compete with you. What do you want to do?"

"We could play a game of Risk. With my dad out of the equation, we could see who's really the better strategist."

"My brain's already aching from all this stuff." He gestured to the thick book.

"We could go for a walk." She wrinkled her brow and scrunched up her face, not looking too thrilled with that idea.

Good, he wasn't either. "That wind is brutal."

She glanced around his little living space. There weren't too many ideas to be had there. "Well, we could watch a movie or something."

"Okay. Let's see what's on."

They sat on the loveseat, and Paul scrolled through the on-demand programming and then the channel guide, finding nothing of interest. "I think this is why I can count the times I've watched Saturday afternoon television on one hand."

Rachel pointed at the screen. "Wait. Go back. How about that piranha movie on the science fiction channel? It starts in five minutes."

"Okay." Just a B-movie, but maybe it would be good for a laugh. "Do you want anything?"

"Water sounds good."

Paul got them each a tall glass of ice water and sat next to her on the loveseat. The piranha flick wasn't half bad.

Rachel pulled her knees up on the loveseat, and Paul stretched his arm around her shoulders. This was good. They could spend the afternoon like this watching the movie and laughing at the low-budget special effects.

Three-quarters of the way through the movie and its increasingly long commercial breaks, Rachel turned and leaned back on the loveseat arm.

She stretched her legs across his lap.

Okay. What should he do with his arms? He laid them across her shins and knees, the legs encased in those silky, shimmery pants-things. Paul stared at her lying there. Beautiful. Her eyes so full of life, her lips so lush. And her tee shirt wasn't some one-size-fits-all garment—it was cut to fit her.

He should've sent her home. Unless she had a whole lot of self-control, they were headed for trouble. Just sitting with her knowing her parents weren't home was driving him crazy.

Paul shifted her legs off of him, leaned over top of her, and kissed her.

Whoa.

She kissed him with more urgency than he'd ever felt from her end of a kiss, and in an instant her arms were wrapped around his neck.

Somewhere in the background the commercials ended and the high-pitched screech that accompanied each piranha attack sounded. He freed a hand to grapple with the remote control and stabbed aimlessly at the buttons with his thumb until the screeching quieted.

Rachel slid down further onto the loveseat, her legs dangling off the side. The loveseat was way too small for...for what? How far could he let this go before it went *too* far? Maybe he should let her decide when to stop. She would know when they needed a breather.

Her fingers played with his hair at the nape of his neck. *Does she have any idea what she's doing to me?* He took his right arm from where it supported his weight above Rachel and slid it between their bodies, searching for a way under that overlong top that she wore. When his fingers finally touched her bare waist, she contracted her muscles, moving away from his hand.

He lifted his head. "You okay?"

She nodded, but her eyes looked doubtful.

"You pulled away. Do you want to stop?" *As if I could.*

"No, maybe slow down a little?" She sounded unsure.

Paul moved to kiss her neck, recalling how beautiful she'd looked standing on his doorstep. Mmmm. Her hair smelled like strawberries.

If she wanted to stop, she'd better say so soon. The possibility of that happening grew slimmer and slimmer with each passing minute.

She sighed and pulled his face to hers. The movement of her lips tickled his skin. "I love you."

Paul remembered hearing those words from one person. A person who would never say them to him again seeing as his remains rested six feet below the earth. Even the memory of those three syllables had faded. He hadn't realized until Rachel spoke them how much he craved those three little words.

He pulled away from her, and as his stare drilled into her green eyes, so filled with affection and desire, the floodgates opened.

"I love you too. I want you. I want to be part of you. Forever."

He kissed her again with a heat he could barely restrain, and though somewhere deep inside he knew it was past time to back off, he fumbled one-handed with the button on his jeans.

.

Chapter 15
Aftershocks

The unmistakable crunch of gravel beneath rubber tires made Rachel's breath catch. Mom and Dad's car! It may not be in sight yet, but in a minute it would be.

Paul's eyes widened.

Rachel sucked in a breath.

Oh, no. If her parents caught them . . .

In a flash Paul's bodyweight lifted, and he adjusted the fly on his jeans.

Rachel sat bolt upright, tugged her shirt down, grabbed her hoodie from the opposite end of the loveseat, and yanked it over her head. She freed her ponytail from the collar and glanced out the window. No sign of the car yet. If she left now she could run around the back of the house and let herself in before her parents or James caught sight of her.

"How do I look?" Her pulse pounded in her veins.

Paul studied her for a second and grimaced. "Your skin is glowing."

Not much she could do about that. She cinched her ponytail tighter and headed for the door with Paul on her heels.

She turned and gave him a quick kiss. "I meant it. I love you."

He stood there dumbstruck, his cheeks flushed and his hair tousled.

She took the three steps down from the guesthouse so fast that her foot caught on the last one, and she stumbled. With a hand to the ground, she steadied herself then ran behind her house.

No sooner had the door slammed behind her than the

car pulled in outside of the house. She couldn't believe she cut it that close. She dashed into the powder room and looked in the mirror.

I look guilty.

Paul was right. Her skin glowed, her cheeks flushed, and what was that mark on her neck? She yanked the band out of her hair and shook it free so that it covered her ears and neck. Then she plopped on the couch, grabbed a magazine, and tried to look nonchalant.

Her dad stepped in the doorway and dropped James's baseball gear in the entranceway. "Miss us much?"

She swallowed hard and willed herself to sound calm. "It didn't seem like you were gone very long."

Dad pinned her with a piercing look as if he were challenging her to look away.

James and her mom came in behind him, and he stepped aside so they could pass. He strolled to the kitchen, found a glass tumbler, and filled it with tap water. After taking a swig, he leaned on the counter. He lifted the glass to the light as if examining what was in it, then lowered it and drank the rest of his water.

Rachel paged through the cooking magazine hoping something would grab and hold her attention.

"Sean called on my cell."

Rachel's gaze darted back to her dad's and she worked to steady her breathing.

"He checks in now and then. Wants to know how things are going with Paul." He set his empty glass in the sink. "He mentioned Amanda is sick. Said they had to nix their plans with Paul today."

He wanted to know if she and Paul had been together this afternoon. Her first instinct was to lie, but she didn't lie. Period. It only led to more trouble anyway.

"Yeah, that's what Paul said. I didn't realize he was even here until after you left, and I saw him."

"So, you didn't know beforehand he'd be here?"

"No, Dad." She tried to keep the patronizing tone out of her voice, but his mistrust grated on her. "Neither of us knew the other was here."

"So, you *did* spend the afternoon together?"

What could she say? She already admitted they had spoken, and there were no set rules about them spending time together. "We watched this cheesy movie about piranhas attacking people." She flipped the magazine page, trying to act casual.

"Hmmm. Did you ever notice how in those movies it's always the couples that are fooling around that are killed off first?" He pushed off the counter and walked toward her.

Rachel swallowed. He couldn't know; there was no way. "I didn't notice. The piranha seemed like equal opportunity feeders."

"Pay attention, Rachel. Horror movies are filled with social commentary."

She needed to end this conversation. "I'm going to read in my room."

She tossed the magazine onto the coffee table and walked to her room, careful not to go so fast that it would seem suspicious. Why was she riddled with guilt anyway? They had only kissed. And, okay, Paul touched her midriff. And he was sort of lying on top of her—no room for Flat Stanley again.

Of course, had her parents been five minutes later, there might have been a whole lot more for her to feel guilty about. She didn't want to think about that.

***

Paul paced the room, biting his lower lip and shaking his head.

What had he been thinking? He hadn't thought. He felt. A riot of crazy, intense emotions: love, desire, exhilaration.

And then there were the other things he literally felt: her skin, her hair, and her entire body under his hands, lips, and fingertips.

She had made it back to her house before her parents stopped the car, but just barely.

If her dad had walked in on them, he'd be looking at the business end of that triple-barrel shotgun right now. Without a doubt, he'd be kicked off their property. What would have happened if Rachel's parents hadn't come home when they did? His own dad wasn't around to care. But what would he say if he were?

He recalled Dad's words—spoken not to him, but Sean.

Three or four weeks had passed since Sean's junior prom. Paul lay in bed, asleep until the noise of three successive door slams and then Dad's voice, angrier than the time Sean had taken Dad's truck for a joy ride without permission—or a license. He couldn't recall where Sean had been that night, out with friends probably, but Dad must've been loaded for bear before Sean returned.

Through two closed doors, his and Sean's across the hall, he heard only snippets of the tongue-lashing. The loudest remarks carried right through the wooden barriers: "What were you thinking?" "You damn well better be," and "Are we clear on this?" The other words were mere fragments gleaned from things said when Dad stood close to the door. "Responsibility," "selfishness," "ashamed," and "sin." The only whole sentences he got, the ones that echoed in his mind now, bursting through his consciousness out of nowhere, were spoken as Dad had opened Sean's door and probably had one foot in the hall. "You don't show a young woman you care by putting her at risk. A man protects her. He's virtuous, not selfish."

The door shut a final time. Nothing but silence came from across the hall. Soon music seeped up through the floor from the basement. Songs that reminded Dad of

Mom. He'd never said that, but it didn't take a genius to figure out. Dad played the same six or seven songs, over and over late at night on anniversaries, birthdays, and whenever something had him down.

Neither Dad nor Sean spoke of what happened, but Sean didn't go anywhere except school and work for an entire month, and Paul never heard mention of his prom date again. Paul's thirteen-year-old self didn't expend energy dwelling on it or deducing Sean's offense. His seventeen-year-old self connected the dots with ease.

The advice Dad would give him about Rachel became crystal clear.

Paul paced and berated himself until his cell phone ringtone sounded. He glanced at the caller ID: Rachel.

"Hey, it's me. Mom says dinner will be ready in forty-five minutes."

Her family might've been in earshot, and she couldn't say more. But he could.

"I'm sorry, Rachel. That never should have happened."

"I feel the same way. See you in a little while." She ended the call sounding as contrite as he felt.

He grabbed his iPod from the end table and put his ear buds in. What would Dad's iPod have to say about this?

"Touching you is easy,
Loving you is hard.
Our minds may say 'no,'
But our hearts say, 'let's go'."

Paul growled, ripped the ear buds out of his ears, and tossed them on the table. He flopped onto the loveseat, the one he'd never look at the same way again, and exhaled.

He'd dwelled so much on what might've happened that he'd forgotten what *did* happen. Rachel told him she loved him. And he told her what he'd known since almost the first month he spent there—he loved her too, and he wanted to be with her forever.

Was it crazy to think about marriage at seventeen? He longed for a normal life with a family to come home to every night. He couldn't imagine anything that would satisfy him more than coming home to Rachel for the rest of his life.

It had been so good to feel her fingers in his hair, her hands on his neck, and her arms around his body. He thought back to the dinner conversation at Sean and Amanda's house last weekend. Amanda read aloud from some relationship book and then tried to get Sean to take a test to determine his "love language." She claimed that hers was "quality time." She suspected Sean's was "words of affirmation," but she wanted him to complete the questionnaire. Paul had thought it was an interesting concept. After Amanda gave him a thumbnail sketch of the five love languages, he hadn't any idea what his was. He would've asked to take the quiz if it weren't for the fact that Sean would rib him about it for the rest of his life. How hadn't he seen it before? His love language: physical touch.

Hadn't his dad claimed he was a clingy child? And even Sean had grown weary of his wanting to wrestle him. He'd never felt more proud than when Dad had patted his back or put an arm around his shoulder and never more godforsaken than when he'd spanked him. No one had ever touched him the way Rachel had this afternoon, with such love and tenderness. How had he gone this long without that, and how could he continue without a steady dose of it?

Chapter 16
Playing by the Rules

The aroma of homemade marinara sauce filled the house. Rachel's belly growled, and she slapped a hand over it. She never did get around to that ice cream she'd planned on downing.

She hoped dinner wouldn't be too awkward.

Paul slipped through the door a few minutes before they sat down to eat. Just the sight of him still wearing the jeans and rugby shirt he'd had on this afternoon caused a sense of euphoria to spread from her head to her toes. Her heart accelerated, the nerve endings in her hands tingled, and it suddenly became difficult to swallow. She feared it would be a long, uncomfortable night.

Rachel felt a soul-deep closeness to Paul that she'd never felt before and a cool distance from her parents that hadn't been there before either.

The conversation at dinner flowed naturally, but Paul avoided eye contact with Dad. Mom invited Paul to stay for a movie, and Rachel and Paul welcomed James to sit between them on the couch; he provided a good buffer. Once the movie was over, Mom ordered James to bed. He dragged his feet toward his room, succumbing to a loud yawn.

Mom straightened the pillows on the couch, grabbed the empty glasses on the end tables, and placed them in the kitchen sink.

"I'm going to read in bed for a while, Linda," Dad said to Mom.

Her parents retiring for the night typically marked Paul's cue to leave. Dad glanced between Rachel and Paul, as if waiting for them to say their goodnights.

"Dad, would it be okay if Paul stayed a while so we could talk?"

Dad cast a look at Mom.

Rachel's cheeks warmed, and for the hundredth time, she wondered if they had an idea what she and Paul had been doing before they arrived.

Seconds ticked by as Dad looked at Mom, shook his head once, and breathed a sigh. Paul's feet shuffled closer behind her.

"Please, Dad. It would mean a lot to me."

Dad let out another breath as he massaged his forehead.

"You'll be right down the hall with the door open, Dad." She smiled sweetly and batted her eyes for good measure.

"Okay, tonight, Rachel," Dad said, "but we're not going to make this a habit."

"No, Dad. We won't be long. I promise."

Her parents headed down the hall, speaking in low tones to one another.

Rachel sat in the middle of the couch and patted the cushion next to her.

Paul sat, ramrod straight, and rubbed his palms on his jeans.

Leaning into his field of vision, Rachel smiled and peered up at him. "Don't worry. Everything's good."

He angled himself toward her and steadied his bouncing knee with his hand. Paul glanced down the hall then looked her in the eye. "Rachel, please forgive me. This afternoon..." His gaze flitted toward the window and then back to her. His sad, guilty expression made her want to skip all the apologies and hug him. "I should never have let it go that far."

"I'm sorry too." She twisted her hands in her lap then folded them together. "Let's face it—I started it. I knocked on your door, I plopped my legs on your lap, and when you asked if I wanted to stop, I, uh, didn't exactly take you up on it."

"Yeah, well, let's say there's enough blame to go around. Still...somewhere in the back of my mind, I knew where things were headed as soon as you walked through my door."

Rachel sighed. "Me too." She dropped her gaze to her hands and then, finding a little courage, searched those blue eyes that she loved so well. "Can I ask you something?"

"Anything."

"Have you ever been with a girl before?"

Paul's eyes widened, and his eyebrows shot up. "You mean have I..."

She nodded as her cheeks warmed.

"No. Why would you think that?"

Rachel twisted her hands in her lap again and tilted her head down. "I didn't think of it before, but you seemed to know what you were doing more than I did." She bit her lip and met his gaze.

Paul shrugged. "Following instinct, I guess."

She had assumed Paul was a virgin, but his confirmation reassured her. For as long as she could remember, her parents had instilled in her that sex was reserved for a husband and wife. Despite how things had spiraled out of control earlier, she agreed with them, in theory. She hadn't anticipated the amount of fortitude required for putting that belief into practice. Still, in her heart, she wanted to wait for her wedding night, and she expected her future husband to do the same.

Paul took one of her hands in his. "I'd better go. I've got that Civil War paper to work on."

"Do you have to? It's only been a few minutes." *That came out way too whiny.*

"I do. I didn't get much done this afternoon." He grinned.

She smiled. "Sorry about that too."

"It's okay." Paul's eyes darted back to the hallway and then his hand caught the back of her head as he pulled her toward him. He kissed her with the self-assurance of a guy who knew he was loved. It didn't have all the fiery explosiveness of this afternoon's kiss, but it felt less tenuous. As he ended the kiss and stroked her hair, his eyes glistened with warmth. "Can I hear you say it one more time?"

She smiled. She knew what he wanted to hear, but seeing his eagerness, she couldn't resist teasing him just a little. "What? Have you ever been with a girl before?"

His hand dropped away, and he narrowed his eyes.

She laughed.

He smiled and tweaked her nose. "No—you know. You're not going to make me beg, are you?"

Tempting, but no. "I love you, Paul."

He kissed her one last time, and only one word described the feeling it left her with: cherished.

"I love you, Rachel."

She walked him to the door, still wishing he could stay a little longer.

"Maybe we can come up with some ground rules." Paul kept his voice low so her parents couldn't hear. "You know, to keep us from crossing the line again."

"Sounds like a good idea. I'll think about it." She gave him one more quick kiss before he jogged down the steps and back to the guesthouse.

***

Rachel genuflected and slid into the pew after her mom. As she lowered the kneeler into place, Paul scooted in beside her. He usually attended Mass with Sean and Amanda, but since Amanda was sick...

Rachel and Paul knelt. She dropped her head onto her hands and forced herself to focus, if even for a minute, on something other than Paul.

Her stream-of-consciousness mental prayer ran the gamut from thanking God for doing well on her algebra test to asking Him to bless her and Paul and seeking forgiveness if they had ventured into sinful territory.

She tried to pay attention to what was happening, but as the priest wrapped up his homily, she realized her mind had wandered, roamed, and wandered some more. She stared at Paul's hand, marveling at how it folded perfectly over hers as it rested on his leg. His freshly-pressed khaki pants creased neatly at the knee. She closed her eyes and concentrated on how it felt to have his thigh next to hers and his hand holding hers so tightly. Was it sinful to be turned on by sitting next to your boyfriend at Mass? She hoped not, because she couldn't help it.

Paul spent the afternoon working on his Civil War paper but returned to Rachel's house before dinner. He and Rachel sat together on the cushions in front of the bay window—out of earshot, but not out of sight of her parents and James.

Rachel pulled her knees up to her chest and spoke softly. "So, we were going to come up with some rules, right?" She pushed her hair behind her ear and hugged her knees tighter. "What have you got?"

Paul gave her a lopsided smile. "Here's the thing. When I try to think of ways to keep my hands off of you, I end up thinking about putting my hands all over you, and I'm trying really hard not to go there. So…I've got nothing."

Rachel smiled. "I'll have to do the thinking for both of us then." She let her knees drop and crossed her legs at the ankle. "I think maybe we should avoid being totally alone together for long periods of time."

"How long is 'long?'"

Rachel shrugged.

"Okay. Exact time to be determined." He unfolded his legs so that they stretched out next to hers. "Anything else?"

"No touching below the waist and above the knee."

Paul took a few seconds to think about that one. "You've got to give me a little more than that. How about, uh, six inches above the knee?"

Rachel glanced down and measured it visually. "Good enough. One more."

"Shoot."

"No hands under clothing."

He leaned his head back against the wall in mock exasperation, and it made a small thud. "You're killing me." He laid a hand over his heart.

"You'll live. I promise." She smiled, took hold of both his hands, and pulled his upper body away from the wall.

"And you think we can do this indefinitely?"

She detected a mixture of resignation and frustration in his question. She tried to match it with confidence. "Of course."

"You sound pretty sure of yourself, Little Miss Tease."

She folded her arms over her chest. "I am not a tease. This is all new to me, and I got caught up in the heat of the moment."

He leaned forward and pried her arms loose so he could hold her hands. "This is new to me too. I *am* sorry. And then again, I'm not. I love you." He leaned in closer and whispered. "I want to make love to you."

They were going to have to come to terms with their limitations somehow. She was barely sixteen, and it was going to be a long wait—one she hoped Paul was willing to endure.

*　*　*

Rachel yanked another weed from the soil and tossed it

onto the growing pile. She peeled off a garden glove and wiped her hand across her forehead. Summer wouldn't officially begin for another three weeks, but the sun's rays already heated her enough to break a sweat.

Paul's shovel sliced another patch of earth behind her. Several seconds of silence passed, then dead leaves crackled. Rachel knew without turning that Paul had tossed a handful of rocks into the brush. They'd been working side-by-side in the garden every chance they'd had for the past several weeks, and his dig, scoop, and toss pattern seldom varied.

The familiarity, ease, and, most of all, the love that had grown between them over the last months awed her. She smiled as she sat back on her heels and spied their small pile of treasures lying in the drying mud: a piece of broken whiskey bottle, a shard of pottery, and a pocket knife. It didn't amount to much considering they spent nearly all their free time digging.

Sometimes, like this afternoon, Rachel tended her fledgling garden while Paul dug around the perimeter. He'd started in a rather haphazard fashion but proceeded in an organized manner, hoping to come across what might be another piece of the wagon. They were close to finding something; she could feel it.

Paul slogged toward her and leaned against his shovel. "I need a break."

Rachel rocked back into a sitting position and tugged off her other glove. "Me too."

Paul grinned and shook his head. "So...she asked you straight out if we'd done it?"

Rachel nodded, recalling in vivid detail the shopping excursion Mom had orchestrated a couple of days earlier. "Yes, and she left me no escape."

Saturday morning the rain had come down in buckets. Paul and Sean went with James and Dad to the indoor batting cages. Mom suggested the two of them do a little clothes shopping. Unlike other girls she knew, Rachel enjoyed shopping with her mom. They browsed, they bought, and they always indulged in frozen yogurt at the mall food court. The shopping trip was ordinary, but the ride home threw Rachel for a loop.

Mom had barely eased the car out of the parking lot when the smile slipped from her face and she bit her lower lip. "Rachel, I know this is uncomfortable, but I have to ask you."

"What?" Rachel couldn't imagine what kind of uncomfortable question needed asking.

Her mom hesitated a second and then blurted it out. "Have you and Paul had sex?"

Rachel's eyes widened, and she stared at her mom, whose attention was fixed on the road. It took a second to make her mouth work.

"Are you kidding?" Rachel's body tensed. Uncomfortable didn't begin to cover it. "No, Mom, we haven't."

It dawned on her that Mom had set her up with both the shopping trip and the ride home. She was held captive in the passenger seat of Mom's Chevy Impala barreling down the highway at 65 mph. Mom was determined to have this conversation whether Rachel wanted to or not.

"I trust you, Rachel, and I know we've talked about this, but in general terms. Before Paul came into your life. I know you care about each other, and the living situation provides more opportunity than your dad and I would like for you two to get in over your heads."

How should she respond? She could clam up and limit herself to monosyllabic grunts while she waited for the awkward conversation to pass, or she could tell Mom the truth. Her mom had never given Rachel a hard time about Paul, and in some ways, she seemed to encourage their relationship.

Rachel breathed deeply. How should she word it? "I'd be lying if I said we weren't tempted, but I want to wait until we're married."

"You've talked about *marriage*?"

Mom's voice came out high and strained. Why did she sound so shocked? Wasn't that what a man and woman did when they loved each other—got married?

"Well, not exactly." They hadn't spoken about it, but she knew that's what they both wanted. "I'll rephrase it. I want to wait until *I'm* married."

"You do, but what about Paul?"

She paused, thinking back over their conversations. They'd agreed things had gone too far, and they should keep that from happening again. She assumed they were waiting for marriage, but she couldn't remember Paul saying that. What *was* he waiting for? For her to turn eighteen? Or until they were "ready"? Whatever that meant. "He wants to wait too...I think. I mean, we haven't talked about it in all that much detail."

Mom's grip on the steering wheel tightened until her knuckles turned white. "Well, even if he agrees you should wait until after marriage, that could be a long time. Good intentions are great, but sometimes things can go farther than either of you expect. I want you to be smart about keeping yourself out of those situations. I know it's hard. Your dad is concerned about how close the two of you have become, so don't be surprised if he lays down the law about you two being alone together."

Mom was trying to help, but it didn't feel that way. It felt like meddling and controlling, and it left Rachel feeling childish and rebellious. "Not that it's any of your business—"

"Stop right there." Her mom took her attention off the road long enough for Rachel to see the anger in her eyes. "I don't like to say it this way, but maybe you need to hear it.

You're sixteen. You're a minor child. It *is* my business."

She wanted to snap back at her mom but bit her tongue. Rachel paused and waited for her anger to subside. "I'm trying to say we have rules. Some things to keep us from going too far."

"Good." Her mom's voice softened and her grip on the steering wheel loosened. "Dad and I want what's best for you. We're not just old fogeys, you know. We were young and in love once too. We don't want you to do something you're going to regret later—for all sorts of reasons."

Rachel relaxed into her seat. She didn't want regrets either. She didn't want to do anything to mar this amazing thing she and Paul had discovered between them.

They approached a stop sign, and as the car slowed, her mom turned to her and smiled. "Rachel, you picked a good one. Paul's handsome, he's smart, and most importantly, he's an upstanding young man."

She had recounted most of the conversation to Paul as they had walked to the bus this morning. If he was still thinking about it, it must've unnerved him as much as it did her.

"I'm glad you were honest with her." The late afternoon sun winked through the leaves overhead. "We don't have anything to hide. Well, not much." He extended his hand to Rachel.

Rachel took it and stood. She brushed the dirt and leaves from her knees and her behind. "I know. It was just...irritating." She reached for his shovel. "I'll dig for a while."

He relinquished the shovel and bent to tighten his shoe lace. "It's her job to watch out for you."

She pushed the spade into a patch of clay and pressed down with her foot.

Paul grabbed the garden rake from where it leaned against the log bench. "Believe me, there are plenty of times I could've used a mother looking out for me like yours does. Be grateful that you have a mother and that she cares."

Rachel's heart twinged. She stopped digging and turned her attention to him. "I'm sorry. I didn't mean to be so insensitive. I shouldn't take her for granted, huh?"

He shrugged. "Just giving you another perspective."

Rachel resumed digging. "And I appreciate it. Really. I guess it kind of hurt that she didn't trust me. Does she think I'm lowering a rope for you to climb into my bedroom at night or something?"

Paul let the rake fall to the ground and came up behind her, wrapping his arms around her waist. "Now, why didn't I think of that? You could unlock the door, and I could slip into the house and between the sheets..." She could feel him fighting a smile as he kissed her hair.

She turned around and reached her hands around his neck. "You're bad."

Paul kissed her, short and sweet. "Not according to your mom. She said I was—and I quote—'an upstanding young man.'"

"Yeah, well, don't let it go to your head." She released him and picked up her shovel.

Paul reclaimed his rake and walked toward a few small mounds of overturned soil.

He hadn't had any luck where he was digging, so Rachel decided to try a little further out along the hillside, hoping she'd find something beneath the coal. She'd lifted a few inches of coal and dirt when she found what looked like a piece of broken brown glass.

"See," she called, "I've found a hot spot. I'm telling you, we're close to something." She tossed the glass aside. She'd add it to their collection later.

"I hope so."

Rachel sunk the shovel less than a foot from where she

had turned up the broken bottle shard.

The ground shifted beneath her.

She planted her feet in the soil to steady herself, but the earth gave way, and the shovel slipped through her fingers.

She slid downward.

Dirt spilled into her eyes and her mouth. She clawed at dirt and air around her, searching for a root, a rock, anything to grasp.

She fell, and her stomach lurched. More dirt hit her face, and she choked on a scream. Then she hit bottom, landing hard on her tailbone, dirt continuing to rain down upon her.

A sharp pain seared her left leg, and she let out a groan. Her knee twisted unnaturally. Blood seeped through her old work jeans around her knee and shin. Above her, only dirt and a small patch of blue sky were visible.

"Paul!" The hoarse scream scraped her throat, and she coughed and spit bits of dirt from her mouth.

Paul didn't answer.

Her heart raced. Panic struck every nerve ending in her body. She cried out his name again, spurring more coughing.

"Rachel! What happened? Where are you?" He came closer, and she recognized an emotion she'd never heard in his voice before—fear.

She shifted her weight hoping to get a better view through the narrow hole. The instant she moved, the pain skyrocketed, and she moaned.

Once the pain subsided, she squinted through the bright hole above her. Paul's head came into view, a shadow blocking what little light she had. He must've heard her cry out in pain.

"Please, Paul—help me! Get me out of here!" Terror consumed her. The small space that trapped her pressed in—cool, dank, and dark. She shivered from head to toe.

A few crumbs of dirt tumbled down and into her hair. Paul backed away from the hole. Where had he gone?

"Paul!" This time a sob caught on the end of his name. "Where are you?"

His face reappeared, and it looked as if he were lying flat against the ground. He probably couldn't see a thing below.

"I'm right here. Hang on. I'm just trying to figure out..."

The panic in his voice matched hers. He didn't say anything for a few interminable seconds. Her anxiety level crept higher and higher until she thought she might lose it.

Chapter 17
Subsidence

"I've got to get help, Rachel." Paul hoped he didn't sound as panicked as he felt.

He'd followed the sound of Rachel's moan and discovered her at the bottom of a hole about twelve feet deep and two feet across. Dirt trickled down the sides of the hole. From where he lay, he could make out Rachel's leg wrenched in an awkward position. Had she broken it? He'd seen that awkward twisted position once before while watching a major league football game. If—*when*—she got out of there, she might need surgery and months of recovery.

"Paul, get me out of here." Her voice cracked, and she cried. The pain and fear in her voice stung him.

More dirt dribbled in on her. What if the whole thing collapsed? "Rachel, don't move. I'm going to get help, and I'll be right back. Just don't try to move, okay?"

"Please don't leave me, Paul. I'm scared." She sobbed.

A stabbing pain ripped through his heart. He hated leaving her, but he had no choice. "I...I have to get help, Rachel. I can't get you out of there by myself." Why hadn't he bothered to bring his cell phone with him?

Paul took off running.

Rachel's parents had taken James to a baseball clinic more than an hour away, so he ran for the drilling site. As he ran, Paul recalled the morning. Rachel's mom sought reassurance about where he and Rachel would be and exactly what they'd be doing while her parents were out. He tried to blend into the wooden paneling in the Muellers' kitchen, wishing they'd be gone a long time. Now he wished they'd never left.

Paul dodged a fallen tree limb as he cleared the tree line and crossed the grassy meadow between Rachel's garden and the drilling site. He dashed through the high grass, which stretched about the length of two and a half football fields. A temporary fence lined the southern and western sides of the site. Paul approached from the northwest, from where he could see three men surrounding a large pipe at the base of the rig. Sean wasn't among them. A yellow tanker truck beeped loudly as it crawled backwards.

"Sean! Sean!" They'd never hear him over the truck backing. He yelled louder. "Sean!" The smell of diesel fumes and dust invaded his nostrils.

He couldn't see Sean yet, but one of the other guys called, "Hey, Porter, your brother."

Sean emerged from behind an above-ground tank, standing on a raised platform about six feet high. By the pinch of his lips and his narrowed eyes, he already sensed that something bad had happened.

Sean gripped the metal rail with one hand, jumped from the platform, and jogged toward Paul. "What is it?"

Paul sprinted and closed the final yards between them.

"Your cell phone." Paul extended his hand, palm up, wiggling his fingers. "Quick!"

Sean whipped out his phone and slapped it into Paul's hand.

Paul fumbled with it, his hands so jittery he had difficulty tapping the numbers. He punched in 9-1-1 and plugged his other ear with a finger to minimize the background noise. It did nothing to muffle the repeated beep as another truck backed up. His gaze locked on Sean, who listened intently, waiting to find out what was going on.

"9-1-1. What's your emergency?"

"I need help. It's my girlfriend. She fell into a hole."

"A hole?"

"A sinkhole or something. She's about twelve feet down, and I can't reach her."

"Is she conscious?"

"Yeah, yeah, but I think her leg..." Paul caught his breath. "...it might be broken, and I'm scared it's all going to fall in on her."

Sean's eyes widened, and he threw his safety helmet to the ground. "Where is she?"

Paul gave the operator the location as he motioned toward the garden room for Sean's benefit. Sean and a couple of the other guys took off in the general direction, but they had no idea that the garden room existed let alone how to get to it. Paul ran behind them.

"Where are you?"

"North. North of Renovo."

"Can you give me your address?"

"Oh, yeah." Paul rattled the address. "There's a gas well here."

"Up on the right," Paul called to Sean. "Behind that fir tree."

Sean and the other guys slowed and studied the ground, stepping carefully through the deep grass.

Paul ended the call and raced ahead, pitching Sean his phone as he passed him. Paul led them under the branches and through the brambles until he reached the garden. "Over here!" he called.

***

Small clumps of dirt rained onto Rachel's head and shoulders, piling on the ground around her. With every ounce of dirt that fell, her heart pounded harder. Rachel gasped for a breath, then another. Her breaths came too quickly, but she didn't know how to stop herself. Her head grew light and her vision fuzzy. She blinked rapidly and gave her head a shake. Was she getting enough oxygen? Was she suffocating? What if the entire thing caved in and buried her alive? Still unable to move her leg, she imagined trying to claw her way through the dirt, and tears rolled down her cheeks.

Rachel had no sense of how long Paul had been gone. Five minutes? Fifteen? What if he didn't come back?

She screamed.

She sobbed.

She turned her heart to God.

"Please, Lord, please don't let me die like this. Please." She rubbed her tears away with her hand. The grit mixed with tears abraded her skin like fine-grit sandpaper. At last voices sounded in the distance.

"Paul?" She craned her neck upward, trying to glimpse him.

His face appeared at the top of the hole, cutting off the light. "I'm back." His voice came out breathless.

"Paul, I'm so scared, and I can't move my leg."

"Help's on the way, Rachel."

"The dirt... it keeps falling."

"I know."

He turned and spoke to someone. What was he saying? If someone else was up there, why couldn't they get her out?

"Are you insane?" Sean's voice, tense and loud.

Paul said something she couldn't make out and then Sean spoke again, not as loud this time. "How is two people stuck in a hole better than one? And what if you cause the whole thing to fall in?"

He muttered something, and Sean's protests stopped.

"Rachel," Paul called. "Lean to the left. I'm going to drop in right next to you."

***

Paul sat carefully on the dirt at the edge of the hole, the dirt crumbling under his weight. His heart raced and his muscles tensed. The smell of fresh earth, a smell he normally enjoyed, but which now choked him, filled his nose and mouth.

Please, Lord, let it hold.

He swung his legs into the hole, then lowered himself as far as he could while still holding on with his arms.

Then he let go.

He landed with a soft thud alongside Rachel. Dirt rolled down on top of them, and he covered his head with his hands.

"What are you doing?" Rachel grabbed his sleeve, tugging him closer.

He shook off the dirt and maneuvered behind her, careful not to touch her legs. He cradled her broken body and let her lean against his chest. A siren wailed in the distance.

"Hang on, Rachel, they're going to get us out of here."

"You okay?" Sean called down to him.

"Yeah. Fine. Great." He shouldn't be sarcastic. The worry etched on Sean's face was genuine. "I'm okay."

Blood soaked Rachel's jeans around her left knee, and her leg twisted in an unnatural direction. It made his stomach roil, and he had to look away.

"How are your legs?"

She groped for his hands to hold onto. "I don't know. My left leg hurts. It was a sharp pain at first, then nothing, but now it's kind of a dull ache. I don't think I can move it."

"Okay, we're going to take care of you. Sean's calling your mom and dad, and the ambulance will be here any minute."

Paul stroked her head. Grime mixed with sweat along her temples, and sandy dirt caked her hair. Her body trembled as she sat propped against him, and she took quick, shallow breaths.

"You're going to be okay, Rachel. We're gonna get you

out of here." He rubbed her trembling arm then held her closer, hoping to warm her. What else could he do?

God, don't let her die.

Paul remembered being ten-years-old and sick. He'd convinced himself the final throes of death gripped him. To his credit, Dad didn't dismiss or laugh at his fears. Instead, he prayed with him. Paul repeated the same prayer now for Rachel.

He whispered into her hair. "Lord, if it be Your will, let this cup pass. Let this cup pass us by."

He wiped dirt and tears from Rachel's face, then kissed her temple. "It's going to be okay," he whispered again and again until he knew by the approach of the loud, shrill siren of an emergency vehicle that help had arrived.

Firefighters clustered around the top of the hole. One, two, at least three of them. Sean's voice was frantic as he told them what had happened.

Paul felt a stab of guilt. He must've scared the tar out of Sean by dropping into the godforsaken hole.

One firefighter's gruff voice boomed over the others. "He went down there with her?" Sean said something, and then the gruff man responded. "Well, as long as he's unhurt, maybe he can help get her out of there."

Rachel had grown quiet, and her hands had turned cool and clammy. Had she lost consciousness? Would that be a good thing or a bad thing? She slouched forward, so he tightened his grip around her waist and scooted closer to her. He shifted his right leg so that she fit snugly against him.

Paul nudged her left leg with his own as he solidified his position, and she groaned.

What was taking so long up there?

As he gazed up at the hole, which despite the falling dirt was still less than a yard in diameter, he glimpsed only the tops of men's heads. He heard only bits of the conversation, but it sounded like they were discussing whether the hole would hold if they attempted to reinforce the opening. Finally, one of the firefighters called to him.

"We're going to lower a light down to you and then some rope. Once you've got it, I'll explain how we'll get you out of there."

Another head hovered over the opening. "Paul, can you tell us anything about Rachel's injuries?"

"Uh. I don't know if she's conscious anymore. She's not moving or talking. Her left leg looks..." He peered over her head at the leg, his stomach tightening with dread. "It's all twisted and bloody. There's blood...it's all over. She's kind of cold and shaking?"

They lowered ropes which were meant to act as a hammock. How was he going to help Rachel into the ropes without injuring her any further?

Paul gently placed her head against the ground. She didn't make a sound. He moved around to get a better look at her. Her skin was pasty white beneath the dirt that smeared her face, but with such little light trickling in, he wasn't sure if that was her true color.

Paul grabbed her around the waist. "I'm gonna get you into this rope hammock. Gentle as I can. Then they're gonna lift you out of here, okay?"

She draped her listless arms around his neck.

He kept his movements slow and steady and tried not to jostle her bad leg as he lifted her into a seated position on the rope sling. He feared hurting her more, but he had to move her. He lifted her legs across the opposite end of the sling.

She winced and cried out in pain.

"We're getting you out of here now." He swallowed back tears. "Sean's up there, and he'll make sure they take good care of you."

She looked at him, but her eyes didn't seem to focus.

He kissed Rachel's forehead. He'd thought when they'd made out on the loveseat that day he knew the depth of true love and its desperation. That experience, as much as it still thrilled him, had nothing on the kind of feelings this anguish evoked.

"Okay. She's in position," he called to the men above.

The men up top adjusted the length of the ropes so that she would come out head first with her lower body trailing. Despite the safety harness clipped securely to her waist, he feared she'd somehow fall and readied himself to catch her at any moment. He assumed they moved at a snail's pace on purpose, so that they didn't disturb the unsettled earth. Here and there dirt fell onto him as they raised her, but it didn't amount to much.

Rachel cried as they eased her legs out and moved her to a stretcher. He wished her parents were there for her, but he hadn't heard them up above yet.

"It hurts...please don't touch it. Don't move it." Her weak voice echoed her distress.

A lump formed in Paul's throat. Couldn't someone reassure her or soothe her?

"Hang in there, Rachel. They're going to take care of you." Sean's voice.

Paul let out a puff of air and relaxed his shoulders. Tack another item onto the list of things for which he owed his older brother. Paul wouldn't forget this one.

"Okay, kid. Your turn." Another rope dropped into the hole.

Paul grabbed hold of it.

"You're going to stand up in it as we pull you out. Got it?"

"Yeah. Okay." He stepped on the two lengths of rope that spanned the bottom and gripped the side ropes with both hands.

"Here we go," one of the firefighters called.

The ropes jerked, and Paul felt himself being raised. His head remained about a foot below the surface when some of the dirt started to give way. He hunched his shoulders to protect his face as soil tumbled over him.

Again, he inched slowly upward.

Suddenly, Paul was falling. He yelped, and his stomach lurched up into his throat. A jerk on the lines stopped his freefall, and he dangled a yard above the bottom. One of the firefighters must have lost his grip on the line.

"Hang tight, Paul," one of the firefighters called. "We've got you."

Paul gripped the rope so hard his knuckles whitened, but in a few minutes, when the dirt had settled again, they raised him out.

Where had they taken Rachel? Paul scanned the area. He zeroed in on two ambulances and moved to break through the small crowd of malingerers, but a strong hand gripped his forearm.

"Hold up there, kid. Let's check you out."

"I'm fine." Paul tugged his arm away and glanced up at the towering man in full firefighter gear. "I'm not hurt. Where's Rachel?"

After giving him a visual once-over to make sure he was okay, the firefighter groused at him for getting down in the hole in the first place. Admittedly, Paul hadn't given much thought to the wisdom of that move. He probably owed Sean an apology, but he couldn't stand Rachel being alone down there, hurt and scared.

Sean pushed his way into the circle of rescue people and hugged Paul. "Come on," he said in a low voice. "I'll take you to Rachel. She's waiting."

"Why didn't they take her to the hospital already?"

Sean shook his head. "She may be beat up, but she was adamant about not leaving here while you were still down there."

Paul jogged toward the emergency vehicles, and Sean

kept pace. "That's crazy. She's bleeding all over the place. She needs medical attention." He understood she was scared and wanted him near, but they were talking about her life here.

"She's getting it. The fracture, uh, cut through her skin they said." He winced. "I guess they figured they could get things started here, and her situation's not so precarious she couldn't wait."

Paul spotted Rachel on a stretcher outside the ambulance doors. A male medic did something to her leg, while a female medic stood near her head. Paul and Sean slowed to a stop, waiting for them to finish with Rachel.

"You sure you're okay?" Sean asked. "Why don't you let them check you out while we're waiting?"

Paul shook his head. "I told you, I'm fine. Where are Rachel's parents?"

"I've left them two messages. It's rolling right to voicemail. Either the battery died or they can't get a signal. I'll keep trying."

"Thanks." Paul wished he had his own phone, but there was no time to go back for it now.

One of the medics stepped away and moved to the front of the ambulance. Clear fluid dripped into Rachel's arm from an IV bag. She appeared to be sleeping. Now that he got a good look at her in the light, it scared him. Dirt streaked her face and hair, but didn't hide her deathly-pale skin. Together with the bluish tint to her lips, she looked like the Goth girl, Leslie, in his American literature class. How much blood had she lost?

"C'mon, Paul." Sean tugged his arm. "It looks like they're almost ready to move her. We'll follow them to the hospital."

Paul nodded, trying to stifle his reluctance about leaving Rachel. "Okay."

Sean had to return to work, so Paul jumped out of his

truck at the emergency room entrance as the EMTs whisked Rachel away. A nurse spoke to both Paul and one of the firefighters, trying to get as much information as possible about the accident. The nurse spoke kindly but informed Paul that while he could wait there for Rachel, they couldn't give him any information about her condition since he wasn't a relative.

"That's okay. Her parents will be here soon."

It wasn't okay, though. He paced the waiting room, walking short laps around the island of plastic chairs in the center of the room. It had been about three hours since the accident. Where were her parents?

The emergency room doors slid open with a whoosh, and Paul spun around. Mr. Mueller raced toward him, his features twisted in worry.

"Paul, what happened? Sean said Rachel's been hurt. That she fell into a sinkhole."

Rachel's mom followed on her husband's heels. Paul let out a breath, his relief so great he hugged her.

"I'm so glad you're here. Rachel and I were digging out behind the garden, and all of a sudden she screamed. When I turned around, I couldn't see her, but I heard her calling. Then I found her. Some kind of hole opened up, and she fell about twelve feet."

Rachel's mom, who he'd always considered remarkably even-tempered, appeared pale and unsteady. "Is she okay?"

"I don't know. They won't tell me anything, but she hurt—probably broke—her leg. I think she lost a lot of blood, and she didn't look so good when they put her in the ambulance." Tears pricked his eyes, but he refused to cry. "I'm worried about her."

Rachel's dad stalked to the admissions desk while her mom remained with Paul. She laid her hand on his arm—a comforting, maternal gesture to which he was completely unaccustomed. He tensed and then, accepting her kindness, relaxed.

"Are you okay, Paul? Were you hurt?"

"I'm okay, ma'am. Just dirty."

"But you're bleeding." She stared at the left side of his chest.

He glanced down at his blood-stained tee shirt. "No, I'm not. That must be...that's Rachel's blood. It must've gotten on my shirt when I lifted her into the sling the firefighters used to pull her out of the hole."

Her hand tightened around his arm, and her eyes widened. "You were in the hole with her?"

Sean must not have explained.

"Not at first. I didn't fall in. I jumped in on purpose. I didn't want her to be alone."

Her mom's eyes grew watery, and she grasped Paul by the shoulders and pulled him into a hug. "Thank you."

She released him and wiped her eyes with the back of her hand. "How long have you been here?"

Paul searched out the wall clock. Before he could guess at how long it had been, Rachel's dad came back.

"She's with the doctor now. The nurse said he should be out to see us shortly."

Paul grew more and more anxious watching Rachel's parents, both of whom looked sick with worry.

Forty-five minutes later, a tall man with salt and pepper hair, wire-rimmed glasses, and green scrubs approached them. In what universe could forty-five minutes be construed as *shortly*?

"Rachel Mueller's parents?"

"Yes." Rachel's dad jumped out of his seat.

The doctor glanced at Paul, as if he wondered if he should speak in front of him.

"Please tell us how Rachel's doing." Mrs. Mueller clutched her husband's sleeve.

The doctor introduced himself and told them that Rachel had been in shock when they brought her in. She was dehydrated and had lost a lot of blood, and they'd given her fluids and a transfusion. Her back and tailbone were bruised, but the main injury was to her left leg, broken in two places.

Each item the doctor ticked off created a fresh ache in Paul's chest.

A tear rolled down Mrs. Mueller's cheek.

Mr. Mueller focused on the doctor, his attitude all business. "What's her prognosis?"

"I think she'll make a complete recovery, but we need to operate on her leg in the morning. She's going to be sore and off her feet for about six weeks. After that she'll be looking at some therapy."

"But she'll be okay?" Mrs. Mueller's eyes lit with hope.

"Yes. Luckily, the rescue team got her out of there quickly. If she had lost more blood, we might be looking at an entirely different scenario."

The doctor told them it would be about a half hour until they got Rachel cleaned up and settled in her room then excused himself to attend to another patient. Another forty minutes passed until a nurse came to let them know Rachel could have visitors.

Mr. Mueller put an arm around his wife and turned to Paul. He bit his lip, as if he were mulling Paul's fate. His tone was terse. "You wait here."

Paul's stomach clenched. Was he serious? He'd go crazy if he had to wait any longer. He needed to see Rachel, to see with his own eyes that she would be okay. The last time he saw her, she looked just shy of death.

"Sir, I-I'd like to go with you." The next words came out just above a whisper. "I need to see her."

The anger in Mr. Mueller's eyes told him he wouldn't budge. "You'll wait here, Paul."

Paul spun in the opposite direction, gritting his teeth and pinching his forehead to keep from exploding.

Her parents followed the nurse a few yards. She stopped and pointed the way to Rachel's room. They nodded and headed in that direction.

Paul stared down the hallway for a full minute. He couldn't believe this. Why did he have to wait? Rachel would want to see him.

This wasn't his fault. Yes, he regretted not having had his cell phone with him, and maybe he could have done better by fashioning a tourniquet or something, but it was an accident.

He plopped into one of the hard orange plastic chairs lining the wall and picked up a magazine. The odor of bleach wafted toward him. Thumbing through the pages, he thought about Rachel and the accident. Nurses talked casually behind the desk, and an assortment of beeps and hums emanated from medical equipment parked in the hall. Paul tossed the magazine onto the table and drummed his fingers on the chair arm. An overhead TV droned the evening news. Twenty minutes later, Rachel's parents returned.

Paul stood, and Rachel's mom shifted her gaze to him. She smiled. "She's okay. They needed to take her for a few tests before surgery tomorrow, so they asked us to step out."

Paul's foot tapped a frantic rhythm matched by his gaze darting about the room. When they brought her back to her room, he would see her. He had to.

Mr. and Mrs. Mueller got cups of coffee and had just sat down next to Paul when Sean came through the emergency room doors. He still wore his work clothes, which were coated in nearly as much dirt as Paul's. He nodded to the Muellers.

"Paul, you okay?"

"Yeah. Just dirty and worried about Rachel."

"How is she?"

Since he had no firsthand knowledge of her condition, Paul looked to Rachel's parents. Mr. Mueller answered.

"She's pretty banged up, and she lost a lot of blood, but she'll have a full recovery. Her leg is broken in two places, and they're going to do surgery on it in the morning."

"She sure had me worried." Sean shook his head. "The rescue people that stayed behind said it looked like that hole opened up after all the rain we had this spring. They said there was a lot of strip mining in the area, and there are some limestone deposits, so it could either be an exit to an old mine or a plain old sinkhole. They're not sure."

"A mine?" Paul hadn't even considered that possibility, but with all the loose coal lying around it made sense.

Sean lowered his voice. "You didn't hear it from me, but if you've got an old mine, some limestone, a wet spring, and you add *fracking* to the mix...well, there's your hole."

"Thanks, Sean." Mr. Mueller stood and extended his hand for Sean to shake. "For calling us. And coming by." Paul would bet he'd even let Sean go back to see Rachel with them if he asked.

Sean laid a hand on Paul's shoulder. "Want a ride home?"

"No. I'm staying. I haven't seen Rachel yet." His eyes darted to Mr. Mueller.

"I figured you'd want to stay. Call me if you need anything, okay?" Sean handed him his cell phone. "You'll need this."

"Thanks. Of all the days not to have it with me..."

"Hey, don't sweat it." Sean squeezed his shoulder. "You got to me in minutes. You saved her." He let his hand drop and dug his keys out of his front pocket. "I'll give you a call in the morning."

"Okay. Thanks, Sean, for everything, but especially for

staying with Rachel until they got me out."

"No problem." Sean said goodbye to Mr. and Mrs. Mueller and left.

Paul dropped back into the uncomfortable seat. Now that the immediate crisis had passed and the adrenaline had worn off, his energy was sapped. He leaned his head back and closed his eyes for a few minutes while they waited.

"What the hell do you two do down there at that garden anyway?" Rachel's dad snapped at him, jarring him out of his relaxed state. "Why do I get the feeling a whole lot more goes on down there than gardening?"

Paul's eyes shot open, and he sat up straight in his seat. "I swear I never laid a hand on Rachel at the garden."

Her dad gave a short, mocking laugh. "At the garden? So where *have* you been laying your hands on my daughter—in the guesthouse? In my own house?"

Mrs. Mueller tugged on her husband's arm. "Ron..."

He ignored her.

Paul bit the inside of his cheek and strove to keep his tone even. "Sir, I love Rachel. I'd never do anything I thought would hurt her."

"Love her? What do you know about loving her? You let her fall down a damn mine shaft! She could've been killed."

"I'm sorry, Mr. Mueller." Paul's muscles tensed and his jaw tightened. "I had no idea there could be a mine under there."

"No one did." Mrs. Mueller gave him a reassuring glance. Too bad her husband ignored her.

Paul doubted there was anything either of them could say that would alleviate Mr. Mueller's anger.

He clenched his fist and glared at Paul.

"I want to see Rachel when they bring her back." Her dad could be as angry as he liked, but it wasn't going to change what had happened or how he and Rachel felt about each other.

"See her?" His voice grew incrementally louder with each word. "You'll be lucky if I ever let you see her again."

Paul became conscious of the stares of the other families occupying the waiting room. He swallowed hard.

"Ron—" Mrs. Mueller tried again to be the voice of reason.

"Linda," he said with a dismissive look, "I don't think you realize the seriousness of this. He's not going to see her tonight. He can wait here until we're done."

A nurse finally summoned Rachel's parents.

Paul fumed with frustration. He looked around the waiting area, searching for something to kick. He stomped outside the ER and thumped his boots against the concrete wall a half dozen times before a couple of nurses gave him curious looks.

He marched back inside and spent the next hour and a half in the hospital visitors' area nearest to Rachel's room, watching reruns of "Jeopardy" and "Wheel of Fortune" while he thumbed through old issues of *Esquire*. He worried himself sick about Rachel to the point that he thought he might throw up. What could he do to get her dad to relent?

A doctor went in and out of Rachel's room a couple of times. A nurse wheeled in a cart with a monitor and an IV rack. Finally, Rachel's parents emerged. They each had dark circles under their eyes, and their shoulders sagged. They looked haggard.

Paul jumped out of the seat. "How is she?"

"She's going to be fine." Mrs. Mueller pressed her hand lightly to Paul's back and gave him a reassuring pat. "She's in some pain, and she's still a little shaken up."

"Are they giving her something for the pain?"

"Yes, but she just got another dose now. I don't think it's kicked in yet."

She pulled Paul into a hug. She felt sorry for him, and it rankled him more. He appreciated her concern, but if she really wanted him to feel better, she'd let him see Rachel.

Paul eased out of her embrace. "Can I go see—"

"Her surgery is scheduled for a quarter to seven tomorrow morning." Mr. Mueller moved toward them. "We need to go and let her get some rest." His tone left no room for discussion.

Paul stepped closer, unwilling to be ignored and denied any longer. "You can't keep her from me."

Her dad drew himself up to his full height and moved so close to Paul that the tip of his shoes touched Paul's boots. His voice brooked no room for discussion.

"She's my daughter. I sure as hell can." He turned and started for the exit.

Paul reeled as if he'd been punched in the gut.

Rachel's mom held back for a moment and gave Paul a sorry look. "I'll talk to him," she whispered as she rubbed Paul's arm.

Paul bit his lower lip and nodded. He let her go ahead of him toward the exit.

No one uttered a word on the way home. As soon as Mr. Mueller put the car into park, Paul jumped out and rushed for the guesthouse. He still might throw up.

"Goodnight, Paul," Mrs. Mueller called. "We'll come get you in the morning when we're ready to leave for the hospital."

Paul lifted a hand to acknowledge her, but he didn't turn around. He slammed the guesthouse door so hard it rattled the windows.

Chapter 18
The First Mystery

Paul leaned against the back of the door and breathed deeply. *Keep it together. Rachel's okay. She's going to be fine.*

He traipsed to the bathroom, stripped off his clothes, and kicked them into a pile on the floor. With the water running, Paul pulled back the shower curtain and stepped into the tub. The hot water sluicing over his shoulders helped ease the tension, and the nausea abated. He gazed mindlessly at his feet as muddy water poured off his body, swirling around the drain. A little pile of silt formed around the stainless steel trap.

Paul eventually realized the room had filled with steam and the pads on his fingers resembled prunes. He dried off, pulled on his sleep pants and undershirt, and turned back the covers on his bed. His St. Paul medal on the nightstand caught his eye, so he grabbed it and fastened it around his neck. It was only half past ten, but exhausted, he crawled into bed.

He couldn't sleep.

His mind replayed the accident. Rachel screamed. He spun around, searching for her, but couldn't see her anywhere. He stumbled forward, tripping on the shovel he'd dropped, and called her name. She cried out, and he followed the sound to the hole. The smell of dirt invaded his senses. Her dad was right. *What if it had caved in on her? What if she had been killed? What if she had broken her back or neck? What if something goes wrong during surgery tomorrow?*

His ability to repress tears apparently came with an

expiration date, and he'd hit it. Even though no one was within earshot, he buried his face in his pillow before the first sob caught in his throat. The thought of losing Rachel, another funeral, tore at his gut.

Paul breathed deeply as he sat up and wiped his face. Slowly, his head cleared enough for him to form coherent thoughts.

"God, please don't let her die. Keep her safe." He punched the pillow and propped it behind him. "God, if she's okay, I promise, I'll take care of her forever. I'll never hurt her." Still uncomfortable, he sat forward and let his arms rest on his legs. "Thank you for letting her make it this far. For being alive. Please, God, let the surgery go well."

He opened the nightstand drawer and pulled out the letter from Dad. Carefully unfolding the paper, he ran his fingers over the widening creases and worn edges. Then he reread it.

Lying back on his pillow, he cleared his throat. "Dad," he squeaked, "why aren't you here when I need you? I am so freakin' sick of being alone."

The closer he grew to Rachel, the less lonely he felt, but if something happened to her... "I love Rachel so much, Dad. I can't lose her...I can't."

Rachel lay in a hospital bed alone and in pain, and he couldn't do a thing to help her. Not a thing. His helplessness irked him. He turned onto his side and repositioned his head on his damp pillow.

Everything outside the window remained still. The crescent moon did nothing to dispel the darkness in the yard. No lights lit Rachel's house. The only light in his room came from the blue glow of the digital alarm clock and its reflection in the mirror above the dresser. A set of rosary beads hung from the upper corner of the mirror.

The brown, well-used beads dangled lazily in the

darkness. Dad's rosary beads. Paul hadn't touched them in the year and a half they'd hung there. Besides a few pictures of his mom, him, and Sean, they were the only item found on Dad.

What do I have to lose?

Paul slipped out from under the sheets and took the rosary beads in his hand. He crawled back into bed, fingering the beads.

When his dad was deployed, he prayed every morning and every night for his safe return. Since Dad's death, he had difficulty praying. Even when he tried, the words wouldn't come. He didn't harbor any anger at God; he just didn't feel anything.

Are you even there? If you love me, why can't I feel it? Does what I feel, what I want, even matter?

God was omnipotent; Paul Porter was not. End of story.

He studied the beads and the little medal of Mary that completed the loop in the chain. She wasn't omnipotent either.

Do you get it, Mary? Were your prayers heard? You had your share of suffering.

Paul couldn't remember the last time he recited a Rosary. The words to the introductory prayers escaped him, so he skipped ahead to the mysteries. He figured God wouldn't mind. The Sorrowful Mysteries seemed fitting, and he struggled to recall what days you were supposed to say which mysteries anyway. He started with the Agony in the Garden. *Couldn't get more appropriate than that.*

He made it to the fourth mystery before he drifted off to sleep, beads still in hand.

Something or someone pounded on the front door. Paul's eyes shot open, and he blinked a few times. Morning already? The pounding resumed, and he climbed out of bed and shuffled to the door. Hadn't he just gone to sleep? No light seeped in from behind the curtain. He opened the door and came face to face with Rachel's dad.

An instant ache formed in Paul's stomach.

"The hospital called." Rachel's dad glanced down, then slipped his hands in his pockets and looked up. "They moved Rachel's surgery up an hour. We need to leave now if we want to get there before they take her in."

It all came rushing back faster than he could process it: Rachel, the sinkhole, the hospital, her leg. Her dad's refusal to allow him to visit her. He'd been half afraid her parents would leave without him this morning. "Yes, sir. Give me five minutes."

He shut the door and sprinted to his room. The rosary beads lay in the disheveled bed.

Paul remembered what his dad told him when he'd fallen asleep during bedtime prayers: "If you fall asleep praying, the angels finish your prayers for you."

This morning, more than ever, Paul hoped that was true. He kicked off his sleep pants and yanked on his underwear, jeans and a tee shirt. In the bathroom mirror, his eyes appeared swollen from sobbing. He splashed water on his face, ran his fingers through his hair, and stepped into his tennis shoes.

Pink streaks in the east mingled with the periwinkle sky. A gray mist hung over the distant mountains. Birds commenced their morning songs from the trees.

Mr. Mueller waited outside his idling truck. He paced back and forth, kicking stones and bending to pick one up and hurl it at the opposite side of the driveway. Mrs. Mueller was nowhere in sight.

Paul strode to the vehicle and leaned against the truck bed a good distance from Rachel's dad. He couldn't deal with any more of the blame and anger directed at him last night.

"Paul."

He shut his eyes and wished away the sound of his name.

"Paul."

Paul turned to face him.

"I apologize for not allowing you to see Rachel last night. I was wrong." He paused as if waiting for a response, but Paul wasn't ready to give any. Mr. Mueller shuffled his feet, but he didn't turn or look away. "I know you care about her, and I'm grateful that you were with her yesterday. If you hadn't been there, she might not be alive." His voice cracked ever so slightly. "So, thank you."

Paul still couldn't muster any words.

"I was worried last night—scared and stressed—and it came out as anger. That wasn't fair to you."

Paul's heart still hurt from the pain of not seeing Rachel last night, but he had to forgive her dad—for her sake as well as his own. "I understand, Mr. Mueller. I was scared too. I still am." Now he'd see how sorry Mr. Mueller really was. "Can I see her this morning?"

"Yes, if her mom gets out here in time."

Thank God. Paul's pulse immediately kicked up a notch or ten. They couldn't get to the hospital fast enough for him if they teleported there.

"Linda," Mr. Mueller called toward the house.

A few seconds later, Mrs. Mueller appeared. "I brought some of Rachel's things—her e-reader, a magazine, and her iPod."

"Let's go." Mr. Mueller motioned them toward the truck.

***

The hospital remained quiet and sleepy. It didn't yet smell like whatever the cafeteria served for breakfast, and silence filled the halls as the nurses finished up their shifts. Rachel had a private room on the third floor. When they arrived, her dad stopped short.

"Paul, why don't you go in first this morning?"

Tears threatened to escape Paul's eyes. He was an

emotional wreck already, and that small kindness almost set him off. "Thank you, Mr. Mueller."

He touched Paul's shoulder and squeezed it. "Son, are you okay?"

One look at his face, and anyone would know he'd done at least as much crying as sleeping last night.

"Rachel needs you to be strong."

"I'll be fine, sir." Paul hoped that was true, that he could keep his wits about him for Rachel's sake.

He yanked open the heavy door and the smell of antiseptic nearly bowled him over. The lights were dimmed, but Rachel sat nearly straight in the bed.

Her gaze lifted to him, and she covered her mouth with her hand. "Paul." Her voice cracked as she said it.

He approached her bed, his heart ballooning, wishing she were well and he could scoop her up in his arms.

A tear ran down her cheek.

"Hey, gorgeous." She *was* gorgeous, beautiful to him in every way, even though her eyes now had dark circles beneath them. He doubted she'd even slept.

"I'm so glad you're here." A tear trickled down the other cheek.

Paul sat on the edge of her bed and held the hand closest to him.

She tried to move toward him, and pain flashed in her eyes. They had cleaned her face and hair, and aside from her pallor, her face showed no signs of her injury.

"I hoped you'd come last night, but you didn't."

He bit his lower lip and cleared his throat. "I was here." He needed to do this without pinning blame on her dad. That wouldn't help anyone. "I was in the waiting room the whole time."

"Dad wouldn't say where you were, only that you weren't hurt. Why didn't you come in?" Her eyes pleaded with him.

The last thing he wanted her to think was that he didn't care, that there was any place in the world he would rather be than with her. Given the choice, he'd go back to the bottom of that pit with her if that were the only way they could be together.

"I wanted to. I really wanted to." Now Paul's voice cracked. He needed to check his emotions. He cleared his throat. "Your dad thought it would be better if I waited outside."

"I don't understand. How could that be better?" Her brow wrinkled, and her eyes filled with unshed tears.

She asked too many questions. He wouldn't lie, but he didn't want to get into this with her now. "Your dad wasn't happy with me last night."

She still wore that look of confusion that left her forehead creased and her eyes so sad. "But Dad loves you, I know he does."

"Well, I wasn't feeling the love last night." Paul lifted her hand to his lips and kissed it. "It doesn't matter. He apologized to me this morning, and I don't think we should waste our time talking about it. I want to know how you're doing."

"How I'm doing?"

She sighed and her eyes glistened. "Paul, when I close my eyes I see dirt. I *smell* dirt. I feel it under my fingertips." Her lower lip trembled.

He swallowed hard and tried to stifle the tears. "I know." He dropped his gaze to her hand and squeezed it. Dirt remained embedded under her fingernails. "I know."

"I was so out of it when they brought me in yesterday. I wanted to see with my own eyes that you were okay. I wanted to thank you." Her tears came now whether she wanted them to or not, and so did his. "Paul, I *needed* you last night."

"I needed you too." His chest burned. He'd never

needed a person like that in his life. He leaned in and wrapped his arms around her as best he could, holding her as she cried. "How's the pain today?"

She took a breath. "Better, but I'm scared."

He stroked her hair. It was soft and clean again, but it didn't have that familiar strawberry fragrance. "They're going to take great care of you, Rachel. I know they are."

"Have you ever been under anesthesia?"

"Once, but I was little. I don't remember it."

"Will you pray for me?"

"Of course I will." He pulled Dad's rosary out of his jeans pocket and opened his hand for her to see it. "I'll say the Rosary for you if you'd like."

Rachel smiled. "Thank you."

"Listen, I don't want to leave, but I'm sure your parents want to get in here and see how you're doing."

He took both her hands in his and kissed them. Then he kissed her cheek, tasting the salty tears that had fallen. He grabbed a tissue from the stand next to her bed and blotted her eyes. His well-intentioned effort proved clumsy, and he handed the tissue to her instead.

"It's going to be okay. I promise."

"Will you be here when I wake up?"

"Absolutely. I'm going to be out there praying on these rosary beads, okay?"

"Okay." She sniffed and managed a smile for him. "I love you."

"I love you too. See you in a bit."

Paul turned and left the room. Rachel's parents waited outside the door. Mrs. Mueller smiled at him with teary eyes. Mr. Mueller gave Paul another pat on the shoulder, took the door from him, and held it open for his wife.

Paul didn't breathe until the door closed again. He stepped to the side and leaned against the wall. He rubbed his eyes and let his fingers slide down over his face, covering his mouth. Refusing to cry, he cleared his throat.

Life crept back into the hospital. Attendants rolled a gurney down the hall, probably to take Rachel into pre-op. His whole life would be wheeled away on that cart, and he didn't think he could bear it.

He turned on his cell phone and called Sean. It went straight to voicemail.

"Hey, it's me. I'm at the hospital. Rachel's okay. She's going into surgery soon." He paused, trying not to let on what a wreck he was. "Call me later."

He walked to the visitor waiting area and dropped some coins into the vending machine. His energy drink clattered as it hit bottom, but when Paul reached into the hinged door to grab it, it lay out of reach. He smacked his palm twice against the machine. It didn't budge. Gripping either side of the machine with a hand, he shook it, hoping to dislodge the small can. No luck. He sighed and depressed the coin return. Nothing.

He dropped into a lumpy chair, ready to watch mindless morning television. The rosary beads bulged in his pocket. He fingered the beads then pulled out his iPod, inserted the ear buds, and closed his eyes.

Bob Marley commanded him not to worry, reassuring that everything would be all right. As if a dead reggae singer would know.

A half hour later, Rachel's parents turned the corner at the end of the long corridor. He paused the music when they approached.

"Paul." Mrs. Mueller had that maternal look. "When's the last time you ate?"

Paul removed the ear buds and jammed them into his pocket with the rosary beads. "Uh, lunch yesterday, I think."

She shot an accusatory look at Mr. Mueller. Paul didn't know why. It wasn't Mr. Mueller's fault; he hadn't had an appetite.

"You need to eat," Mr. Mueller said. "You're no good to Rachel if you let yourself get run down. Let's get something in the cafeteria, and then we'll stop at the chapel."

He still wasn't hungry, but he welcomed a distraction from his worries and the shiny, happy people on the morning shows. "Okay."

Paul forced down the rubbery eggs and greasy sausage on the Styrofoam plate in front of him. Rachel's parents seemed oddly unconcerned as they talked about James's Little League games, scheduling the car for inspection, and something going on at church.

For the first time, Paul noticed James's absence. "Where *is* James?"

"He went home with a friend after we got Sean's message yesterday. He spent the night. We'll get him on the way home today."

Paul nodded and glanced at the clock. "Won't Rachel be coming out of surgery soon?"

"Not for another hour probably." Mr. Mueller wadded his napkin on his plate. "You done? We can head over to the chapel."

Paul took a last swig of the orange drink that passed for juice and carried his tray to the counter.

The chapel was located on the wing opposite the cafeteria, below Rachel's room. The morning sun lit the altar as it filtered in through the stained glass windows. The simple, nondenominational chapel brought more comfort and peace than the visitors' waiting area.

They slid into the first pew, first Mr. Muller, then Mrs. Mueller, then Paul.

"Would you like to pray together?" Mrs. Mueller must have caught Paul pulling the rosary beads out of his pocket with her peripheral vision.

"I'm a little rusty with these, but sure." He held up his dad's worn, brown beads.

"They don't look like the beads of someone who's a little rusty."

"They were my dad's. You know what they say about there being no atheists in foxholes." He hoped mention of his dead father would be enough to end that line of conversation. It was.

Mrs. Mueller led the prayers in an even, soft voice.

"In the name of the Father, and of the Son, and of the Holy Spirit."

"Amen," Paul and Mr. Mueller said together.

They managed to get through all the Glorious Mysteries—it was Wednesday, and Mrs. Mueller *did* know which mysteries were for which days.

"Let's go upstairs and see if we can find out how Rachel's doing." Mr. Mueller raised the kneeler.

They waited in the visitors' area closest to the operating room, enduring an unending stream of vapid talk shows until Rachel's surgeon found them.

He addressed Rachel's parents, and they immediately stood. Paul stayed seated, but anxiety wreaked such havoc on his system that he nearly burst out of the chair. The surgeon talked in hushed tones, and Paul couldn't hear a word he said. After a few minutes, Rachel's parents thanked the doctor, and he left through a set of double doors.

Paul stood.

Mrs. Mueller smiled. Rachel's parents' relief was palpable as they relayed the information to him.

Mrs. Mueller hugged him. "Rachel did great."

Paul could breathe again. *Thank you, Lord.*

"When can we see her?"

Mr. Mueller gathered his wife's sweater, her magazine, and his coffee. "She's in post-op now. They'll bring her back to the room in a few minutes. We can wait for her there."

They walked down the long corridor, which now bustled with doctors, nurses, staff, and visitors going this way and that. Paul hesitated as they approached the door. Would her dad want him there with them or was he going to go all Mr. Hyde on him and make him wait outside?

Her dad clapped Paul on the shoulder and nudged him toward the door. "I think Rachel would like to see you there when she wakes up." Dr. Jekyll it was. "She'll want to know the people she loves were here waiting for her."

Wow. Something had changed her dad's thinking since last night. Maybe Rachel's mom got to him. Maybe he had a change of heart. Whatever it was, Paul was grateful. He told Rachel he'd be there when she awoke, and that's where he'd be. "Thank you, sir."

They didn't wait long before a couple of attendants wheeled her in and transferred her to the bed, awake, but groggy. Rachel's parents moved to her bedside while Paul hung back towards the foot of the bed.

"The doctor said it went okay." Her voice was raspy, and she cleared her throat. Her mom handed her the bottle of water the nurse had left for her, and she sipped from the straw.

"I'm glad you're all here." Her eyes settled on Paul for a couple of seconds, and she smiled. "Where's James?"

"At school." By the time her mom answered, Rachel had closed her eyes.

Her mom patted Rachel's hands where they lay on top of the sheet and blanket. "We should let her rest."

Paul had never seen Rachel sleep. Even in a shapeless hospital gown, her hair pulled back, and Band-Aids on her hands and arm, she looked beautiful.

Rachel's okay.

He praised God, and he thanked his dad too. Somehow, Paul felt like he had something to do with it.

Chapter 19
Homecoming

"Thanks for the ride." Paul slammed the car door shut and waved goodbye to one of his work buddies. His muscles ached from a long, late Friday at the orchard, but he jogged to the emergency room entrance. Since it was late, he signed in at the desk according to policy. The woman behind the Plexiglas scrutinized him as he signed his name and pushed the clipboard in her direction.

He smiled and hoped she wouldn't ask his age. He still had almost two months until his eighteenth birthday, and he didn't want to get tossed out since he was still a minor.

She took the clipboard and flipped it in her direction, then smiled and said, "Have a good night."

Paul strode through the quiet halls and took the elevator to Rachel's floor. For the past couple of days, Mrs. Mueller spent most of the day with her. In the evenings, Mr. Mueller had taken James and Paul in to see her for a couple of hours. Paul sat alongside her bed and held her hand while she talked to her dad and James. It felt awkward at first, but by the end of the first evening it had become the most natural thing in the world.

The door whooshed open, and Paul stopped for a second as his eyes adjusted to the darkness in her room.

Rachel slept in the semi-reclined bed. Her hair hung in a loose braid over her left shoulder and onto her lavender sleep shirt.

He hadn't thought how he'd get home, and now that he was there, Paul decided to spend the night. At least Rachel would see him in the morning. He couldn't wait for the doctor to release her so she could come home.

He pulled out his cell phone and texted Mrs. Mueller, telling her he worked late and not to worry. Then he texted Sean and asked him to pick him up at the hospital in the morning.

He grabbed an extra blanket from the plastic bag in the nook beneath the nightstand and flopped in the boxy, cushioned chair next to her bed. He pulled the blanket around him and leaned his head on the top of the wooden chair.

Despite the discomfort and the occasional noise from the nurses' station, Paul slept.

"Paul?" Rachel's voice was a groggy whisper.

"Hey." He rubbed the sleep from his eyes with his knuckle and glanced at the time on his cell phone. Three in the morning. "What're you doing up?"

The dim glow from the parking lot crept between the vertical blinds, casting soft light on her smiling face. "When did you get here?" Her eyes brightened, and he marveled at how much better she looked every day.

"After work last night. You were asleep."

"I'm glad you're here. I hate this place at night. I get so lonely." She glanced around the dimly-lit, sterile room and pulled the covers toward her chin.

"You don't have to be lonely tonight. I'm staying. Now, go back to sleep. If your dad hears I kept you up all night, he'll skin me alive." He winked at her so she'd know he wasn't really worried.

Some time he'd tell her about this week. His relationship with Mr. Mueller had gone from good to bad to better than ever before. Maybe he was trying to make up for the way he'd shut Paul out the night of the accident, but he'd spent the rest of the week treating him like another son. Their conversations on the way to and from the hospital had been relaxed, and he couldn't dismiss how good it felt to have a father-figure in his life. His behavior earlier in the week notwithstanding, Ron Mueller was the kind of man Paul wanted to be—a loving husband, a devoted father, and a loyal friend. He was hardworking, honest, and generous. And his daughter could make every nerve ending in his body come alive with no more than a look.

"Come hold me." Rachel patted the bed.

A whole new side of Rachel had been revealed to him this week. Her vulnerability made his heart ache with love for her. He'd never felt such a strong desire to guard and protect anyone or anything. She handled her forced dependence with trust and grace, and her reliance on God and her family beguiled him. He witnessed an intimacy among them—with each other and with God—that he longed for and missed. When had he become such a loner?

"On the bed?"

"Yeah, there's room." Rachel scooted to the side and turned down the covers for him.

Paul shoved aside his blanket and, still in his dirty jeans and tee shirt, kicked off his shoes. He climbed in alongside Rachel, careful not to disturb her healing leg. Lying on his back, he wrapped his arms around her, letting her rest her head on his chest.

Despite how many times he touched Rachel, her softness always caught him off guard. Even the crisp smell of the clean sheets couldn't quite overcome the scent that was all her. He kissed her head and stroked her hair, and in no time her breathing became soft and even.

He closed his eyes.

What seemed like moments later, Sean's voice rasped in his ear. "I hate to wake you, man, but you've got to get to work."

Paul opened his eyes and blinked a few times, trying to identify his location. Sunlight streaked between the vertical blinds.

Rachel sighed against him in her sleep, and peaceful warmth flooded over him. As much as hated to leave, he did have to go. He shifted her off him and onto the other side of the bed.

Rachel woke and repositioned herself, sitting up. "Hi, Sean." She pushed stray strands of hair behind her ears.

Was it wrong that Paul took an inordinate amount of pleasure in the fact that she hadn't mentioned Sean's good looks once since they'd first kissed? Instead she told Paul with regularity how handsome he was.

Paul slid out of the bed and repositioned Rachel's covers. He glanced at the clock. They'd be bringing her breakfast tray in a half hour or so.

Sean walked to the foot of the bed. "How's your leg coming along?"

"Good, but not great. The doctor thinks I need a day or two of rehab before I go home."

"You scared me half to death when they lifted you out of that hole." Sean shuddered at the memory.

Paul relived the terror of the EMTs lifting Rachel into the ambulance, half–conscious, her skin and hair streaked with blood and caked with dirt.

"Me too." Paul folded the blanket he'd used and laid it over the chair. "I don't want to think about it." He smoothed out his clothes and ran his hand through his matted hair.

Sean looked him up and down. "Did you come here straight from work?"

"Yeah, and you've got to get me back there by eight o'clock."

"When's the last time you shaved?"

Paul rubbed the stubble on his chin. "Uh, day before yesterday maybe?"

He returned to Rachel's bedside and bent to kiss her goodbye. He sensed he'd pulled back a little sooner than she'd have liked.

Her eyes fluttered open, and she bit her lower lip. "I like it." She reached up and ran her fingers along his jaw.

He leaned over and kissed her once more. She couldn't come home soon enough for him.

With a hand behind his head, she whispered into his ear. "Thanks for staying with me last night. I love you."

"I love you too."

Sean tapped the foot on her good leg. "Take care, Rachel." He opened and held the door.

Turning into the hallway, Paul assessed how grungy he felt after having spent the night in his dirty clothes.

Sean didn't speak until they reached his truck. "Want to stop for coffee?"

"Yeah. And food."

"I should've known. Do you have money?" Sean dug his wallet out of the glove compartment.

"Enough."

"Yeah, right." Sean peered into the billfold and shoved the wallet in his rear pocket. "If you didn't have to work, I'd bring you home and make pancakes for you and Amanda."

Paul raised his brows as Sean buckled his seat belt. "Since when do you cook?"

"Since I married a woman who doesn't." Sean laughed as he started the engine and moved his hand to the gear shift. If it bothered him that his wife didn't cook, he didn't let on. She liked reading. Maybe Sean ought to get her a cookbook.

He didn't immediately shift the truck into gear.

Why are we sitting here? Why doesn't he go?

Sean turned to him. "Paul, be careful with Rachel."

Paul opened his mouth to speak but hesitated. *Was this about the accident? Or something else?* "What do you mean?"

"I walked in on a pretty cozy scene. The two of you

sleeping together. What am I supposed to think about that?"

It *was* cozy. It felt so good to have Rachel lying against him.

"I mean, consider the consequences of your actions. If Dad were here, he'd give you the whole lecture on why you should save sex for marriage. I'm not Dad, but the older I get, the more I see how many things he was right about. If you love her like I think you do, take things slow, okay?"

Uncomfortable under Sean's stare, Paul glanced out the window. Sean had never broached this topic with Paul before—at least not in a serious manner. Should he take it seriously too, or could he play it off? He and Sean had done serious more than either one of them liked, especially since Dad died.

Paul held a hand up in surrender. "Okay. Not to worry. We'll be back under her parents' watchful eyes soon."

Sean shook his head, kicked the truck into reverse, and peeled out of the parking space. "Yeah, well, a year ago, I had to push you to even tell her you liked her, and now I'm worried you're going to make me an uncle before I'm even a father."

"Uncle Sean...I kind of like the sound of that." Paul lifted the left side of his mouth in a half grin. He could make Sean squirm.

Sean jerked the truck to a stop at the intersection. "Me too, but I don't want to hear it until at least nine months after your wedding day, got it?"

Paul studied his face, trying to gauge Sean's seriousness. His gaze didn't waver.

"Relax. We didn't do anything. We were just sleeping. In fact, we didn't even kiss until I went to leave." The absurdity of the conversation struck him. "She just had surgery. And do you think we'd want our first time to be in a hospital bed?"

That put a smile on Sean's face. "I don't know. How much of a horndog are you?"

Finally, some levity. "Well, I do have this serious hospital fetish. Nothing sexier than a girl in a hospital gown and the smell of institutional antiseptic."

Sean tapped the wheel with his thumbs. "Yeah, well, maybe keep that picture in mind when she's back in her hidden bed of roses."

No roses grew in Rachel's garden, but Paul didn't quibble. He got the point.

***

Paul ran from the bus stop to the house. The afternoon sun soaked through his shirt, heating his shoulders. Sweat gathered at the back of his neck and under his arms. A cloudless, blue sky reflected the simple joy and hope that filled his heart.

Rachel's parents expected to have her home before he arrived from school. Even crazy Merrill couldn't drive fast enough for Paul.

His shoulders sagged with disappointment when the house came into view and their truck wasn't in the driveway. The discharge must have taken longer than they had expected.

His phone vibrated in his pocket, and he pulled it out. A three-word text from Rachel's mom: *On our way.*

Not sure what else to do, Paul walked toward Rachel's garden. He hadn't been down there since the accident. It would be a long time before Rachel could tend it. He thought a bouquet of fresh-picked flowers might cheer her.

Paul crossed under the branches, through the brush, and into the garden. The emergency vehicles had torn up huge swaths of groundcover and left deep tracks filled with mud. Most of the flowers lay trampled and dead.

Police tape wrapped around a cluster of trees marking the area where the hole remained, its maw gaping. Paul gave it wide berth. Rachel's dad had mentioned getting a load of fill down there next week. The sooner, the better.

A corner of the garden remained untouched, and Rachel's shears still lay next to the log bench.

Paul cut the remaining blooms to make a beautiful, colorful bouquet for Rachel. Its sweet fragrance reminded him of her.

As he stepped back onto the path, Paul spotted the truck in the driveway and jogged to the house. Breathless, he knocked and waited for a reply.

"C'mon in," Mrs. Mueller called.

He hid the bouquet behind his back and opened the door.

Rachel sat on the couch, her mom adjusting pillows behind her back and under her foot.

"You comfortable, honey?"

"I'm good, Mom. Thanks."

Rachel's hair lifted in a high ponytail, and she wore a Gallitzin Academy tee shirt and sweat pants with a soft brace around her left knee and lower leg.

She grinned at Paul and rolled her eyes as her mom fussed over the position of her leg.

Paul's smile spread from ear to ear as he brought the bouquet from behind his back and presented it to Rachel.

"Thank you. They're beautiful." She sniffed and rotated the bouquet, examining each flower. "Are these from my garden?"

"What's left of it." He hated to tell her, but she would have to find out sooner or later. "The garden's pretty messed up, but I was able to salvage these for you."

"Mom, could you put these in a vase for me?"

"Sure, honey. I know just the one." Her mom took the flowers. "How was your day, Paul?"

"Good, Mrs. Mueller. Just long."

Paul sat and took Rachel's hand. "Welcome home."

"It is *so* good to be back."

Rachel's mom returned with a vase and settled the bouquet in the center of the coffee table.

"Paul, Rachel needs to rest." She made a brushing motion as if she could sweep him out the door. Paul understood Rachel needed to take it easy, but couldn't he sit with her while she rested?

Stifling his protest, he forced himself back to the guesthouse and spent the remainder of the afternoon staring at his laptop, trying to proofread his Civil War report.

He ate dinner, as usual, with Rachel and her family.

"James, get your glove," Mr. Mueller said after dinner. "Let's throw the ball around for a while."

James pulled on his shoes and ran out the door. Mr. Mueller grabbed a ball cap from the top of the coat rack and fit it on his head.

"Paul, we'll be inside in a half hour or so, then I've got some reading to do for work. Give a holler when you're ready to go, and we'll come help Rachel get into bed. And not too late, okay? She's had a long day."

"Yes, sir." Paul tried to swallow his surprise. "Thank you."

Mrs. Mueller had again made Rachel comfortable in the living room. Paul sat on the couch next to her. Neither spoke until her parents moved out of earshot. Rachel grinned and took his hand.

"I guess Dad thinks you're too much of a gentleman to take advantage of me while I'm recuperating." She leaned toward Paul and whispered. "He doesn't even suspect that I might try taking advantage of you."

He suddenly realized how much he'd missed her teasing. "Man, it's good to have you back."

Rachel giggled. "Seriously, Paul, I'm not so fragile I'm going to break. You can touch me."

He glanced at her leg propped on a pillow atop the coffee table, then at their intertwined hands, and finally settled his gaze on her eyes. "I'm sorry. I don't want to hurt you."

"It'll hurt more if you don't make a move on me than if you bump my leg."

He cocked an eyebrow. "Is that so?"

"Yes, that's so. I'm pretty sure the surgery hasn't affected my lips."

Had Rachel ever been this bold before? He didn't think so, but he couldn't say he didn't like it. "I'll be the judge of that." With that, Paul kissed her, really kissed her, for the first time in what felt like an eternity. Had it only been a week? If he knew a way to press *pause* on life, he'd have done it right then. There was something both frustrating and liberating about her parents being just out of view and earshot. He enjoyed kissing her without worrying about what might happen next.

He pulled back and rubbed her nose with his. "Yeah, I'd say your lips are working fine, but I think we should test them out regularly, just to be sure."

"Whatever you say."

Ordinarily, Paul scoffed at such corny conversation, but this time it didn't bother him one bit.

Rachel leaned back and adjusted her leg.

He sat back as well, still holding tight to her hand.

"My dad had to wait a long time with me this afternoon while all the paperwork got straightened out. We had a chance to talk." She squeezed his hand and blinked away tears. "He told me the doctor said if I hadn't been rescued so quickly, I could have bled to death."

"I know." He hated to think about it, but things could have ended badly.

"How can I ever thank you for saving my life?"

A sudden melancholy settled on them. Eyes on her, he

dipped his head and smiled, wanting to lighten the mood. "Well, I can think of a couple ways..."

Rachel's smile was all sweetness, and the hint of a blush came to her cheeks. "I'm serious, Paul. You saved my life."

"I think you're being a little dramatic about it. I wasn't even thinking, I just reacted. In fact, I ticked off Sean, and even the rescue squad seemed angry with me, especially the one guy."

She took her free hand and laid it over their folded hands. "Well, you can act like it was nothing, but it wasn't. I want you to know how grateful I am."

Paul shrugged a shoulder. "I guess I'm uncomfortable with you making me out to be a hero when to me it was kind of selfish."

She wrinkled her brow and tilted her head in question. "Selfish how?"

"I don't want to live without you. I *can't* live without you."

She didn't seem to know how to respond.

Did I say too much?

They *were* young, and maybe she wasn't as sure about him as he was about her. "Rachel, I didn't mean—"

She shook her head. "No, I'm just...I don't know. I don't want to ever be without you either, Paul." She turned her gaze away from him toward the window where pink clouds turned a mottled gray as the sun set. She looked tired.

"I don't want to wear you out on your first night home. I've got some studying to do anyhow, so I'll get your dad."

"Okay." She must have been exhausted; she didn't even ask for five more minutes. "I love you."

He kissed her forehead. "I love you too. I'm so glad you're home."

Chapter 20
Serpent in the Garden

Rachel leaned forward and grabbed the remote control. She flicked the TV off, sunk back into the couch, and sighed. She scanned the room for something of interest. The small stack of books on the end table: read. The crossword puzzle book: filled. School work: complete. Rosary beads and prayer book: done that. Library book on knitting: boring. She had thought teaching herself a useful, sedentary skill might be entertaining. Instead, she'd found it tedious and frustrating. Learning from a book wasn't going to cut it.

She stared out the window. Sunlight filtered through the green, leafy trees, and the leaves bobbed in the breeze. Wispy clouds dotted the brilliant blue sky. Here and there, a puffy cloud hung above the tree line.

If only she would be done with these crutches. *One more week.* She might go stir crazy before then. The weather had been glorious, but the furthest she could get was the porch, and that was only with assistance. It felt like years since she'd been able to get around like a normal person. The doctor kept telling them her recovery was "on pace," so she tried to be a patient patient.

Rachel glanced at the wall clock. Paul would be back from school soon, and he had a rare day off from the orchard. Her mom would be home from her errands at roughly the same time. The only boredom-buster on her list: sleep. With a sigh, she nestled her head into the top of the couch cushion and closed her eyes. Pathetic that her only relief from monotony was unconsciousness.

It didn't feel like any time had passed when fingers

poked either side of her rib cage. Her eyes popped open, and she jerked upright, gasping.

"Wake up, sleepyhead." Paul sat next to her, the grin on his face a mile wide.

"Don't you ever do that to me again!" Suppressing a grin, she swatted at his shoulder.

He leaned away, avoiding her weak retaliation. "What? Can't have you missing out on a beautiful day like this." His eyes darted to the enticing late spring weather outside.

Rachel's lips pursed in an angry pout. "You scared me near to death."

"Sorry."

She glared, forcing a truthful admission from him.

"Well, I'm sort of sorry. Actually, it was kind of fun."

She huffed a sigh. "You want to watch a movie?" She'd had a romantic comedy in mind for a couple of days. Watching it with Paul sitting close to her sounded good.

He glanced outside again, obviously itching to enjoy the fresh air and sunshine. "What is it, some chick flick?"

"No, it's...okay, yes, it's a chick flick, but it's a really good one.'

Paul shook his head. "Never seen one. Not about to start now."

Rachel's eyes widened. "Never? Not one? No *Sleepless in Seattle*? No *While You Were Sleeping*?"

"Uh-uh."

"Paul Porter, you just gave me a mission." With a knowing grin, Rachel grabbed for the pen and paper on the end table. "I'm making a list."

"Please, no." His voice lowered into a pleading groan. He tugged her arm, keeping her from grasping the pen and sending it rolling onto the floor.

After a flash of irritation, she gave up, then took his hand. She rubbed it back and forth with her fingertips and leaned in as if she were going to kiss him. "Paul..."

His Adam's apple bobbed as he swallowed.

She batted her eyes, glanced down, and then up into his eyes. "I didn't know your mom," she said softly, sweetly, "but I'm confident she would be grateful to me if I exposed you to a few low-testosterone movies."

He yanked his hand out of hers and bit back a smile. "Maybe some other time. It's too beautiful out there." He nodded toward the window. "Once the peaches ripen, I won't get free days like this. I'll be working dusk to dawn. I'm taking you outside." He leaped off the couch and strode to the porch.

Plastic and wood scraped across the porch floor as he re-arranged the furniture. Paul opened the storm door and fiddled with the closing mechanism until it remained open. Returning to the couch, he took her hand and pulled.

"On your feet, Rachel."

She pushed against the couch and stood, but before she'd gotten her balance, he placed one arm gently behind her knees and scooped her up. Her stomach tingled as her feet left the ground.

He carried her out the door and deposited her on one of the plastic chairs.

"Uh, thanks. I guess." She scooted back in the chair and propped her leg on the low table he'd set in front of her chair.

Paul closed the door, then walked to the railing and pointed down the sloping hill. "Your garden is waiting for you down there." He gazed toward the tree line.

"It's a jungle, isn't it?" It would be almost as much work as when she first started the garden, but she couldn't wait to sink her hands into the cool earth and inhale the familiar floral fragrance.

"Yep." He sat in the chair he'd placed next to hers. Eyes registering concern, he bit on one side of his lower lip. "Are you okay with going down there again—once you're back on your feet?"

"What do you mean?" The sooner she got back to her garden, the better.

He shrugged. "I don't know. I thought maybe you'd be thinking about the accident, afraid it might happen again."

Her heart lifted. He really cared about her.

She shook her head. "When you fall off a horse, you've got to get back on again and ride, right? Besides, Dad said it's all been filled in, and he had an engineer come and check everything out. It's all sound."

He exhaled and nodded. "Yeah, he did. There shouldn't be anything for you to worry about. To tell the truth, I'm kind of eager to see if we can find any more stuff down there. Remember, we found those pieces of bottle and the pocket knife before you fell."

Rachel squinted into the sunlight then closed her eyes for a couple of seconds, enjoying its warmth on her face. She opened them again and looked Paul in the eye. "I'm game, so long as I can tame the wilderness down there first and get it looking like a respectable garden again."

***

Rachel sank the shovel into the ground again and stopped. She took a deep breath, inhaling the scent of her remaining wildflowers wilting in the August heat. The wild honeysuckle she'd planted as a ground cover had spread beyond her rough garden borders. The black-eyed susans and purple coneflowers thrived despite the near-death experience endured by most of the garden. She brushed her wrist over her forehead, wiping away the sweat. The humidity had to be near a hundred percent. She glanced up, looking between treetops at the dark, anvil-shaped clouds amassing. The gray thunderheads blocked the noonday sun. A warm breeze tickled the stray hairs on her damp neck beneath her ponytail, and the smell of rain pervaded the air.

It hadn't taken Rachel as long to get the garden in

shape as she had anticipated. Heavy equipment had rolled over and destroyed much of it, guaranteeing those plants wouldn't grow back this year. But, with a strong dose of tender loving care, some hardy plants survived.

Finally, Rachel had the garden pretty much where she wanted it, so she decided she could afford to spend the morning digging. Her injury and subsequent rehabilitation had nixed her plans for a summer job. Paul worked at the orchard early each morning and generally until late afternoon, sometimes longer.

Turning her attention back to the dirt, she dug about seven inches below the surface when she unearthed an unusual-shaped rock. She dropped to her knees and using her fingers, dug out a small piece of soft, dull golden metal-like rock. Its size was no bigger than a quarter, but instead of being round, it had blunt edges on one side, as if it had been broken off the corner of a larger object. She slid it into her shorts pocket as the clouds thundered.

After tucking her shovel behind the log bench, Rachel half ran, half walked toward the house, barely beating the torrents of rain that licked at her heels. Her leg and knee were healed and better every day, but they still weren't at one-hundred-percent strength.

She made it inside the door as the warm rain pounded the roof and pelted the windows. The thunder rolled into the distance after a short while, but the rain continued off and on throughout the early afternoon. She couldn't help but feel sorry for Paul on days like these. He had probably been drenched.

Rachel tugged the band out of her damp hair and looked about for something to do. Her mother had taken James to a friend's house before running errands, and her dad was at work. Ambling through the kitchen, she looked for a treat. Finding none, she decided to bake a double batch of chocolate chip cookies.

The cookies cooled on wire racks by mid-afternoon, and Rachel decided to surprise everyone by cooking dinner. The prospect of making soup had always intimidated her, but while she may not have been a gifted or experienced cook, she could follow a recipe. She threw together a big pot of lentil soup, which she left to warm inside the Dutch oven on the stovetop.

Dinner and dessert done, she grabbed the remote control, plopped onto the couch, and turned on the TV. She scrolled through the hundred or more stations on the channel guide but found nothing interesting. She was about to turn it off when something about the scene playing behind the channel guide caught her eye. It was the piranha movie she and Paul had watched in the spring. They never did see how it ended.

Paul was never far from her thoughts, but now she wouldn't be able to think of anything but him. Placing the pot of soup in the still-warm oven, she decided to walk to the orchard to hang out with Paul until he was done working.

She strolled to the end of the driveway, stopping here and there to pluck some Queen Anne's lace or pick up an odd-shaped rock. She turned left up the road about a half mile, then down the long drive to the orchard. How good it was to be up and moving again. As she neared the long rows of cherry trees and then peach trees, she spotted a few workers, one on a stepladder, picking peaches. She recognized Paul right away. He had his ear buds in, so he wouldn't hear her approach. It was a perfect opportunity to surprise him.

***

Thank God the rain had stopped. Maybe if the sun stayed out, he'd dry out before he went home. A generator kicked on in the distance, and he nudged up the volume on his iPod. Led Zeppelin's "Fool in the Rain." *Funny, Dad.*

"Why don't you show up and make it all right?" he whisper-sung as he scanned the tree above him for more ripe peaches. The hair rose on the back of his neck. He had the strangest sensation he was being watched, and he adjusted the volume back down. Turning on the ladder, he saw her, the person who could bring a smile to his face faster than any other. He popped the ear buds out of his ears and let them dangle around his neck.

"You sure are a sight for sore eyes." His rainy, miserable day had just gotten a whole lot better. He planted his feet on the outside of the ladder, slid down, and reached for her.

She stopped a foot short of him. "Ugh. You're sopping wet."

His hair had started to dry, but his tee shirt clung to his chest and arms. The rain had soaked his jeans, turning them midnight blue and making them feel ten pounds heavier.

Rachel's gaze lingered on the wet sleeve that clung to his biceps. He hadn't thought much of it, but he supposed he had added muscle picking and hauling peaches. All the shoveling in her garden probably didn't hurt either. "Do I pass inspection?"

"Absolutely." Her gaze slid to his. "I'd hug you, but I don't want to get all wet."

"It's just rainwater." He grabbed her hand before she could get away and pulled her in close to him. The cool dampness touched her dry shirt and bare arms.

Rachel squealed. She stroked his arms beneath the wet cotton of his sleeves.

"The worst thing about this job is working in the rain, but do you know what the best thing is?"

She squeezed his arms, and it started to get to him—in a good way.

"Free fruit?"

"No. It's mindless work, so I can think about anything I want. That means I can spend *all* day thinking about you." His gaze locked on hers, and he gave her a quick kiss. "And us." He kissed her again and felt that familiar burning rush in his chest that made him think that given enough time kissing her, he would probably explode.

A few others worked in the orchard, so there was no guarantee against prying eyes, but they weren't Rachel's parents' eyes, so Paul figured he could do about anything short of ravaging her right there under the peach tree without anyone so much as batting an eye. Tempting.

She stepped back and reached overhead for a piece of low-hanging fruit. "May I?"

"It'll cost you."

She took two steps backward. "How much?"

With a gleam in her eye, and her feet braced to bolt, she took another step backward with the peach protected behind her back.

"I'll have to extract a pound of flesh."

With that she took off, and he was on her heels. It was good to see her run and move. He didn't know how she withstood the unbearable amount of restrictions on her activity over the last couple of months.

All healed or not, his legs were longer, he was faster, and in a second or two he would bring her down. He reminded himself this wasn't Sean, and he needed to go easy if he was going to tackle her.

He got an arm around her waist, and she screamed and stopped in her tracks.

He collided with her, sliding on the wet grass and falling partly on top of her. He landed hard on his elbow. "Ow!"

She wriggled her arm out from between them and held up the unbruised peach. "It's still mine."

He rolled off of her onto his back, rubbing his elbow with his opposite hand.

She moved onto her side. Grass stained her shorts and tee shirt. "Are you okay?" Her brows pinched together.

He'd only taken a hit to his funny bone, but he had one last chance to turn this to his advantage. He cradled his elbow against his chest and groaned.

Kneeling over him, she repeated with more urgency. "Paul, are you okay?"

He wasn't much of an actor, but he faked a grimace.

Still holding that blasted peach in her hand, she grew closer.

He grabbed her again around the waist and rolled her onto her back so that he was lying on top of her again.

The instant he saw her beneath him, he knew this had been a big mistake. He couldn't goof around with her anymore without it turning into this. Too much energy, too much proximity, and in this case, too much privacy. With Sean's admonition still swirling in his mind, he wouldn't let anything happen today, but he couldn't let her go without—he captured her lips with his.

If that first kiss at Sean's wedding uncorked the dam holding him back, this kiss was demolishing it. She was so free, so alive, and so vulnerable there underneath him. His body was on sensory overload. The smell of rain and peaches lingered in the air as his hands and lips made their way over her warm, damp skin and, God help him, she moaned.

She gripped the back of his wet tee shirt.

A muffled plop of sorts came from the grass alongside him.

The peach.

It wasn't much of a motivator to pull his lips away from her skin, but it would have to do. He sat back on his heels, grabbed the peach, and held it up in victory. "Got it!"

She tried to pout, but it gave way to a smirk. "Only because you cheated by kissing me like that."

If he didn't get out of this situation quick, he was going to kiss her again. And he may not stop there. Her hair was loose, and it splayed all around her in the grass, right over a...

"Rachel, don't move." His voice came out shaky. "There's a snake by your head."

"Yeah, right. You've already got the peach. I concede." She blew a few loose hairs from her face and huffed.

A black rat snake at least a yard long uncoiled next to her, its head slipping beneath her hair as its smooth body parted the grasses and leaves in its path.

"I'm not kidding, Rachel. It's not poisonous or anything, but you don't want it to bite you."

"That's the best you've got? There's a snake in my hair?" She propped herself up on her elbows, and the movement caused the snake to retract and still.

"You don't believe me? I'll prove it to you." He scanned the area, trying to find a fallen branch he could use to prod or lift the snake. Nothing. He wasn't afraid of snakes, but he had a healthy respect for any wild animal and preferred to keep his distance. Paul inched his hand forward and grabbed the snake behind the head, lifting it for Rachel to see. Its lower body twisted and swung in the air.

Rachel shrieked and leaped to her feet.

Paul slung the snake into deep grass several yards away.

Rachel stared into the grass and brushed her left arm as if trying to remove any traces of snake.

"I tried to tell you."

"It sounded ridiculous. I thought you were messing with me."

"Yeah, well, I was messing with you all right." He grabbed her around the waist and pulled her close. "That's probably why we didn't see the snake in the first place."

She smacked his arm.

A motor, rumbling like a lawnmower, came their way. Jorge, one of the seasonal workers, trundled over the uneven ground.

"Pablo, Mr. Shalamon say to go home. Another storm is coming." Jorge jutted his chin to the sky, indicating the dark cumulus clouds amassing in the west. "Go now and beat the storm. I punch clock for you."

"Thanks, Jorge."

He grabbed Paul's nearly-full bushel basket, loaded it into the back of the cart, then waved as he took off down the lane.

Paul glanced at Rachel. "You think we can beat it?"

Thunder cracked in answer.

"Truthfully? No, but we can try."

They set off at a quick pace, but in less than a minute the heavens opened in a torrential downpour. Since they were already soaked to the bone, they slowed and walked at a normal speed. Dripping wet, Rachel's hair seemed much longer. At least it covered most of her back; otherwise he could see straight through her light yellow shirt to her bra. He wished he had something dry he could give her so she could return home with some shred of modesty. He reached for her hand, and when she took it, she smiled at him through the rain dripping down her hair and lashes onto her face.

"The look on your face when I held up that snake…" He shook his head and laughed. "Priceless."

She used their connected hands to jab him in the side. "Oh, hey, I almost forgot. Speaking of priceless…"

She let go of him and reached into her shorts pocket. She twisted her hand against the damp denim and pulled out a small object, holding it in her open palm for him to see. "Look what I found this morning." She gave him a few seconds to examine it. "I was digging behind the log bench, almost near the slope when I found this."

Paul blinked the water from his eyes and focused. He turned the quarter-sized golden rock over in his hand and rubbed his thumb across it. The rain slowed to a drizzle. He wiped the rock with the underside of his shirt. It was mostly dull, but the rain revealed some shiny spots. "This might be real."

"And it might be a funny-colored rock. Did you ever see that episode of 'Little House on the Prairie' where Laura and her friend spend all this time panning for gold, and they're all proud of themselves because they think they've found treasure? Laura has all these daydreams about being rich, they haul a wheelbarrow full of their gold to the banker, and it turns out to be Fool's Gold. That's how I see this going."

Paul returned the rock to Rachel, and she shoved it into her wet pocket. "First of all, I've never seen *Little House on the Prairie*. Remember, no mother means no chick shows. I watched shows like *Walker, Texas Ranger*. Second, we test it. You can do an acid test to tell if it's real gold."

"I don't think we should get our hopes up. Even if it's real, this may be all we find."

Paul stopped walking. "Rachel, do you know the price of gold per ounce?"

Rachel took a few steps then stopped and turned to him. "No."

"It's more than a thousand dollars, at least. C'mon, you're not the least bit excited about this?"

"I had no idea it was that much." She shrugged her shoulders and started walking again. "I want to be excited, but it seems too good to be true."

"So do you but you're real, aren't you?" He wasn't just saying that. For the first few months after he met her, he waited for some major flaw to be revealed—he'd discover she was manipulative, bossy, or a liar. None of that had proven to be true. She wasn't perfect, and neither was he, but they were pretty darn good together.

She spread her arms and said, "With me, what you see is what you get." She wrapped her arms around herself again, probably remembering her soaked shirt.

"It's okay. I'm not looking—at least I'm trying not to. We should get back and get dried off. I'm starving too. I wonder what your mom made for dinner."

"She didn't make dinner. I did." Her eyes beamed with pride. "Before I came to see you, I made a pot of soup and baked chocolate chip cookies."

"No way. Cookies? I'll race you. I'll even give you a head start."

Rachel took off, and they reached the house neck and neck. He showered and dried off at the guesthouse and went back to Rachel's. Her soup was good, and the cookies were even better. After dinner, her mom and dad sat around the table talking with James while he and Rachel used the laptop in the living room to Google "how to tell if gold is real." Paul pulled up a bunch of hits on how to do it.

"Here." He scanned the page. "Rub on an unglazed porcelain tile. If it makes a black mark, it's not real. A magnet should not be attracted to it. It won't dissolve in acid."

"Dad has a piece of tile in the shed, and you can get a magnet from the kitchen."

"Okay, and if it passes those tests, I'll see if I can get some hydrochloric acid. There's a guy that comes out to the orchard and does something chemical with the composting system. He might know how to get some."

"I'll be right back." Rachel jogged to the shed, and Paul loped to the kitchen to grab a magnet off the refrigerator. James had left the table, but Rachel's parents seemed engaged in a serious conversation.

"Ron, I know what you're saying, but maybe we should get it over and done with," Mrs. Mueller said. "They'll give us something for it, and it's not as though you or anyone else is going to use a parcel of land that small for anything."

"It's the principle of the thing, Linda." Mr. Mueller pounded his fist on the table. "This is our property, and no one is going to steal it out from under us."

"But what's worse, them taking a small piece and compensating us—"

"Under-compensating us."

"Or," Mrs. Muller continued, "taking it by eminent domain?"

Paul headed back into the living room. Who wanted their property and what for?

Rachel sauntered into the room with a small square of gray ceramic tile. "Let's take this outside." She grabbed the small rock, Paul grabbed the magnet, and they left by the back door.

"I heard your parents talking about someone trying to buy or take part of their property. Your dad seems pretty juiced about it. You know what's going on?"

Rachel sat on top of the picnic table and stretched her legs out on the bench. "Sort of. About a year ago, Dad got a letter from the state saying they want to run a natural gas pipeline through here. Then in the winter, they made an offer on part of the land. Dad would have to get it subdivided and sell, but he said they're not even offering half of what it's worth. So, he won't sell it."

Paul sat next to her and rested his elbows on his knees. "I heard them talking about eminent domain though."

"Yeah, now the state says if Mom and Dad won't sell, they'll take it anyway. I think they'd give them something, but Dad wants no part of it." She held the piece of tile out for him.

"Is there anything he can do about it?" Paul sat up and took the tile. He scratched the rock diagonally across it, leaving behind a golden yellow smudge. He did it again.

Still no black mark. He held the rock out to her, and she gave a swipe with it too.

"Well, he has a lawyer, but if the state tries to take it by eminent domain, that's it. My parents can appeal, but that might not stop it from happening."

Paul stared at the tile. "Are you seeing this?"

"Yeah. I'm not getting a black mark." She handed him the rock and the magnet. "Here, you try the magnet."

Paul took the rock in one hand and the magnet in the other. He tapped the magnet against the rock, waiting to feel a pull. Nothing. Again. Nothing.

"This could be real." He knew she was skeptical, but he couldn't keep the excitement out of his voice.

"Let's wait and see how the acid test turns out. And, Paul, let's not say anything to anyone about this yet. Not even Sean or my parents. The less people we look like fools in front of the better."

"Agreed." He searched her face for a trace of the enthusiasm he felt. She stared back, her eyes serene and her expression blank. "You're awfully pessimistic about this, aren't you?"

"I'm being realistic. Finding interesting artifacts is one thing. How many people do you think find buried treasure? Next to none."

Buried treasure. He hadn't thought of it like that. It did sound far-fetched. "You're probably right, but you've got to let me dream a little." Finally, he was able to coax a smile out of her.

"Dream away. Check it out with the compost guy. If that's good, I think we should take it to a jeweler."

They didn't talk about the gold for the rest of the evening, but it lingered in Paul's mind. What if it *was* real gold? What if there was more of it?

After Paul said goodnight to everyone and stole a long, slow kiss on Rachel's front porch, he returned to the guesthouse and opened his laptop. He searched "treasure," "gold," and the name of every little town he could think of in a ten-mile radius. Half a dozen searches later, he was rewarded with a link to an eight-year-old article from *Treasure Trove* magazine.

Paul scrolled down through the ads for metal detectors and gold test kits to the article. He couldn't blink or breathe until he got to the end.

Chapter 21
Eureka!

Paul scrolled up and re-read the story for the third time. An amateur treasure hunter from about fifty miles south of the Mueller's house crisscrossed three states multiple times searching for supposed lost treasure. A wagon-load of gold had gone missing between Wheeling, West Virginia, and the Mint in Philadelphia during the summer of 1863.

A Union Army lieutenant in charge of the expedition diverted the convoy's course north to avoid the battle at Gettysburg in early July. The lieutenant fell ill, and one of the soldiers went for help. When he returned ten days later with a rescue party, the camp was empty. The men, the wagons, and the gold—all gone. The convoy, comprising two wagons, eight soldiers, and more than two dozen fifty-pound bars of gold, was lost in the wilderness of Pennsylvania. The rescue party discovered the body of the lieutenant buried in a shallow grave nearby.

The treasure hunter relied on a map he purchased at a pawnshop in Williamsport, Pennsylvania, for his exploration.

Paul clicked on the blurred image of a black-and-white map to enlarge it. James could draw a better map. Stick-like trees dotted the center along with a body of water, probably the Susquehanna River. A mountain range framed the upper left corner opposite a big, fat X. A small arrow pointed to the X. Paul squinted at the text beside it.

He sounded it out. "Aboard mihe? Ab...abandoned mihe...abandoned mine."

Abandoned mine? Paul pushed away from the screen and let the information sink in. The path across northern

Pennsylvania wilderness, the Union Army wagon, the hole Rachel fell in, the gold...it all added up. He pulled the small rock from his pocket and turned it over in his hand. "Unbelievable."

His heart pounded. He wanted to call Rachel, but she wouldn't have a cell phone in her room—her mom insisted they stay charging in the kitchen all night to be sure they weren't in use after bedtime. He didn't want to wake her whole family. He'd have to wait until morning.

***

Paul dressed as soon as the sun crept above the horizon. He jogged over to Rachel's house and knocked on the door. No one responded, so he twisted the knob. Locked. He knocked again, louder this time. Finally, the deadbolt turned. Rachel's dad opened the door, sleepy and unshaven.

"Good morning, Mr. Mueller." Paul squeezed by him and darted into the kitchen, his laptop under his arm.

Mr. Mueller shuffled behind him then stopped, rubbed his eyes, and ran a hand over the stubble of his beard. "Paul, it's barely six o'clock on a Saturday. What are you doing here? Why are you even up? Is something wrong?"

Paul peered around the dark living room, wishing Rachel were already awake. "I need to talk to Rachel, sir."

"Son, if you can wake her, by all means, talk to her all you want. I'm going back to bed." He turned and shuffled down the hall toward his bedroom.

With his laptop still at his side, Paul followed Rachel's dad down the hallway, stopping at Rachel's bedroom. Conscious that Mrs. Mueller and James still slept, Paul kept his voice to a loud whisper. "Thanks, Mr. Mueller."

Mr. Mueller didn't bother to lower his voice. "Uh, Romeo, I'm sleepy, not stupid. I'll wait here while you try to wake her. If you can do it, and she doesn't bite your head off in the process, you can have your conversation in the living room."

Paul nodded. Carte blanche access to Rachel had been too much to ask.

He'd only glimpsed Rachel's bedroom a few times. Her parents didn't allow them to be in there alone. Rachel lay on her side, her hair in disarray and fanned over the pillow. Her lips parted, and she sighed. If he weren't there to tell her something important—and her dad weren't hovering nearby—he would've loved to watch her sleep, stroking her long, silky hair. He was on a mission, though, so he sat on the edge of her bed and gently shook her shoulder.

"Rachel...Rachel, time to get up."

She opened her eyes and blinked twice. She stared blankly, as if in a dream. "How did you get in here?"

He recalled joking that he should sneak into her bed at night but resisted the temptation to tease her. "It's morning. Your dad let me in." He opened his computer on his lap.

"He *what*?" Her voice rose both in volume and in tone as she propped herself up on her elbows.

"Shhh," he whispered with a finger to his lips.

She pushed her hair behind her ears and spoke more softly. "My dad let you come into my bedroom while I was sleeping?"

Paul grinned. "He's lurking outside the door." The web browser was taking forever to open. "I need to talk to you. Come out to the living room with me?"

Rachel glanced toward her window. Light seeped in around the edges of the curtains. She sat up, and the sheet fell from her shoulders, revealing a silky pink camisole with spaghetti straps and lace trim. The fabric hung loosely over her soft curves.

Interesting. He thought her more of a long sleep shirt kind of girl. It wasn't an unpleasant surprise. Paul struggled to refocus and deliberately averted his eyes to clear the vision from his mind. How long could it take to pull up the *Treasure Trove* story?

"Uh, do you want me to step out while you get dressed?" Could he just ask her to cover up? Not that he didn't like what he saw, but now would not be a good time to give in to temptation for myriad reasons.

"Oh." She glanced down at her chest. "Would you hand me my robe? It's behind the door."

He set the laptop on the bed and retrieved the matching silky pink robe from its hook. "Here."

She swung it around her shoulders and tied it in front. "What's so important that you couldn't wait a couple hours until everyone was up?"

"I'll show you. C'mon."

She pushed the covers off and pulled the robe down to cover her legs.

He grabbed his laptop and strode toward the living room, nodding to Mr. Mueller as he headed toward his own bedroom. Rachel's bare feet made hardly a sound behind him.

He sunk into the couch and adjusted the computer on his legs. The page had finally loaded, and he turned the screen toward Rachel, who had slid in alongside him.

"What am I looking at?" She adjusted her robe, making sure it covered everything it should.

"It's an article from *Treasure Trove* magazine. Scroll down to the part about the gold being transported to the Philadelphia Mint around the time of the Battle of Gettysburg."

The glow of the screen lit Rachel's face as her eyes shifted from side to side, skimming the article.

"Well? What do you think?" His knee itched to bounce up and down, almost of its own volition. He stilled it with his hand, barely able to contain his excitement.

Rachel tilted the screen back and stared. "It's kind of

uncanny. You think our little hunk of gold came from that?"

"Maybe. It's hard to see on here, but look at this map." Paul took control of the laptop, clicked on the map, and angled the screen back toward her.

Rachel studied it for a few seconds. "Oh, come on, that looks like one of the treasure maps James draws."

"I know, I know. That's what I thought too, but look at what this says." He pointed at the screen. "Abandoned mine. Don't you think it all fits? The location, the wagon wood, the gold, the mine?"

Deep in thought, Rachel dropped her gaze to her lap. Her brows knit together as she considered the puzzle pieces he put together last night. "I guess it could."

"So, do you feel like doing some digging this morning?" It was fun sharing a secret with her, especially one this big.

She smiled. "I get the feeling I can't say no."

He shook his head. "No, not an option. Get dressed and meet me outside." He kissed her cheek, closed his laptop, and nearly skipped to the kitchen door.

Rachel headed for her room, passing her dad as he plodded down the hall toward Paul and the kitchen. He was still unshaven, wearing only pajama bottoms and an undershirt, but his eyes appeared less sleepy now. "Did you talk to her?"

Paul stopped as he neared the door. "Yep. We're going down to the garden to work."

Her dad shook his head. "Well, if I had any doubt, I guess I don't anymore."

"What do you mean?"

"Only love would make that girl get out of bed so early." His lips twisted in aggravation, and his brows knit together.

Paul smiled. "I'd like to think so." The possibility of discovering treasure worth an obscene amount of money might have something to do with it too.

"Waffles in, uh..." He glanced at the wall clock. "Half an hour?"

"Oh, that's okay. I'm not very hungry."

Rachel's dad laid a hand on Paul's forehead as if taking his temperature. "Hmmm. Feels normal. You've lived here, what, eighteen months? I've never known you *not* to be hungry outside of the first day Rachel was in the hospital. What's going on, Paul?"

"Nothing really. At least not yet. Just eager to get to work, sir." Paul suppressed a grin and ignored the look questioning his sanity. If they found more rocks and they turned out to be the real deal, they'd have plenty to tell Rachel's dad later.

***

"I'm starting to feel like one of the Seven Dwarfs." Perspiration trickled beneath Rachel's hair, tickling her neck. She scrunched her shoulders as it dripped down her back.

"Huh?" Paul didn't stop digging. He was relentless in searching for the supposed treasure. They'd been digging for two weeks since he showed her the article from the treasure hunters' magazine.

"You know, 'We dig, dig, dig, dig, dig, dig, dig from early morn till night.'" So, her singing wasn't impressive. "You can't tell me you haven't seen *Snow White and the Seven Dwarfs*. I know it's got a princess, but it is *not* a chick flick."

"You can rest easy. I've seen it." He stopped digging and leaned against the shovel handle. "Maybe we're not looking in the right place, or we're skimming the surface. That gold is somewhere; we just have to find it."

She plunged the shovel into the soil again, her heel and body weight pressing it deeper into the ground. A metallic clang reverberated through the shovel.

"Did you hear that?" A surge of optimism struck her. "What do you think—tin can, piece of an animal trap?"

"Let's see." Paul dropped on all fours and dug with his gloved hands. In several minutes, he unearthed what looked like a larger version of the small golden rock Rachel had found. Much larger. It measured at least a foot long and ten inches wide. A huge smile spread across his face.

Rachel tried to lift it. "I can't get it. It's too heavy."

Paul pried it free and hoisted the bar into his arms. He shook his head, his eyes wide and gleaming. "Geez. It must weigh forty pounds.

"Oh, my gosh, Paul." A tidal force of giddiness hit her, and her stomach tingled in anticipation. "Do you think this is real?"

"Why would someone mold it into a bar if it wasn't real?"

"What do we do with it?" Rachel brushed away several patches of dirt caked to the bar's sides.

Paul glanced around the garden. "I think we ought to store it at the house somewhere and look for more. Once we think we have it all, we can decide what to do next. Get it tested, I guess. We'll need to tell your parents."

They continued digging but found nothing more that day. Over the next week, they discovered eleven more bars, all with similar dimensions and weight.

Transporting them from the garden to the house was a challenge. Rachel couldn't carry them by herself, so Paul loaded them onto a wheelbarrow, which they hid in the garden the best they could. During the day, when everyone was out or otherwise occupied, Rachel wheeled it up to the house covered with flowers, dirt, or whatever she could find. Then, under the cover of darkness, Paul took the gold bars and hid them in the guesthouse loft.

At the end of the week, confident that they'd found all

there was to discover, they took a break from digging. Rachel's garden didn't need tending, so she took her e-reader beneath the shade of the big elm tree that grew at the edge of their yard. The midday August air was stifling, even in the shade, and every couple of minutes her head bobbed. She reread the same passage at least six times. Giving up, she turned the e-reader off and leaned her head against the rough, cool tree trunk.

The storm door squeaked.

"Rachel. Paul's on the phone for you," Mom called from the back door.

Paul never called from work, and it was early for his lunch break.

Rachel stood, brushed off her shorts, and jogged to the house. She took the phone from her mom and held it up to her ear as she headed back into the yard. "Hey, what's up?"

"The biology guy—actually he's a chemist, I think—he was here today, and I showed him the rock. He's not a metallurgist or anything, but he thinks it's gold."

Rachel stopped walking. "Are you kidding me?"

He laughed, his exhilaration and excitement contagious. "Honest to God, no, I'm not kidding."

Rachel paced around the picnic table. "What do we do?" She had hoped it was gold, but deep down she wouldn't allow herself to believe it. People didn't just find gold lying around no matter how much they wished, prayed, or dug.

"I don't think we should do anything yet. Let's sit on it a couple of days, and then we'll talk to your parents and Sean about having it appraised."

"Do you think it's safe?"

A few seconds of silence elapsed. "It's been buried underground for a hundred and fifty years. I don't think a couple more days in that loft are going to hurt it."

"Oh, my gosh, Paul. This is big. Huge."

The excitement in his voice raised her pulse. "I know. I'm stoked."

***

Rachel closed her eyes, but sleep didn't come. The air was so sticky the sheets clung to her damp skin. She kicked them off and lay under the ceiling fan, lifting her camisole away from her chest in a vain effort to cool her skin. Even the hum of the cicadas' steady rhythm couldn't lull her to sleep.

She still couldn't believe it was real. That rock, those bars, were gold. Everyone harbored a secret childhood dream of finding buried treasure, didn't they? Look at James, who made treasure maps and planted X's everywhere, especially in places they weren't wanted. He was just a kid, but as Paul had discovered when he found that online magazine, there were grown men equipped with metal detectors doing essentially the same thing.

Tomorrow was Friday. By some miracle Paul was off, and her mom had promised to take them to the pool. Saturday he'd probably work ten or twelve hours, but Sunday would be free. They'd decided that they would talk to her parents and Sean about the gold over dinner on Sunday. Only two more days, and they could share their secret.

Chapter 22
On the Brink

Mom stepped on the gas as the light turned green, zooming from zero to forty in three seconds. She glanced at the dashboard clock for about the twentieth time. Mom was way stressed.

She'd been fifteen minutes late in picking up Rachel and Paul from the pool, and she was supposed to pick up James from a friend's house five minutes ago.

Mom glanced at her in the rearview mirror. "Rachel, I'm going to drop you and Paul off at home. I need you to preheat the oven for me and start a pot of water boiling for dinner."

"Okay. What time?" She would rather go home and start dinner than ride around in her damp bathing suit anyhow.

Mom glanced at her through the mirror. "A quarter after five. Set it to 375 degrees."

"I could throw together a salad too, if you want."

"Already done. It's in the refrigerator, but thanks. Oh, and Paul—" She found Paul in the rearview mirror. "I think there's a load of your clothes in the dryer."

"Okay. Thanks. I'll get 'em."

Rachel slipped her foot out of her flip-flop and placed it on Paul's foot. He continued to gaze out the window as if he didn't notice, but he slid his foot out of his flip-flop too, and wiggled it back beneath her foot.

They had gotten adept at playing footsie and holding hands in ways that didn't draw attention from the front seat. He looked at their feet then took her hand, turned it over, and traced the letter "I" on her palm with his index finger. It tickled, and Rachel struggled to keep from either giggling or pulling her hand away. He continued tracing a heart and then a letter "U."

When he was done, he peered at her from the corner of his eye.

Tempted to stare at his tan skin and bare chest, she bit her lower lip and averted her gaze. Even the religious medal she'd given him, which he seldom took off, looked downright sexy on him. She turned their hands over and used her finger to trace two words on his palm: "Home alone."

***

Paul gazed at his palm and bit the inside of his cheek. Did he read that right? He knew Mr. Mueller was going to be late tonight. What was she suggesting?

He raised his eyes to hers, and her smile gave him both the answer he sought and all the encouragement he needed. His heart rate accelerated.

While they were horsing around in the pool, he had been keenly aware that only the thin fabric of his low-riding trunks and her navy and white polka dot tankini separated them. Plenty of girls at the pool wore significantly less, making Rachel's suit modest by most standards. Still, it was a swimsuit, sleek material designed to hug her body, cover the essentials and not much more.

Mom screeched to a halt in the driveway. "Everybody out. Don't forget about the oven and the water, Rachel."

"I won't."

Paul slammed the car door behind them. "Man, she's in a hurry." He stared as Rachel's mom backed up and pulled away, his heart hammering in his chest. Another couple seconds...one...two...and they were alone.

"Yeah, she is." Rachel fiddled with the house key. By the time she opened the door, her mom's car was out of sight.

Rachel entered the house first, Paul a step behind her. The late afternoon sun beat down, its sweltering hotness pouring through the door and the old window seals. The window shades were pulled low to block the late afternoon heat, creating shadows along the walls and a quiet stillness. Judging by the humidity, the air conditioning unit in the living room couldn't keep pace with the rising heat index.

The keys jangled in Rachel's hand as she stepped into the dimly-lit room. Paul grabbed her hand and pulled her back toward him.

The keys fell to the floor with a clatter.

Her body slammed into his, and before she could say anything, his lips captured hers. Without breaking their kiss, they shuffled forward, and he set his iPod on the table behind the couch. Pushing the beach towels they had dropped out of the way, he eased Rachel onto the cool vinyl floor.

The St. Paul medal swung freely around his neck, dangling above Rachel's chest. Paul tugged it over his head and set it on the floor. He was pretty sure St. Paul frowned on what was about to happen; no sense bringing him into this.

The strawberry fragrance of her hair and the earthy, herbal sunscreen on her skin pervaded his senses, intoxicating him. Her scent, the taste of her lips, and the silky softness of her skin...Paul let it all carry him away.

Rachel ran her fingers through his hair, and his scalp tingled at her touch. She tilted her head so Paul could kiss her neck.

"Paul, how old do you have to be to get married?" Her voice was all breathy.

"Huh?" *What did she say? Get married?* He trailed kisses up and down her neck. "Uh, sixteen." He started on the other side of her neck. "In Pennsylvania, sixteen."

"For real?"

"Mmm hmm. Need parental consent if you're under eighteen."

"You've looked into this." Her tone shifted from breathy to wondrous.

His lips lifted in a half grin. "I may have Googled it." His gaze met hers and the heat in her green eyes pushed his heart rate sky high.

Rachel wound her fingers through his still-damp hair, pulling him closer to kiss him again.

His breath caught.

"And remind me again...why are we waiting..." He detected a note of pleading in her voice. "...to have sex?"

"Nothing coming to mind right now." That was the truth. How could he think at a time like this?

"Paul, I love you. I want you so bad I feel like I can't breathe."

"I love you too." His heart stilled. He stopped kissing her and drew back. By some miracle, Paul recognized the moment for what it was—their last chance for turning back before they reached the point of no return.

I'd be a fool to stop now. She wants me, and I love her.

Yet something didn't feel right. Well, physically it felt as right as that plunge into the cool water from the fiery pavement had felt this afternoon, but in every other way, not so much. If they didn't stop, there would be sweet relief, satisfaction, and...

"Rachel..." He needed to say something now. Otherwise, he was pretty sure he was moving into territory where words were superfluous.

"Tomorrow morning, when we're not hot, and wet, and totally turned on by each other, are we going to be sorry we made love, or sorry we didn't?"

Rachel's body relaxed beneath him. She averted her gaze but didn't answer. She didn't have to. They would both regret going any further.

Paul rolled over and lay on the floor, staring at the ceiling while massaging his forehead with his hands.

Rachel sat up, adjusting her swimsuit up and down in the appropriate places.

"Thank you." Her voice was soft and meek, more chastened than he'd ever heard it.

"For what?" He smacked both hands hard against the bare floor and pushed himself up in one deft movement. "I didn't give you what you wanted, but I still managed to break all of our rules."

"For having enough self-control to stop when you did. Most days we can kiss, and I can walk away and be cool with it. And then there's days like today that I can't stop thinking about you, and kissing doesn't seem like enough."

"That's pretty much how I feel all the time." *Every freakin' waking minute. And some of the sleeping minutes too.*

Paul grasped Rachel's hands and pulled her to her feet. Releasing her, he bent and picked up his medal, pulled it over his head, and paced around the room, hoping his heart would stop pounding out of his chest. In his peripheral vision, he could see Rachel combing her hair out with her fingers. When he turned, her eyes were trained on his body. His cheeks, already flushed, burned.

Rachel's head snapped in the opposite direction, but not before he recognized the look of innocent curiosity she wore. His embarrassment dissolved into something else—guilt and then shame. His curiosity about her body was anything but innocent.

Rachel walked to the kitchen, lifted a pot out from under the sink, and began filling it with water. She looked at him—this time into his eyes. "I want to be with you, Paul, but I always thought I'd wait until I was married. What if I got pregnant?"

Paul stopped pacing. "I know...I get it." He'd thought he'd wait until he was married too, but he'd realized lately that was a default position. Was he convinced it was the best way or the only right way? He wasn't sure anymore. He needed some counsel. "Hey, maybe we should go to confession. Maybe we need a shot of grace."

She smiled. "Confession?" She blinked and her smile faded. "Did we sin? We didn't go through with it." She lifted the pot from the sink and carried it to the stove. The lid hit the top of the pot with a clatter.

"No, but…" Did they? Where was the line? How far could they go without it being a sin? He *did* know that even if he hadn't yet *gone all the way* in real life, it happened with frequency in his daydreams. Not only was his love teetering on lust, but it was becoming a source of other temptations as well.

Rachel pulled a saucepan from the cabinet and set it on the stovetop. "I can't ask my parents to take us. My mom would be all over that, and my dad would never let us be alone together again."

Paul let out a deep breath. Had their actions alienated her from her parents? He didn't want that. She was so blessed to have them. Still, he understood her fear. "You're right, I guess. Maybe I can get Sean to take me. Go separately. Or we can wait until school starts and make an appointment with the chaplain, but I'd rather go sooner than later."

A few minutes of silence passed between them. Rachel turned on the burner and the oven and approached him. Taking his hands, she swung them back and forth with hers, a mischievous, playful look in her eyes. "You know, the fact that you stopped makes you even more irresistible to me."

"Don't even go there, Rachel." Paul yanked his hand from her, snatched a pillow from the couch, and whipped it at her.

It caught her in the side, and she yelped.

He grinned. "I've got to get my stuff and get out of here."

In the laundry room, he grabbed an armload of his clean clothes from the dryer, and slung them over his arm. He stooped twice on his way toward the door to retrieve a wayward sock.

"Here," Rachel called as she disappeared into the laundry room. "Use this basket."

He waited a minute until she returned with a white plastic laundry basket and set it in front of him.

"Thanks." He dropped the clothes into the basket then grabbed his iPod off the table and put in his ear buds.

He hefted the laundry basket into his arms and forced his feet to move toward the door. He touched his iPod. "You Can Look But You Better Not Touch" blared in his ears.

Really, Dad? You didn't even like Bruce Springsteen.

Paul strolled back to the guesthouse, all the frustration and irritability melting away.

Chapter 23
Fraternal Correction

Paul lay on his bed, his hands clasped behind his head, staring at the ceiling. He'd given up even trying to get his mind off Rachel and what they'd almost done.

"Hey." Sean's voice called to him from the door. "You home?"

"In here," Paul said, not moving from the bed.

Sean sauntered into the bedroom and leaned against the door jamb. "What's wrong with you? Other than it feels like it's a thousand degrees in here."

"Nothing's wrong. Just thinking."

"About what?"

Paul sat up on the bed and crossed his legs. "Can I ask you something?"

"Sure. Let me get a chair." He glanced down at his tee shirt smeared with grease in spots. "I'm filthy. That's what you get when I come straight from work." Sean grabbed a wooden chair out from under Paul's kitchen table, dragged it to the bedroom doorway, turned it around, and sat so that he could rest his elbows on the back. "Okay. *Something's* bothering you. Shoot."

Paul breathed in and tensed. Maybe this wasn't a good idea. This wasn't the kind of thing he talked about with anyone. Ever. He needed advice though, and Sean was all he had. He exhaled and blurted it out. "Did you and Amanda have sex before you got married?"

Sean rubbed a hand over his face. "That's kind of personal, isn't it?"

"Yeah, it's just—" Paul stared aimlessly at the bedspread. How much should he say? He could keep it general, as if he was just curious.

Sean's face grew serious, and his eyes drilled Paul for the truth. His knuckles went white where his hands clasped together. "Dammit, Paul—did you get Rachel pregnant?"

Paul's head darted up. "No, but—"

"How can you be sure?"

Uh, cause we haven't had sex. Yet. Sweat beaded behind his neck, only partially from the heat. He should never have started this conversation. "Listen—"

"Mr. Mueller would kill you, you know."

Heck with it. He needed to say it aloud to someone. He scooted to the edge of the bed, where he sat face to face with Sean. "Yeah, but, Sean, I love her. I *ache* for her." This was harder than he thought. "We were goofing around together at the pool, and I think it sort of built up and overwhelmed us."

Sean swore and dropped his head onto his hands. "Listen..." He sat in silence a half minute, then stood and slid the chair back to its place in the kitchen. "We need to have this conversation. Go tell the Muellers you won't be around for dinner. We'll get something together."

"You're seriously not going to lecture me, are you?"

"I don't lecture, but we need to talk."

Paul slid his feet into his flip-flops, and went next door while Sean called Amanda to let her know his plans.

The truck rumbled as they accelerated on a winding hill. Trees zipped by, reminding Paul of his first glimpse of this place he now thought of as home. Then, the trees had been barren and lifeless. Now, verdant foliage hid their bark-covered skeletons, making the hills and valleys come alive.

"How's work?" Sean glanced from the road to Paul and back again.

"Okay."

A few silent moments ticked by, punctuated by the shifting of gears.

"Hey, there's a new Marvel movie coming out at Christmas? Did you hear?"

Paul tried to focus on the question. "Huh? No. Hadn't heard."

Sean let out a sigh and repositioned himself in his seat. He tapped his hand against the steering wheel. "I was thinking we'd go hunting one weekend in September. You up for it?" His gaze flicked to Paul again.

Paul grunted as he considered whether that was something he wanted to do or whether he'd rather hang out with Rachel. "Maybe. Something's wrong with my .22 though. Last time I used it, I lined up the sight, but it shot off to the left."

"Huh. I'll have to get someone to take a look at it." He turned the truck into the Hardee's drive-thru. "Think about it, okay? I'd like to go."

"Yeah. Sure."

A few minutes later, after plopping the hot, greasy bags in Paul's lap, Sean drove to the nearest neighborhood park. They carried their dinner to an empty picnic table in the wooden pavilion. It took several minutes for Paul to find a table that wasn't either dotted with bird poop or acorn-shell fragments left by squirrels. He settled on a table in the rear corner and pulled their food out of the bags while Sean bought their drinks, his cell phone up to his ear.

"I love you too," he said and ended the call.

"Here's your Sprite." Sean put the drink down in front of Paul and sipped his Coke. "I put this conversation off way too long. I apologize. This was Dad's job. Did he ever talk to you about sex?"

Paul unwrapped his sandwich. "When I was about twelve, he did, but it was just kind of a biology lesson. At least that's what I remember. I might have tuned out or forgotten the rest."

Sean sat across from him and fiddled with the foil

wrapper while he stared at his sandwich. Paul smiled as he thought how difficult he could make this for his brother if he wanted.

"Let's pray." Sean bowed his head, and they said a quick grace before digging into their burgers and french fries.

"Amanda's confident I'm going to say the right things to you. I'm not so sure." He bit into his burger and wiped the corners of his mouth with a paper napkin.

Paul stopped chewing. "You talked about this with her?" He loved his sister-in-law, but his cheeks burned at the idea of her being privy to the kind of personal things he was about to share with Sean. He forced down the wad of sandwich in his mouth. "How much of this does Amanda need to know?"

"I've only told her that we needed to talk about your relationship with Rachel. And that's all she's going to know. This is between us."

He took a breath and nodded. "Okay. Cool."

Paul thought back over the months since he and Rachel had first gotten carried away while watching that stupid piranha movie. They had respected their rules, and though it seemed contradictory, he found that having some boundaries made him feel freer. They had a code of conduct, and as long as they honored it, they could be loving and affectionate with each other and neither of them worried about things getting out of hand. It had worked well until today.

Paul shoved a couple of fries in his mouth, chewed, and swallowed. "So, you and Amanda didn't wait to...y'know ...*did* you?"

Sean nodded as he finished chewing. "Yeah, we waited." He sipped his drink. "But there was someone else before Amanda. It wasn't anything like you and Rachel. I didn't even love her. I could give you a bunch of excuses, but I slept with her." Sean clenched his jaw, his regrets evident in the grim set of his lips. "She was the first, and I could never take that back."

"Does Amanda know?"

He nodded. "She didn't say much, but I know it hurt when I told her. I never want to see that look on her face again."

"Rachel and I..." *Why is this so hard?* "...we haven't..." He should be proud they hadn't, right? Then why did he feel embarrassed about it? "...we haven't had sex...yet."

Sean blew out a breath and leaned back. The tension left his face, and he almost smiled. "When you said what happened after the pool, I assumed..."

Paul shook his head. "No. I stopped. For some crazy reason, I stopped before—"

"I promise you, you won't regret stopping." Sean grabbed a packet, ripped it open, and squeezed ketchup onto his wrapper. "I know waiting's not easy, believe me, I do, but most things worth doing aren't. You've just got to find something else to do together. When she's weak, you've got to be strong, and vice versa."

This wasn't what Paul had expected.

Sean must have seen the consternation on his face. "What's the matter?"

Paul took a long drink then rattled the ice in his cup. "I was hoping you'd tell me to go for it."

Sean chuckled. "No such luck, bro." He reached over the table and patted the side of Paul's head a couple of times, giving him a good swat before he relented.

Paul remembered when Sean was twelve, before he had a cell phone, and girls started calling the house and hanging up. Eventually, they got bolder and asked for Sean amidst fits of giggles and laughter. Finally, Dad had to answer the phone and tell them that Sean couldn't come to the phone, and they could talk to him at school the next day if they wanted.

As they got older, the number of girls throwing themselves at Sean increased. They became brazen too. Paul figured if Sean could resist all that temptation—with one exception—even through his engagement, then he could too.

Sean polished off his meal and shifted gears. "The first time Dad was deployed, he talked to me a long time about responsibility and how I had to be an example to you and all this stuff. First, it terrified me. And then, after I got used to the idea, all I wanted was for you to look up to me—to be cool in your eyes."

Paul grabbed a fry and traced a circle in the ketchup as he thought about what Sean was saying. He *had* always looked up to Sean and considered him the epitome of coolness when they were kids. He had never known what Sean thought about that.

"I'm afraid with this conversation, any last vestiges of coolness I've clung to will be gone. Hopefully God will keep me from saying anything too stupid and give me the words you need to hear."

Sean crumpled up his hamburger wrapper and threw it and a used ketchup packet in the empty bag. "Okay. You do know how a girl gets pregnant, right?"

"Dude, I'm eighteen, not eight." Paul took one last rattling suck on his straw.

"I meant besides the obvious. People have some weird ideas about what they think is safe." He made little air quotes as he said *safe*. "On the flip side, you and I both know there are plenty of other things you could do that won't result in a pregnancy. I know I was on you about not getting her pregnant, but that's because that has the most obvious repercussions for you, her, and the baby. That doesn't mean all the other stuff is okay. When I say you should wait, I'm talking about all of it."

Paul tried as hard as he could not to smile, but he

couldn't help himself. Sean's leg was bouncing at a fast clip, and he had run his hand through his hair so many times it would be oily by the time the conversation ended. "I'm sorry. I've never seen you as totally uncomfortable as you are right now."

Despite his discomfit, Sean proceeded to go through every physical, emotional, and spiritual consequence he could think of from having sex before marriage. And then, with a little more gusto than Paul would have liked, he went on to talk about how great it was once you were married. He answered every question and objection Paul had with patience and aplomb—even the personal questions about his own experience and behavior.

When they had exhausted the topic to his satisfaction, Sean rose from the bench and walked the sack of burger wrappers and his drink container to the garbage can. He came back to the table and sat.

"I should tell you how damn proud of you I am. And grateful. You could've made these last couple of years a living hell for me, but you didn't. You do well in school, you work hard at your job. Rachel's a sweetheart. Dad would be pleased."

Paul shook the remaining ice in his cup. "Thanks." He wanted to say more. To tell him what a great brother he was. How he always had and always would look up to him. How Dad would be proud of him too. But he knew if he said all those things, he wouldn't be able to keep his emotions in check. Already his eyes stung with tears. Maybe it was something left over from when they were kids, but he always worried that being emotional in front of Sean would do two things—make him look weak and add to Sean's burdens.

Sean glanced at his watch. "I've got to get home. I know you heard everything I said tonight, and I know you and Rachel want to wait until you're married. I'm just concerned that your reasons for waiting seem like everyone else's reasons. You want to wait because that's what Dad would want or Rachel's parents would kill you, or the Church says it's a sin. That's all well and good, and it's kept you from crossing the line so far, but I think it's going to be easier for you if they're *your* convictions you're acting on, not someone else's. You've got more than two years to wait—at a minimum, if you marry her after she graduates from high school. Until then, it only takes one moment of weakness and everything changes."

"I know." It was a sobering thought. Paul got up from the table to throw his trash away. "I'll think about what you said."

"Good. Pray about it too." Sean drummed his hands on the table. "And confession first thing tomorrow morning. Be ready."

Paul rolled his eyes not so much at the prospect of confession, which he and Rachel had already discussed, but at Sean's bossiness.

The drive back was quiet. Sean put on the radio and seemed relaxed now that he had said what he thought Paul needed to hear. Paul didn't say it, but his esteem for his brother didn't diminish that night—it rose exponentially.

Paul leaned back in the seat as his co-worker Luke pulled his parents' minivan precariously close to the Mueller's truck and came to a stop. "Dude, you sure you have a license?"

Luke scowled. "I sure do, two weeks now. Which is more than you can say."

He had him there. Paul needed to talk to Sean about that again.

Paul angled his right hip up and slid the cell phone from his pocket. Almost midnight. What had he been thinking? He'd been exhausted when they'd clocked out at 8:30. When Erik and Luke had suggested going out for pizza after work, he should've just said no. Instead, he'd spent the past three hours sitting in the corner of a grimy booth, eating greasy pepperoni pizza. His face felt oily just from sitting in the place.

What was Rachel doing? Probably in bed reading or sleeping.

Paul popped open the door and stepped out. "Thanks for the ride, man. See you next week."

"Later, dude." Luke waved.

Both hands on the wheel, buddy.

Paul made sure Luke didn't clip a vehicle or building on the way out. Once he'd gotten the van turned around in the driveway, Paul dragged his weary bones toward the guesthouse, eager to shower and sleep.

"Paul!"

He startled when Mr. Mueller called to him from the porch. He sat on the top step. The only light came from inside the house where Mrs. Mueller left the light on over the kitchen sink. What was he doing sitting outside alone this time of night?

"Come sit for a while." He scooted to the side, making room for Paul.

Paul crossed the yard, climbed the porch steps, and lowered himself onto the cool concrete. The cicadas buzzed in the trees and the crickets chirped from the cracks and crevices around the old porch and foundation where they found dark, damp hideouts. Clouds covered the crescent moon Paul glimpsed on the ride home.

Mr. Mueller looked up and down Paul's dirt- and sweat-stained tee shirt and faded, ripped jeans. "You look like you worked hard enough to earn a beer. I'd offer you one, but I can't. Would you settle for a Coke?"

It sounded good, especially after the heavily-chlorinated tap water he'd had at the pizza shop, but he didn't want anything to interfere with the sleep he needed. "Do you have anything without caffeine?"

"Hang on." Mr. Mueller hoisted himself from the stoop, strode into the house and returned a minute later with a brown sixteen-ounce plastic bottle.

"Thanks." Paul glanced at the label, unscrewed the cap, and took a long drink of the decaffeinated sweet tea.

Four empty beer bottles lined the picnic table behind them, and Mr. Mueller had a fresh reinforcement in his hand. The design on the front was familiar to Paul; his dad drank the same kind.

Mr. Mueller took a drink, set the bottle on the step between his feet, and cleared his throat. "So, Paul, what are your intentions with Rachel?"

His chest tightened. Intentions? What was this, 1860? "What do you mean, sir?"

He motioned generally to the side with an unsteady hand and arm, referring to some kind of amorphous future. The stout obviously impaired his gross motor skills. "Where do you see yourself in five, ten years?"

"I, uh..." Paul's mouth hung open, unable to wrap around a single word. What kind of test was this? He sucked in a breath. He could only offer the truth. "I'd like to marry Rachel, raise a family, and grow old with her." Something about Mr. Mueller's obviously-impaired state set Paul at ease, allowing him to speak freely. "She's the best thing that's ever happened to me." Just getting it out in the open lightened the tension, and he said more than he intended. "You have a beautiful, wonderful daughter."

"You sound pretty sure."

"I am." He said it with confidence. Not a shred of doubt clouded his mind or his heart.

"I was sure about Rachel's mom too. I was sure about a lot of things." He stretched his legs out in front of him and raised the beer bottle to his lips again. "I thought when we bought this place, we had it made. It was our own little piece of earth, and no one could take it away from us. Now the government's going to take what it wants anyway." He slurred the word government.

Paul hid a grin. So *that* was what all the beer was about. "Didn't your lawyer say you could appeal?"

He waved his free hand in a dismissive gesture. "We could cut some kinda deal. But I've got no leverage, no bargaining power. They have nothin' to lose, and I have everything to lose." He shook his head and tapped his hand against the bottle in an erratic rhythm.

The wheels in Paul's brain turned, gathering speed as a nugget of an idea germinated. "That may not be true, sir." He wished he had a chance to talk to Rachel about it first, but considering Mr. Mueller's current state, now was the time.

"What do you mean?"

"Well, you know how you've asked what Rachel and I do down at the garden room?"

Mr. Mueller nodded.

"Uh, it's not all gardening."

Mr. Mueller stamped his foot on the step again and dragged his wrist across his forehead. "Aw, listen...I don't want to hear your confession, son, but if you're going to tell me that you and Rachel—"

"No." Paul's head shook furiously. "No, that's not what I'm saying." He didn't want any misunderstanding on that point. "We're not going down there to make out—I mean, there might be the occasional kiss, but what I'm trying to tell you is we've discovered something down there. It started out as little things, you know, a hunk of wood, a piece of a metal trap, a couple shards of a whiskey bottle and a knife."

"How's that going to help me keep my property?" Four beers or not, he suddenly seemed sober.

"We think we found gold." The night sounds grew unnaturally quiet, as if Paul's statement had stunned the world into silence.

Mr. Mueller stared through the darkness for a minute.

Paul stood, moved in front of him, and emboldened by the man's semi-drunken state, perhaps, met his gaze straight on.

"Gold?" He smacked his beer bottle down against the step and chuckled.

Relieved to see the glass hadn't broken, Paul nodded. "Yes, sir."

"What? A gold pendant?" He laughed again and drained the bottle.

Did he think Paul was an idiot? "No, gold bars. A dozen of them. Big ones."

"And you think they're real?" He sounded doubtful. Who wouldn't?

"I'm convinced of it, although we'd like to have a jeweler test them. We haven't figured out yet how to have that done. We just found them last week, and we think we got it all."

Mr. Mueller leaned forward and his gaze sharpened. "Where are they now?"

"In the guesthouse. Do you want to see them?"

"Hell, yeah." Mr. Mueller stood and grabbed the railing to steady himself.

Leaving their bottles on the porch, they semi-staggered—Mr. Mueller from too much beer, Paul from too little sleep—to the guesthouse. Paul unlocked the door and stepped inside. Mr. Mueller followed, his footsteps shuffling over the uneven ground.

Paul entered the hallway outside his bedroom and pulled down the trap that led to the loft. He grabbed a small wooden stepstool from his bedroom and placed it under the door. The extra step allowed him to hoist himself up into the small loft. His muscles tensed and ached as he used his arms to support his body weight. He steadied himself on the support beams, spotting his bed as he glanced down through the hole and hoping this wouldn't take long.

The bars lay side by side across wooden beams in individual burlap sacks like a line of bundled babies in the hospital nursery. Very heavy, very valuable babies.

Using both hands, Paul picked up one of the bars and eased the burlap sack into Mr. Mueller's arms. "It's really heavy, Mr. Mueller."

Mr. Mueller teetered on the stool, and Paul reached down to steady him.

Don't fall. I don't want to have to explain this to Mrs. Mueller.

"I got it, I got it." He grunted as he repositioned it in his arms then stepped down and started toward the kitchen table.

Paul jumped down, clearing the stool and hitting the

hall floor with a thud. He loped sleepily toward the kitchen, where Mr. Mueller grappled with the opening of the sack.

"Go ahead and take it out. Rachel talked to Mrs. Mueller about having Sean and Amanda over for Sunday supper. We planned on telling all of you about it then."

Mr. Mueller nodded, his features taut and his gaze drilling into the sack before him. He stretched the drawstring, reached in, and, while Paul held the sack open, pulled out one of the dull gold bars. With his eyes still glued to it, he turned it over, ran his hand down it, even sniffed it.

"Holy..." He stopped short. "Damn, Paul." A crazy grin stretched across his face.

Paul laughed.

Mr. Mueller glanced at him. "We've got to get this tested."

"Before we found the bars, Rachel found a little nugget. We tested it with a magnet and by scratching it against a tile, and it reacted like gold. I had a guy from the orchard do an acid test on it. He called Wednesday and said nothing dissolved."

Mr. Mueller continued to run his hand over the bar. "And you found this down by the garden?"

"Yes."

"Behind the tree line?"

"Yeah."

Mr. Mueller stared at him. His expression fell. "Paul, that tree line is the property line. This was found on state property."

Paul swallowed though his mouth had gone dry. They were trespassing? That couldn't be good. "We...we thought it was your property."

"Tomorrow we're paying a visit to my attorney." He no longer sounded like a man who'd had five beers. He didn't sound angry either. Just determined.

"But, it's Sunday, Mr. Mueller. We've got church and—"

"I know. Phillip O'Donnell goes to ten o'clock Mass. We'll meet with him after." He pulled the burlap sack back around the bar and cinched it shut.

"Paul, I need to talk to you about something more precious to me than whatever this might be." He gestured to the gold bar and then glanced at the empty chair across from him. "Have a seat."

Uh-oh. Rachel wouldn't have confessed what had almost happened, would she? He couldn't know...could he? Paul sat, suddenly not as tired as he'd been a minute ago. The greasy pizza in his stomach flopped around, and a burning sensation climbed up his esophagus.

"I'd have to be blind not to see what's going on between you and Rachel. Do you love her?"

Paul's heart pounded against his ribcage. "I do."

"And she loves you?"

"Yes, sir." Paul's throat constricted. *Where was that iced tea?*

"This is going to be awkward, but I've put it off too long. Dereliction...dereliction..." He couldn't seem to think of the words. "...of duty. I love my daughter, and I've come to think of you as another son. I expect you to be honest with me."

Paul nodded, wishing Mr. Mueller would get to the point. His knee bounced uncontrollably under the table.

"I know what Rachel told her mother, but I'd like to hear it from you." He pointed at Paul, his eyes glassy yet determined. "Is...is my daughter still a virgin?"

The blood drained from Paul's face, and he jerked back. Wow. No beating around the bush. Shouldn't he have asked Rachel rather than him? He breathed, relieved that he could give an honest answer. One that wouldn't get him killed.

"Yes, sir."

Mr. Mueller leaned back in the chair and sighed. Then he straightened and folded his hands in front of him. "No matter how closely we try to guard Rachel, I'm sure the two of you have had sufficient opportunity, so I'm assuming you've made a conscious decision to abstain."

It was a statement. Paul wasn't required to answer, was he? Because, for his part, he wasn't absolutely certain.

When Paul didn't disagree, Mr. Mueller continued.

"If, on the other hand, you two feel incapable of delaying sexual gratification, no matter the reason, I'm not sure there's anything my wife or I, or Sean for that matter, can do to stop you."

Had Sean spoken to him? Paul's hand formed a fist, which he tucked under his arm. Sean said their conversation the day before was between them. If he found out Sean had said anything to Mr. Mueller, he'd kill Sean. Beat the living daylights out of him and then kill him. Slowly. No matter how much bigger he was. Paul and Rachel hadn't done anything. There was no reason to go to her parents.

"If...If you two want to do..." His cheeks reddened. "If you want to have sex...you'll find a way. I want you to consider something, though: if you can't say 'no,' what does your 'yes' mean?"

"I'm not sure I understand, sir." Exhaustion pressed in on him from all sides like a trash compactor, and his ability to comprehend diminished. Mr. Mueller was talking in circles.

"Have you ever used a spring trap? An old-fashioned mouse trap?"

"Yeah. Sure." Setting the traps was an annual tradition in their Maryland home. As soon as the first frost hit, the little rodents found their way in through the basement and up along the heating pipes. Paul had pinched his fingers a dozen times while baiting and setting traps.

"Once the mouse trips the trap, nothing can stop it. It snaps. It's a trigger mechanism; there's no control. The fact that the trap has snapped doesn't mean it snapped at the right time or that it caught the right thing. It only means one thing: it was triggered.

"That's the way some people are with sex. I trust that you and Rachel know better than that." He paused and drilled Paul with a stare that made his heart race.

Through sheer determination, Paul held his gaze.

"Be smart. Savor this precious gift you've been given only at the right time and in the right way. So when the trigger is released—when you're married, if that's where this is headed—"

"It is, sir." Paul may not have been sure he wanted to wait for marriage, but he knew with one-hundred percent certainty that it wasn't a casual thing. He'd marry her right now, if he could.

Mr. Mueller shook his head and continued. "Then what happens next isn't an inevitable release—a snap. It's a decision to love. It means something. It's treasured."

Paul didn't know what to say. He needed time for that to sink in.

"You know, back when this all started, I was bent on keeping the two of you apart. Rachel's mom convinced me that by not allowing you any opportunity to be together, we would set the trigger—the proverbial backfire. She convinced me that it's best to give the two of you some freedom—within reason, of course—to be together."

Paul felt as if he'd been called to the principal's office. He expected Mr. Mueller to hand him a suspension and leave a blot on his permanent record.

"That said, it would be foolish to put yourselves in a position where you are tempted beyond your ability to resist." For the first time, he cracked a smile. "I'm not *that* old. I remember what it's like. My high school sweetheart,

Julie, man, she was..." He rubbed a hand over his chin. "Well, never mind." He cleared his throat. "The fact that we haven't laid down many hard and fast rules doesn't mean it's a free-for-all. She's underage, and I expect you to behave as the Catholic gentleman you are."

Paul nodded. Everything seemed a little fuzzy. He wasn't sure what was expected of him. If they had to have this conversation, he would have preferred it to have been when he wasn't struggling to keep his eyes open. Mr. Mueller kept talking, but Paul only picked up about every third word. His green plaid cotton shirt moved in and out of focus.

At the sound of his name, Paul jerked to attention. By the tone of Mr. Mueller's voice, he guessed it wasn't the first time he'd said it. "Sorry. I was okay until I sat down. I should stand." He pushed back from the table and stood. "What were you saying?"

Mr. Mueller stood too, a big smile creasing his face. Was he laughing at him?

He moved around the table and clapped Paul on the shoulder. "Go to sleep, Paul. I ought to go to bed too. I had two beers too many."

Paul wasn't aware of him leaving, but he was gone. He would have found the whole exchange about the gold and then Rachel strange and nerve-wracking if he weren't so beat. He didn't take a shower. He didn't even take off his clothes. His head hit the pillow, and he fell asleep.

***

Paul thought he had just closed his eyes when a pounding at the door woke him. Sunlight filtered through the sheer curtain on his window. Morning already? His alarm clock read 8:00 a.m. The knocking started again, reverberating in his head. He dragged himself off the bed, still in his sweaty, dirty clothes from yesterday, and opened the door.

Sean stood on the other side, clean-shaven and dressed

in crisp khakis and an orange Polo, looking like he walked off a Land's End catalog. He held a paperboard coffee cup in one hand, and the rich aroma of coffee with the hint of vanilla wafted in the air.

"Hey, breakfast and Mass, remember?" Then, after he took a good look at Paul, "Did you sleep in your clothes?"

"Yeah." The word scraped over his throat, rough and hoarse. Even his voice wasn't functional yet. He cleared his throat and tried again. "Yeah."

Sean walked past him through the open door and into his living area.

"You stink."

"Thanks."

"I thought you were supposed to be a morning person."

Paul followed Sean into the living area. "I am when Mr. Mueller doesn't keep me up talking until after one o'clock."

"What?"

"It's a long story." He remembered traces of last night's conversation—sitting on the steps sipping their drinks, showing Mr. Mueller the gold bar, and then Mr. Mueller asking point blank if Rachel was still a virgin. His cheeks grew warm, something that hadn't happened the night before. Maybe it was a good thing he had been so worn out. "Oh, he wants me to go to Mass with them and then go talk to his lawyer."

"His lawyer?" Sean's face contorted. "I'd ask you if Rachel was pregnant, but not that much could've changed since the other night, unless he caught you two—"

"No." Gosh, what was *with* everyone? He did occasionally concern himself with things other than the thought of having sex with Rachel. Not often, but still. "It's nothing like that. It's a property matter. I'll explain it later."

"Then go shower. We'll swing back and get Amanda, go to breakfast, and meet up with the Muellers at church."

A shower sounded good. His clothes were stiff and uncomfortable, and Sean was right—he stank. Some cool water would go a long way in waking him up too.

He started for the bathroom, took a few steps, and stopped. A suspicion he hoped was untrue niggled at the back of his mind. "Hey, Sean?"

Sean stood sipping his coffee next to the kitchen table. "Yeah."

"You didn't say anything to Rachel's dad about, y'know, what we talked about Friday, did you?" He pulled his tee shirt over his head and wadded it into a ball. It reeked of sweat and greasy pizza.

Sean set his cup down. "No. I said it was between us, didn't I?" Minor irritation laced his words. "I would've told you if I thought he had to know."

"Okay. Cool." Paul turned back toward the bathroom, unbuttoning and unzipping his fly as he went. Good. He'd have hated to kill his own brother.

***

Paul sat next to Mr. Mueller on the opposite side of Mr. O'Donnell's neat-as-a-pin desk. Sean had driven everyone else home after Mass while Mr. Mueller drove Paul to meet with Mr. O'Donnell. It had only taken ten minutes, but Paul feared he'd fall asleep in the warm truck.

Mr. O'Donnell's office filled the first floor of a new plaza that had sprung up alongside the highway. The lobby was neat and sparsely decorated with a bland watercolor landscape flanked on either side by two artificial Ficus plants. New carpet smell tickled Paul's nose.

"I could put on a pot of coffee, if you'd like." Mr. O'Donnell shuffled to a credenza along the far wall.

He was a short, round man with a pleasant face. He struck Paul as a genuine guy. What kind of lawyer did that make him? He was an agreeable enough sort of fellow that he consented to meet them at his office on Sunday instead of going out to brunch or something.

Thinking the coffee might perk him up, Paul leaned forward. "Oh, that'd be—"

"That won't be necessary," Mr. Mueller blurted out. "We're anxious to get started."

Well, so much for a little pick-me-up.

Mr. O'Donnell adjusted the blinds, toning down the brightness from the midday light. He shrugged out of his suit jacket and draped it over the back of his chair, then sat.

"Okay. You said you have some new information regarding the state's attempt to take your property for its gas line." He steepled his fingers and waited.

"Last night," Mr. Mueller started, his tone terse and exasperated, "I learned from Paul that he and my daughter have made a discovery on what they thought was my property, but actually belongs to the state."

Mr. Mueller looked at Paul, as if expecting him to chime in.

"Uh, yeah, so Rachel has this garden there, and we literally stumbled on an old piece of wood that we think came from a Civil War wagon. We did more digging and found some old junk—pieces of metal and glass, a knife— that kind of stuff."

"I see." Mr. O'Donnell scratched a note on a yellow legal pad.

"Then Rachel found a little rock that looked like gold. We tested it and think it's gold, but we haven't had a professional check it out."

"Tell him how much gold you found, Paul." Mr. Mueller stared at Mr. O'Donnell, his brows raised in anticipation.

"A dozen full bars. They're at least forty pounds apiece."

Paul expected surprise or amusement, but Mr. O'Donnell's expression registered...nothing. A complete blank.

"And how deep did you and Rachel dig to get this possible gold?"

"It varied, but I'd say around eight inches down."

Rachel's dad perched on the edge of his seat, but Mr. O'Donnell wouldn't be rushed. Finally, he spoke.

Chapter 25
From Lemons to Lemonade

Paul pressed his lips together, wide awake now, and his hands gripped the armrests of his seat.

"Ron, I'm not sure how this helps your case." Mr. O'Donnell swiveled his chair and pulled a thick, hardbound book from the shelf behind him. He plopped it on his desk and thumbed through the pages.

He read, "Any person conducting a field investigation on any land or submerged land owned or controlled by the Commonwealth, without first obtaining a permit from the state's museum commission, commits a third-degree misdemeanor."

The book closed with a thud. "Paul and Rachel, if convicted, could be fined up to $2,500, face jail time, or both. You can dig a couple of inches into the soil, but being that they went down eight, they violated the law."

Jail time?

Every muscle in Paul's body tensed. He turned to Mr. Mueller, expecting to see a mirror image of his own distress.

Mr. Mueller's expression remained neutral, and for the first time, he had no reply.

"Listen, it's not all bad," Mr. O'Donnell said quickly. *This was him trying to be reassuring?*

"If you can verify that this gold is real, we may be able to strike a deal. It could be of considerable value, and without Paul and Rachel having discovered it, the state wouldn't have any knowledge of it. With the budget deficit the Commonwealth is facing, you never know. You get the stuff tested, and we'll get together later in the week."

He shuffled the papers on his desk and set them in neat piles. Still the only one filling the vacuum he'd created when he'd mentioned prison time, he continued. "I'm sorry I can't stay. My wife and I are going to visit her mother at the nursing home today. I'll make some notes and email them to my secretary. You get back to me when you know more."

With that, he shooed a stunned Paul and a sober Mr. Mueller out the door.

Paul's need for sleep had vanished, and the words "jail time" reverberated in his head.

"Mr. Mueller, you have to believe me. Rachel and I had no idea we were on state land. We weren't trying—"

Mr. Mueller stopped in front of his truck and grabbed Paul's arm, stopping him both from speaking and walking. "It's okay, Paul. Let's get this gold tested, and then we'll figure out the rest. I have a good feeling about this."

Paul jerked his head back. "You do?" The pitch of his voice rose to a near-girlie sound. He had expected Mr. Mueller to tear into him.

Mr. Mueller held tight to Paul's arm and whispered. "If that gold is real, the price of gold what it is, the state will be all over it. It's in our possession, and that's our bargaining chip—for my land and to keep them from filing any charges against you and Rachel."

"Uh...bargaining chip?" Paul's jaw slackened. How could Mr. Mueller be so optimistic after Mr. O'Donnell was so grim?

Mr. Mueller thumped Paul on the back and reached to open the driver's side door. "Let's go home and tell everyone the good news."

***

Rachel stretched out in the wooden lounge chair on the shaded half of the porch, reading a dystopian novel. The spunky heroine could sure kick some butt. Her ear buds dangled around her neck as she listened to old Taylor Swift music. She swatted at the water beaded above the scar on her leg. Evidence of James's last run-by with the water gun. She'd feigned outrage at his ambush, but in truth, the cool water felt good.

When would Paul and Dad ever get back? And what were they up to? They'd only said they had a meeting with his attorney after Mass. What that had to do with Paul, she couldn't figure out. If it were anything legal related to Paul, why wouldn't Sean be included? Of course, Paul was a legal adult now that he'd turned eighteen. It couldn't be about the gold, could it?

Dad's truck rumbled up, scattering gravel beneath it.

Rachel sat upright.

Dad sprang from his seat while Paul fumbled with his seat belt.

Bounding for the porch, Dad whistled a tune as he went. On his way to the door, he tapped her knee and flashed a grin. "Hey, Rach. How's it going, honey?"

He breezed into the house as Paul plodded up the steps.

"What's with him?" She nodded in Dad's direction.

Paul shook his head. "Your dad's got me kind of confused."

His gaze grazed her shorts and tank top, but instead of the appreciation she usually saw on his face, he looked envious. It was stifling hot, and Paul was still dressed for Mass. He collapsed into the chair next to hers.

"So, what's all this Secret Squirrel stuff going on with Mr. O'Donnell?"

"Where do I start?" Paul ran his hand through his hair and opened the top three buttons of his dress shirt, flapping the fabric to let in some air.

"I got home about midnight, and your dad was out here on the porch having a few beers." He kicked off his loafers and removed his socks. "He asked me to sit down and have a drink with him."

"A beer?" she squeaked, her eyes wide.

"I wish." His head dropped against the chair back. "He gave me an iced tea. I think he just wanted someone to talk to. First he was asking about us, but then he started talking about this gas pipeline thing and the state." He leaned back in the chair and fanned his shirt out a couple of times.

Rachel tried to avoid staring at his bare skin.

He turned and lowered his voice. "I know we weren't going to tell your parents about the gold until today..." He swallowed and searched her gaze. "...but I felt like your dad needed to know."

Rachel bolted upright in her chair. "You told him?" She dug her fingertips into her forehead, forgetting the sweaty moisture that clung there, then wiped her fingers down her shorts. They were supposed to tell everyone together. They shared the discovery, and they should share the glory too—if there was any glory.

"Yeah, I'm sorry. I wished I could've talked to you about it first, but he seemed so dejected, and, I don't know, I thought it could help somehow."

She relaxed against the back of the chair. "That's okay. We were going to tell them anyway." It was done. No use making a big deal about it. "I don't understand how it could help with the gas line problem."

A stream of ice-cold water smacked her upper arm.

She squealed and jumped from her seat, turning in time to see James push off the ground with his forearms and sprint around the side of the house. She let out a growl. "I'm going to kill him."

Paul sat up, scanning the yard in either direction. "Man, I'll pay him to hit me. I'm dying out here." He unbuttoned his cuffs and rolled up his sleeves.

Rachel giggled. "You look ridiculous, you know." Sleeves and pant legs rolled up. Shirt undone. Bare feet. He needed to put on some shorts. He could leave his shirt off, and she wouldn't mind. Not one bit. "Why don't you go get changed?"

"I will. In a minute. Where were we?"

Conscious that James could be lurking and eavesdropping, she sat and lowered her voice. "I was asking how the gold could help with the gas line thing."

"Yeah. Right. I don't really know. Your dad was saying he didn't have anything to bargain with, and I thought somehow the gold could help—its value, us knowing the location. I didn't really think it through."

A warm breeze blew, and she scooped her hair and lifted it above her neck. "Okay. I think I get what you're saying. So, why the rush to the lawyer?"

"Well, here's the thing." He tugged at his shirt as if he was going to free it from his pants then gave up. "Your dad told me that the garden isn't even his property. Your family's property ends at the tree line."

She let her hair fall around her shoulders and squinted. "It does?"

"Apparently, we've been digging on state land."

"The gold was on state land?" That couldn't be good.

"Yeah...so, after interrogating me about our sex lives, your dad finally let me go to bed and said that I'd be visiting his lawyer with him this morning."

Rachel shot out of her seat and grabbed Paul's arm. "Whoa, whoa, whoa. Our *sex lives*? How did *that* come up?" Paul grinned, but she couldn't see what was so amusing. Her heart thudded louder than the song of the cicadas buzzing from the trees.

Water sprayed across Paul's face and shoulders. He jerked away, scrunching his face then scrambled to his feet and leaned over the porch rail. "You'll be sorry when I catch you, James."

He turned to Rachel, winked, and mouthed, "That felt sooo good."

She covered her smile with her hand as James taunted them and ran back in the direction he'd come. She sat again, and Paul did too.

"Keep your voice down. He's sneaky, and he listens. If he eavesdrops...I know he's little but he knows, sorta, about, you know...about sex. He might think—"

One side of Paul's mouth lifted in a grin. "You think he'd tell?"

"I know he would."

"Listen. I'm trying to tell you, it doesn't matter. Your dad asked me straight out last night."

Her eyes grew wider and bigger. "Asked you what?"

"I think four or five beers gave him the nerve to ask me what he's wanted to know—whether we've had sex. He was relieved to know we hadn't."

She rolled her eyes. "Well, yeah." Her arm dropped back to her lap.

"He did take the opportunity to talk about why it should stay that way." Paul rubbed a hand over his eyes, dragged his sleeve across his forehead, then closed his eyes. He had said this morning at church how tired he was. She elbowed him twice during the homily when he nodded off.

"I think he said something profound about a mouse trap and a decision to love, but that's when I started to zone out on him."

A mouse trap? That made no sense. "Zoned out? Kind of like you're doing now?"

"Hmmm?"

Okay, he needed sleep, but she needed to find out what happened with the lawyer. She jabbed a finger into his ribs, and his eyes snapped open. "So what did Mr. O'Donnell say?"

Paul yawned and straightened in his seat. "Well, that's the other thing. Right away he says that we were digging illegally, and we can be fined and go to prison, yadda, yadda, yadda."

"Wait a second. You don't say, 'go to prison,' and then 'yadda, yadda, yadda.'"

"I know. I practically, uh, wet my pants when he said that, but your dad brushed it off."

"I don't get it."

"Me neither, because Mr. O'Donnell is negative about the whole thing. I'll bet your dad thinks we can make a deal with the state for his land and this gold."

Rachel bit her thumb. A deal? "So, what else did my dad say about the gold?"

"I showed it to him last night, and he said we need to get it tested, which we were going to do anyhow."

The screen door creaked behind them, and Rachel jumped. The door closed with a loud crack, and Dad stepped onto the porch.

He held a tall, frosty glass in each hand. "Lemonade?" He offered one to each of them. "I'm taking a day off from work tomorrow, and you two are coming with me to see a precious metals appraiser in town."

Paul gulped half his drink in one tilt of the glass. "I have to work tomorrow."

"I'll call and explain that you have an urgent matter to attend to with me." He stood there a moment, hands in his pockets, grin on his face, watching them drain their glasses. "Any idea how much that gold is worth? Assuming it's real."

Rachel placed her cold, half-empty glass against her neck. "I didn't do the math. Didn't you say it was, like, a thousand dollars an ounce, Paul?" She glanced at Paul, and he nodded. She suspected he'd done the math.

"Rachel," Dad said, crouching in front of them. "Gold is thirteen-hundred dollars an ounce. It could be worth millions."

Every thought fled from her mind. After a few seconds, she realized her jaw hung open.

Paul's eyes were half closed, but a smile lit his face. Then his eyes blinked open. "Sir, I've gotta tell Sean."

Dad nodded. "You're right." He stood and stepped back to the screen door and called, "Linda, when are Sean and Amanda expected for dinner?"

Her mom called back, "Five o'clock."

Dad laid a hand on each of their shoulders. "Big day tomorrow, kids."

Rachel smiled at him and turned to Paul. His eyes were closed and his breathing soft and even. He was asleep.

Chapter 26
Click and Double-Click

Paul's hand bumped Rachel's as he took the last of the dirty dishes from her and stacked them alongside of the sink. Somehow, her presence made mundane chores bearable.

She gazed at him from beneath her long lashes and smiled.

He winked, then rinsed and loaded plates while Rachel wiped the kitchen table.

Meanwhile, Rachel's parents, Sean, and Amanda discussed the possible implications of his and Rachel's discovery.

Paul smiled recalling how Sean's eyes nearly popped out of his head at the news that he and Rachel may have discovered millions of dollars in gold. If he had been sipping his water, he would have done a spit-take. Sean had been less excited about the discovery being on state property and more on the knowledge that Paul could be charged with a misdemeanor.

Once the table was cleared and the dishwasher running, Paul and Rachel retreated to the living room. The conversation had shifted from their discovery to home buying and mortgages. Oblivious to everything in the next room, James waved his Wii controller wildly as he navigated Mario and Luigi through a skeleton-littered desert terrain.

Rachel sat on the cushion in front of the bay window, and Paul sat opposite her, their legs tangled together. Her shoulders lifted and fell as she sighed. "I guess by this time tomorrow, we'll have a better idea where we stand." Her voice sounded pleasant enough, but her smile seemed forced, and her eyes held a look of pleading.

He moved his legs so that his feet rested against Rachel's hip. "Are you okay with all this, Rachel?"

Her smile dissolved, and she shrugged. "This might sound crazy, but I'm a little sad. We had this big, beautiful, exciting secret, and now it's just a legal jumble."

"Well, there's a chance we'll get to keep something. Even a little bit would be a lot. And if it solves your dad's issue with the state and its pipeline, that's good too." He nudged her with his foot. "I don't think they're going to throw us in jail. Can you imagine how that would play in the media?"

He made a rectangular shape with his thumbs and index fingers, as if framing a movie marquee. "Teens Jailed for Finding Lost Gold." He wrinkled his nose. "They'd look like a-holes."

Leaning forward, he took her hands in his. "Rachel, whether we get any money or not, or we're fined or whatever, you and I did something historic. We uncovered a lost treasure that's been missing for almost 150 years. How cool is that?"

A genuine smile lit her face. "I guess you're right. It *is* pretty incredible." Her smile waned, and she interlocked her fingers with his. Her gaze fell to her lap. "Can I admit something to you?" She sounded almost guilty.

He nodded. What could she have done?

"A part of me wishes we had taken the gold, cashed it in and run away together." Her gaze shifted to their hands and then back to his eyes. "But I know it wouldn't be that simple, and we wouldn't have any peace anyway, taking something that's not rightfully ours." She paused. "It would be fun for a little while though, wouldn't it?"

Finally, he understood. You couldn't take something that didn't belong to you without repercussions. Bits and snatches of jumbled conversations ran through his mind, coalescing into something that started to make sense. Dad telling Sean a man is virtuous, not selfish. Sean telling him if he loved Rachel, he should take things slow. Mr. Mueller reminding him that sex was a gift to be savored at the right time and in the right way. His mom's letter urging him from beyond the grave to "spend your life loving and living so that we can spend eternity together."

Rachel's voice broke through his thoughts. "Paul? Are you still with me?"

He blinked and refocused on her. "Yeah. It's just what you said made me think of something else."

"What?"

He released her hands and straightened, pulling his knees toward his chest and gazing out the bay window. How hadn't he seen it before? His heart sped up as his soul filled with exhilaration.

He glanced toward the dining room, making certain everyone was out of ear shot. "I wanted to make love to you on Friday. I *really* wanted to." He raised his eyebrows and gave her a devilish smile.

Her eyes widened then darted to James. He hadn't heard. He busied himself jabbing the Wii remote toward the TV, grunting and talking to himself.

"I mean, we had the opportunity and definitely the desire. But it wouldn't have made us happy. For a little while maybe, but it's like the money." He ran a hand through his hair. "It's like...it's like taking something that's not rightfully ours. Yeah, we love each other, but doing that before we're married—is that love? I mean, the real deal—I'd *die* for you, see you in heaven, kind of love? It's ...it's risking our hearts and our souls...and a baby. I know we've always said we wanted to wait, but it's like it all just clicked for me."

Searching Rachel's eyes, he tried to get a sense of

whether she agreed with him or thought he was nuts. Not getting a sense one way or the other, he blathered on.

"Rachel, you mean the world to me. I want to do things *right* with you. If that means we've got to wait..." He paused, taking a deep breath and realizing the ramifications of his newfound convictions. "...*years* to be together like that, after we've made all the promises before God and our families, then so be it."

Rachel's unblinking gaze remained steady.

Have I disappointed her somehow? Maybe she doesn't want to wait after all.

Finally, she took his hands back in hers. "Why am I thinking about money when I've already hit the jackpot with you?" She lunged forward and hugged him.

He sighed, relief pouring over him followed by the humbling knowledge that he was far from a "jackpot," and just because he "got it" now, it wouldn't make living it easier. He still craved her kisses, her touch, her body... They'd have to take things one day at a time.

Still careful with her legs, he propped them on his lap and scooted closer. He stroked her cheek with his fingertips. "Have I told you today that I love you?"

She shook her head.

"I love you."

"I love you too, and no matter..." Her voice cracked, and she cleared her throat. "No matter if we get a penny from the gold or not, I feel so blessed."

The background conversation, the videogame noise—everything fell away but Rachel. He kissed her as if they were the only two in the world.

Loud and insistent throat-clearing—Sean's—came from the kitchen. Not so subtle.

Much as he hated to, Paul ended their kiss. "That was probably my cue to get out of here." He glanced toward the kitchen, where everyone but James now stood. "It looks like Sean and Amanda are leaving too. I'll see you in the morning."

After a round of 'goodnights,' Paul walked out with Sean and Amanda. Locusts and cicadas hummed and a dog barked. He savored the quiet, the peacefulness. The contrast between this place and their home in Maryland still struck him. Back home the soundscape included car and airplane noise, emergency sirens, and eighteen-wheelers and their brake retarders. A shot fired in the distance, and he remembered what he wanted to ask Sean.

"Hey, my .22 is still not hitting the mark. It's veering left, I think. Can you take it and have it checked out at a gun shop?"

Sean lifted his head from where he nuzzled Amanda's neck. "Yeah, I forgot about that. I'll stop by sometime tomorrow morning and grab it. I'll bring it to the gun shop on my lunch hour."

"Thanks. You were talkin' about hunting, and one of the guys at work mentioned shooting pheasant some time. It's been a long time since I shot game."

"No problem. I need to stop by the place anyway." He grabbed Amanda and squeezed her to him. "The little woman here has never held a gun in her life, and I think it's about time she got ed-u-cated." Sean drew out the word as if he were anything but educated.

Amanda punched him in the chest, but she didn't move away, and the look she gave Sean reminded Paul that they were still very much newlyweds. Not only were they free to show their love physically, it was expected. He felt a stab of jealousy. That would be him and Rachel. In time. A long, long time.

Paul meandered to the guesthouse intending to shower and go to sleep. Instead he lay beneath the thin cotton sheet, staring at the ceiling while his mind raced with questions. What would they learn at the appraisal tomorrow? Any chance it wasn't gold? And if it was, what would the state do once they found out? Would Paul and Rachel get a reward? Jail time?

Wish you were here, Dad. Most of the time since Dad's death, he felt like he was floundering. And the better he got at floundering, the more he felt like he was betraying his father. Dad would want him to be capable and independent, but the thought of not needing his dad anymore scared him almost as much as needing him did. The only constant, the only thing he was sure about in life, was Rachel.

With a tinge of guilt, he realized he should be able to say that about God. Maybe he needed to make more room in his life for Him. If Dad *were* here, that's where he'd point him. Paul was sure of it. He'd been praying at night again and in the mornings, but now he put his heart into it. It settled his anxiousness, but did nothing to help him fall asleep.

He reached for his phone. No text messages, no email. He did have a Gmail account. True, he only used it for social networking and online shopping, but sometimes a message from an actual human ended up mixed in with the spam. Since he couldn't sleep anyway, he might as well get up and check that one too.

Thirty-five new messages. Sure enough, sandwiched between a male enhancement ad and a Nigerian money laundering scam, sat a message from what looked like a real name. The sender was "Richards, James" from a Yahoo! address.

Hi-

I hope I've found the right Paul Porter. My name is Capt. James Richards, and I served in the 42nd with your dad. I'm on leave and passing through the northern PA area this week. I have some personal items of your dad's that he wanted you to have. I'd like to deliver them in person. I'm traveling through New England now, and, if you're the right guy, I'll send you a message when I'm nearby.

Capt. Jim

A thrill shot through him. More of Dad's belongings? He'd never heard of Captain Richards, but that didn't surprise him. He'd never known the guys his Dad had deployed with. Dad only mentioned a couple of them by name.

Paul typed a quick reply.

You've got the right Paul Porter. Thanks for getting in touch. Let me know when you are in the Williamsport area. You can reach me on my cell at 570-555-1971.

Paul

He deleted the spam email but left the laptop on and the email open in case another message from Captain Richards came through. He crawled into bed and lay for a short time wondering what things of his dad's Captain Richards might have. In no time, he fell asleep.

Chapter 27
Au

"Rachel, c'mon!"

Rachel rolled over, buried her face in her pillow, and groaned. How many times had Dad called her now? She was excited about the appointment for the appraisal this morning too, but the bars would have the same value at nine o'clock that they would at eight o'clock.

The smell of coffee finally lured her out of bed. She didn't drink it, but the aroma was warm, familiar, and delicious. The steady murmur of her parents' conversation carried down the hall as she dressed then headed to the kitchen for a quick bowl of cereal.

Paul met Rachel and her dad at the door, and they piled into the truck for their visit to Larry, the precious metals expert on the opposite side of town.

Though Larry's little bungalow looked quaint and countrified from the outside, on the inside, elegant displays lined the walls. Larry was a talented jeweler who specialized in custom jewelry using various precious metals.

Rachel admired the necklaces and rings in the glass cases, especially a beautiful aquamarine stone displayed alongside silver and turquoise jewelry.

Paul peered into the case from over her shoulder. "You like it?"

"The Native American stuff, not so much, but that one ..." She tapped the glass above the one she meant. "*That* stone is beautiful."

"It is. I can't say I've ever spent much time thinking

about jewelry, but this guy does good work. What do you think it costs?"

"I don't know, but we're not here to window shop anyway."

Standing at the counter, Dad motioned for Rachel and Paul to join him. They'd called ahead, so Larry had been expecting them.

Rachel had imagined a greasy guy with slicked-back hair who spent his weekends at gold-buying events at local hotels, but a balding, bespectacled middle-aged man approached the counter. "Good morning. Can I help you?"

"Larry?" Dad asked. "I spoke to you on the phone about testing some gold."

"Oh, yes—Ron, right? You said the bar you brought is rather heavy. Why don't you bring it around to the back door? That's where my workshop is."

Rachel followed Dad out the door and stood by as he and Paul hefted the heavy gold bar from the rear of the truck. Dad carried it through a small, chain link fenced-in backyard toward Larry's shop. It smelled like dog dirt, but she didn't see a dog.

Soft rock music came from an old boombox in a tidy workshop filled with various lamps and an assortment of pliers and mallets. An array of intricate tools lay neatly-arranged on a table against the far wall.

Dad slid the burlap sack onto the workbench and drew the heavy bar out of the bag.

"Wow," Larry said, peering above the frames of his glasses. "You kids *found* this?"

She opened her mouth to answer, but Paul beat her to it. "Yeah. We dug it up."

Dad rested a hand on her back. "I'm sorry, this is my daughter, Rachel, and her boyfriend, Paul."

Huh. Dad had never called Paul *that* before. She bit her lips, hiding her smile.

"Good to meet you." Paul shook Larry's hand.

Rachel extended her hand too, but Larry had moved on to examining the bar. Her opinion of him nose-dived.

"Well, it looks authentic. Let's test it out." Larry brought out a small machine, which he identified as an ultrasound. He applied some gel to the top of the bar and slid what he called "the probe" along the length of the gold.

"I don't see any impurities," he murmured as he worked. He used a small rag to wipe off the surface, reapplied gel and began again.

"It looks like an air bubble here." He pointed to the small color screen attached to the probe. Larry wiped the bar a final time, returned the probe to the ultrasound, and switched it off. He took off his glasses and laid them on the table. His gaze shifted from Paul to Rachel and then her dad, his stoic expression giving no indication of his conclusion.

Rachel's pulse quickened, and she became conscious of every breath.

"What you've got here is solid gold."

Paul gasped, and a nervous laugh erupted from Dad.

Rachel fought her own wave of disbelief. "You're... you're positive?"

Larry grinned. "I'm certain. Let's weigh it." He hoisted the bar onto an electronic scale behind the counter. It didn't look like it could hold something so heavy, and Rachel feared it would break.

"I'd say...forty-nine and three-quarters pounds."

"And the value of that?" Dad asked. His fists clenched and unclenched.

Paul leaned on the counter, his eyes wide.

Rachel reached for his hand and squeezed his fingers.

"I'd say a little over a million dollars."

"A million dollars?" Rachel and Paul echoed in unison.

"At today's rate, I'd say so," Larry said, his voice not

betraying even a hint of excitement.

Dad blew out a breath. "Whew...wow." He turned to Paul and Rachel, excitement brimming in his eyes. "I need you to give me that appraisal in writing, Larry... and we've got eleven more bars in the truck. We'll need written appraisals for them too."

They were talking about a dolly or something to bring them in, but Rachel tuned out everything else. She had been riding around in a truck with her dad, her boyfriend, and about $12 million in solid gold. That she and her boyfriend Paul dug up.

Un-freakin'-real.

Paul turned and leaned back on the counter, shaking his head.

Larry ambled into the retail area of the store to retrieve something for the written appraisal.

"Well," Dad said, "I don't know about you two, but I'm nervous as hell carrying this stuff around. We're going straight from here to Mr. O'Donnell's office."

A half hour later, Larry had performed the ultrasounds and weighed all the bars. Written appraisals in hand, they headed to Mr. O'Donnell's office. Thank God it was a short ride.

Chapter 28
Mutiny

Paul reached for Rachel's hand as they stood in the waiting area of Mr. O'Donnell's office. Mr. Mueller marched up to the secretary's desk and introduced himself.

The secretary, a plump older woman with an updo so high it resembled a beehive hairdo, sat behind a large, immaculate desk. Paul glanced at her nameplate, which displayed an unpronounceable Eastern European last name with more consonants than he thought should be allowed by law.

"Mr. O'Donnell is in. I'll see if he's available to meet with you." She gestured toward a row of leather-backed chairs lining the wall. "You can take a seat." She picked up the phone and swiveled toward the credenza behind her while Paul, Rachel, and Mr. Mueller sat.

A minute later, Mr. O'Donnell emerged from his office, straightening his necktie and tugging up his belted brown pants. "Ron, back so soon?"

Mr. Mueller stood. "Yes. Do you have a few minutes?"

"I can make a few minutes for you. Come in." He motioned for them to step into his office.

Beehive-Do cast a wary glance at Paul, then swiveled away from them toward her unused desk calendar.

Mr. Mueller urged Rachel forward with a hand to her back. "Phil, you remember my daughter, Rachel, and you've met Paul."

"Rachel, nice to see you." Mr. O'Donnell extended his hand to Rachel and then to Paul. "Good to see you again, Paul."

"I don't want to take too much of your time," Mr. Mueller said. "We just came from having the gold appraised. We have in our possession..." He glanced at Rachel, then Paul. "Twelve solid gold bars weighing about fifty pounds each with an estimated total value of more than $12 million."

Paul grinned, impressed that he'd delivered the news without a burst of giddy laughter. The amount was staggering. Beyond belief.

For the first time, honest-to-goodness emotion played across Mr. O'Donnell's face. His eyes widened and his chin sagged. "Dear God. I never thought it would be real." He sunk into his chair, which let out an embarrassing sound akin to flatulence.

Paul stifled a grin and tried to resist the feeling of smug satisfaction. He'd had his doubts too, but his gut instinct had proven true. "I don't think any of us did at first, sir."

Mr. Mueller sat and nodded for Rachel and Paul to do the same. Mr. Mueller scooted his chair forward several inches. "Twelve million dollars-worth of gold recovered illegally on state property."

And like a popped balloon careening to the floor, Mr. Mueller's sober statement brought them all back to *terra firma*.

"Yes," said Mr. O'Donnell, his lips a grim line. "Therein lies the rub."

Mr. Mueller propped an elbow on Mr. O'Donnell's desk. "Here's my thinking, which you pretty much said yourself yesterday. This is our bargaining chip. Clearly, the gold does not belong to us—for several reasons—but mainly since it was not found on our property. We will turn over the gold to the rightful owner, the state, I presume..."

"So long as..." Mr. O'Donnell prompted.

"So long as they quadruple the offer on my land and offer Rachel and Paul a finder's fee of, say, five percent."

Mr. O'Donnell leaned back in his chair and tapped his pen against the desktop. "Well, we can make the request, but to be honest, I think you're aiming a little high. I'd say we should expect maybe triple the value and a one percent finder's fee."

Paul manipulated the dollar amounts in his head. One percent of $12 million was $120,000. It wouldn't make them rich, but it might put them both through college with a little extra to get them on their feet.

He cleared his throat and raised a hand. "Uh, hey..." They'd left out a critical detail. "And no criminal charges filed against us." Paul glanced at Rachel, and she nodded.

"Yes—full immunity." Mr. Donnell leaned forward and made a note on his lined yellow notepad.

Was it a fair deal? Paul had no context, no experience for evaluating it. He fixed his gaze on Mr. O'Donnell's desk while the men spent the next few minutes discussing an urgent meeting with the state conservation department attorney. His mind wandered to the six hundred pounds of gold weighing down the Mueller's truck. What were they supposed to do with it? How did you keep something like that safe?

Mr. O'Donnell must've been considering the best place for the gold as well. He called Beehive-Do and instructed her to contact the bank and make arrangements for the safe deposit of the gold. "Call about a police escort too," he added.

Several minutes later, a sharp knock sounded on the door, and Beehive-Do stuck her head and towering hair in the room.

Paul suppressed a laugh at her gaudy earrings. How hadn't he noticed them before? They looked like miniature Christmas bulbs. Only it was August.

"Mr. O'Donnell—a police escort will be available in an hour. Would you like me to confirm it or would you rather move the gold now?"

The lawyer's gaze shifted to Mr. Mueller for an answer.

Mr. Mueller sighed. "We're only a few miles away. The sooner we get it to the bank, the better, as far as I'm concerned."

"Okey dokey, then," Beehive-Do said. "I'll let the bank know you'll be there shortly. Security will be on hand when you arrive."

Paul caught a furtive smile on Rachel's glossy lips. She turned toward him and tugged her ear lobe. She had noticed the Christmas bulb earrings too.

He smirked and turned his attention back to the desk before he broke into laughter.

They wrapped up their conversation, and Mr. O'Donnell escorted them to the waiting area. Movement caught Paul's eye. Beehive-Do sat with her back to them, her earrings bobbing as she whispered emphatically into the phone. Must've been a personal call.

She swiveled around, placed a hand over the mouthpiece, and bid them goodbye before turning back to her call, a stern look in her eye. Paul pitied the party on the other end of the phone.

Once he and Rachel climbed into the truck's back seat, Paul checked his cell phone to see if Sean had texted him. Had he remember to picked up his .22 and take it to the gun shop?

Sean hadn't sent a message, but Captain Richards had.

Heading into Williamsport. Not familiar with the area. Can you meet me at the Little League Museum parking lot at eleven o'clock?

Paul checked the time on his phone. 10:48 a.m.

"Mr. Mueller, we're going to pass the Little League Museum, aren't we?"

"Yeah, why?"

"Can we stop at the parking lot there? There's this Captain Richards, a friend of my dad's. He's been trying to get in touch with me. He has some of Dad's things. He's passing through this way, and he says he can meet us at eleven o'clock. It should only take a minute." He glanced at Rachel, who peered over the seat at the covered gold in the flatbed behind them.

"Please, Mr. Mueller. I just saw his message now."

Mr. Mueller shook his head. "No, Paul. With all this gold, I want to go directly to the bank."

"Me too, sir, but I'm afraid I won't get another chance to get Dad's stuff."

Mr. Mueller was probably right. What were some of Dad's things worth compared to $12 million? The monetary value of Dad's stuff wasn't what motivated him, though. It was the personal value. He grasped at any tangible tie to Dad he could find. He hadn't thought there was anything else until Captain Richards' email. What if he had a message for Paul, and that's why he was delivering the items in person? To have something, *anything*, of Dad's was priceless.

The truck hit a small pothole, and the valuable load in the back thudded. Mr. Mueller swore under his breath. "Can't he mail the stuff to you?"

"I don't know. For some reason he wants to do it in person. He said Dad wanted me to have whatever he's got." The more Paul thought about it, the more he itched to learn what it was. Could it be a personal message like the letter from his mom?

"Please, Mr. Mueller. You don't even have to turn off the engine. I'll jump out, get whatever Captain Richards has, and get back in so we can go to the bank. No one knows what we're carrying back there anyway."

He glanced at Rachel, hoping for a sign of support, but her gaze remained fixed on her dad. Paul couldn't fault him if he said no, but what was the harm? It would only take a minute or two.

Mr. Mueller glanced at Paul in the rearview mirror and sighed. "All right, Paul. But it has to be quick. I'm not playing around with this cargo."

The tension building in Paul's shoulders diminished. "Thank you, sir."

He texted Captain Richards, *On our way.* His heart stirred as he wondered what the man had for him.

Minutes later they swung into the upper parking lot of Little League headquarters. The narrow lot opened into a small flag plaza. A giant American flag billowed in the breeze. Would he ever look at a flag and not recall the one they'd received at Dad's funeral? Unlikely.

The sunlight brightened the red geraniums dotting the flowerbeds. A few cars were parked near the museum entrance, but no one waited to meet them.

Behind the museum and gift shop, a steep drop off led the way to a baseball stadium and several additional fields as well as housing facilities for the annual world championship competitors.

"Let's check the lower lots, near the fields," Mr. Mueller said. "We'll swing around, and see if he's down there. It's almost eleven. If he's not here in five minutes, we're leaving."

"Okay. I really appreciate this, sir." *C'mon. Be on time.* Maybe Captain Richards hit traffic.

They pulled into one of the lower lots adjacent to the stadium, but, again, no one waited.

Paul texted again. *In the stadium lot. Where are you?*

A split-second later, Paul's phone buzzed.

He read the incoming text. Tightness seized his chest, and his mouth went dry.

Right here. I see you. I'm sure your mom will want to see this stuff...

He gripped the vinyl seat back and reached forward, coming up behind Mr. Mueller.

"Mr. Mueller..." Terror rang in his voice. "Something's not right. We need to go."

A banging sounded on the window.

Paul jumped and spun to the window.

A teen with a thin gray hoodie pulled over his eyes rapped on the window with a—with a pistol. He motioned for them to get out of the truck.

"What the hell's going on, Paul?" Mr. Mueller was angry, but there was no masking the fear in his voice too.

"I-I don't know. Something's not right."

The short, swarthy young man outside the truck rapped again. "Everybody out. Now."

Mr. Mueller turned to Paul and Rachel. "Do what he says. No amount of gold is worth getting hurt."

Or killed. He didn't say that, but Paul guessed what he was thinking.

Rachel's cheeks paled, and when Paul grabbed her hand, it was cool and shaky.

"It'll be okay," he whispered. At least he hoped it would.

Mr. Mueller cracked his door open and stepped out, hands in the air.

Paul opened the other door, and with a final glance at Rachel, led her out of the back seat.

The young man smiled, revealing a shiny gold cap on one of his incisors. "I'm Captain Jim. I understand you've got quite a cargo here." He motioned toward the truck bed with his gun. "Treasure, aye?"

Captain Jim laughed at his feeble attempt at humor. "Think you're treasure hunters, do you? People digging up buried treasure should beware of pirates."

His high-pitched laughter reminded Paul of a flock of chickens, nervous and ready to scatter.

Captain Jim looked them all over, as if trying to assess his next move. The way his gaze lingered on Rachel made Paul want to vomit.

"I'll take the pretty little thing." He grabbed Rachel's arm and yanked her hand from Paul's grip. Then he motioned to Paul and Mr. Mueller with the gun. "You two move the booty into my trunk." He inclined his gun toward a little gray Chevy that Paul hadn't seen before. "You give me the gold, I give you back this little cutie, and we'll all be on our way."

Paul's mind raced. Who was this guy? How did he know about the gold? About Dad? And how could he get Rachel away from him?

As if he could read Paul's mind, Mr. Mueller grabbed him by the elbow and led him to the rear of the truck. "Stop thinking, Paul. Do what he says, and he'll let Rachel go."

Captain Jim still had one hand on Rachel, who twisted under his grip. The other hand remained on his gun, aimed alternately at him and Mr. Mueller.

What if this guy had no intention of letting Rachel go? Cooperating with this lowlife wouldn't guarantee her safety or theirs.

Paul measured the distance between them visually—maybe three yards. It would take only seconds to get to Captain Jim.

Paul took Mr. Mueller's advice—he stopped thinking.

He charged across the lot, intent on knocking Captain Jim off his feet. Captain Jim's eyes widened with shock. He'd expected compliance, not rebellion. Had he ever held anyone at gunpoint before?

Paul braced for impact and the possibility of a bullet to his gut.

Captain Jim, rather than firing, released Rachel and lifted his hand in the air.

Paul rammed into Captain Jim's midsection.

At the same moment, tires screeched and a door slammed somewhere behind him.

Rachel screamed.

Two gunshots sounded.

Someone cried out.

Pain seared Paul's skull. And everything went black.

Chapter 29
Oasis

Heat came at Paul in waves. Dry and intense like the warmth from a wood-fired oven. It mixed with gritty dirt that stung his cheeks and eyes. An ocean of sand rose and swelled before him. Wind whistled as it kicked up the grains lapping at his face and arms.

From a distance, a man called his name.

Who was it? And where was he?

Paul squinted through the stinging sand...then he saw him.

Dad.

Wearing his familiar Army fatigues and boots, he strode toward Paul, immune to the sand blowing between them.

"Paul!"

A smile spread over Paul's face as joy filled his heart.

Everything stilled—the wind and the sand. The lull and silence made him think of being in deep space. Only relentless heat filled the void.

He opened his mouth to call to Dad, but no sound came out.

Urgent desperation drove Paul to charge to Dad, hug him, and tell him how much he missed him. But his feet wouldn't move. They were as impotent as his voice.

Dad walked steadily toward him, expressionless, but hale and hearty.

Paul's frustration grew nearly to the point of tears when a sudden sense of peace filled him, replacing irritation with contentment. He knew, somehow, that Dad understood all that he wanted to say. And that Dad loved him.

Dad stopped a yard or so in front of him. His gaze took in all of Paul. His lips turned up in the slightest of smiles, and Paul sensed his approval.

"Have patience, Paul. What you've discovered with Rachel is genuine."

Paul comprehended the words, but not their meaning. Although Paul had mentioned her a couple of times, Dad had never met Rachel. And how did he know about the gold?

"Protect it. Cherish it. It will withstand every test."

Unable to speak, Paul stared and listened.

"Don't trade everlasting love for finite pleasure."

Dad wasn't talking about the gold at all.

"Tell Sean he's done good. And to take care of that grandbaby of mine."

Paul tried to nod but couldn't.

Dad smiled, a real smile this time, then faded into the endless dunes behind him, disappearing before Paul's eyes.

The tide of sand receded.

The heat abated.

Another voice called to him, this one soft and feminine.

Now, finally, he could speak.

"Mom? Mom?"

A hand rubbed his shoulder. "Paul, it's Amanda. We're at the hospital." She stroked his arm. "Are you okay?"

No, not Amanda. *Mom.* It had to be her.

He batted his eyelids a few times, the intense light immediately forcing them closed. A couple more blinks, and his eyes opened.

A pretty blue-eyed, strawberry blonde stood at his bedside. Amanda. She grabbed his hand in hers. "You seemed agitated. Like you wanted to say something." Her voice was gentle and low.

He did have something to say, didn't he? The dream, if that's what it was, slipped further away every second, and he couldn't remember why he wanted to speak.

His gaze roamed the room, taking in vertical blinds hanging in front of a large window, a vinyl chair, and bare, white walls and tiled floor. "How long have I been here?"

"A couple of hours. Do you remember what happened?"

"What happened?" What was she talking about? Within seconds, fragmented memories returned.

"The guy, the pirate. He wanted the gold." The gleam of his gold tooth flickered in Paul's mind. "He had Rachel, and I went after him. Then he must've...he hit me on the head with something."

Amanda smiled. "Good. You remember." She patted his hand and squeezed it. "He hit you with the back of his gun. It wasn't loaded."

The whole scene flooded his memory. He shot upright in the bed, pushing aside the blanket and sheets, his head throbbing. "Is-Is she... " He couldn't get his question out fast enough. "Is Rachel okay? Mr. Mueller?"

"Relax. They're fine. You were the only one hurt."

Relieved, he sunk into the bed, rubbing his aching head.

"They're at the police station with Sean. They'll be here as soon as they can."

Sean hadn't been there. It was just him, Rachel, and Mr. Mueller. "Sean? Why Sean?"

"He went by your place to get your gun, remember? Your laptop was open, and a message from Captain Jim came through. It must've been before he texted you. Sean knew it was a setup."

"How?"

"Sean talked to your dad's buddies after the funeral. There was nothing of your dad's left. You already have all his stuff."

He tilted his head into the pillow, staring at the ceiling. What a fool he'd been. He should've checked with Sean in the first place.

"Seems like neither of you have your cell phone when you need it. He'd left his at the work site. He used the app on your laptop to track your phone. That's how he found you at the Little League headquarters. Just in time too."

The screeching tires. The door slam. Must've been Sean. "What do you mean, just in time?"

"Well, a second after that guy pistol-whipped you, Sean shot him in the calf with your rifle, and Rachel's dad pinned him to the ground."

He blew out a breath. "So, he didn't get the gold?"

"No."

Paul rubbed his forehead. His entire head ached, front and back. He closed his eyes to block the glare of the fluorescent lights overhead. The throbbing at the base of his skull made Amanda's explanation hard to follow.

There would be time to clear up the details later. He needed to see that Rachel was okay. "You said they were at the police station, right? How long do you think—?"

The door to his room swung open, and Sean strolled in.

Sean grinned. "Look who's up."

He approached the bed and grabbed Amanda from behind, wrapping his arms around her waist and kissing her hair and cheek.

Paul cleared his throat. "Hey, I'm the injured party here."

He got no response.

Amanda turned toward Sean, kissed his cheek, and whispered something in his ear.

"I'll be back, Paul." She let her hand fall from Sean's waist. "I need a restroom break. And a snack."

Paul tried to straighten in the bed, but his head protested, and he leaned back against the pillow. He sat motionless for a moment as a wave of nausea passed. "I guess I owe you."

Sean plopped in the chair alongside his bed. "Yeah,

well, I'll put it on your tab. I'm glad I got there when I did."
He leaned forward and rested his elbows on his knees.
"You okay?"

"I guess. My head hurts like hell, though."

"I imagine it would. Doctor doesn't think you have
anything more than a mild concussion though. You'll be
fine."

Paul tried to recapture his dream, but he could no
longer feel the heat or the sand, and the image of Dad
already grew fuzzy. Internally, he repeated what Dad had
said to commit it to memory. Had it only been a dream?

One way to find out.

"Sean, is there something you want to tell me?"

Sean wrinkled his face. "I'm glad your stupidity didn't
get you killed?"

Paul tried to smile. "Thanks for the love, but I meant
news about you. And Amanda."

Sean shrugged. "News? I got nothin'."

Maybe it was an ordinary dream. Maybe thoughts of
pregnancy were bubbling in his subconscious from the
conversation he and Sean had last week.

Or maybe Sean was withholding information.

In the course of their talk, he'd told Paul he and
Amanda weren't doing anything to prevent a pregnancy.
They were hoping to have a bunch of kids.

"I've gotta ask you something. Is....Is Amanda
pregnant?"

Sean's eyes widened. "Did she tell you that?"

"No, Dad did."

Sean's brow crinkled, and his eyes narrowed. "What do
you mean, 'Dad did'? The doctor said you had a mild
concussion, not that you were delusional."

"Just before I woke up, I was dreaming, and I saw Dad
out in the desert." A lump grew in his throat. He swallowed
and took a deep breath. "One of the things he said to me

was, 'Tell Sean he's done good. And to take care of that grandbaby of mine.'"

Sean stood, hooked his thumbs in his jeans pockets, and stalked to the foot of Paul's bed. "How could you know that? She took a pregnancy test two days ago. We weren't going to tell anyone until she saw her doctor."

"It's what he said in the dream."

Sean was going to be a dad—a great one. And Paul would have a little niece or nephew. His heart swelled. The amount of joy that knowledge brought surprised him. "Congratulations."

Sean glanced up from where he'd been studying the bed sheets. "Yeah, thanks. We're thrilled, it's just, that's weird. What else did Dad say?"

"Not much. Something for me about Rachel and then what I told you."

The door swung open, letting in a strong food aroma—real food of the non-hospital variety. Paul got a whiff of the onions and his stomach roiled. The stronger smell of chili quickly overpowered the onions.

Amanda, Rachel, and Mr. Mueller came through the door. Mr. Mueller filled the tray at his bedside with four white paper sacks.

Rachel rushed to the bed and threw her arms around Paul. She looked unhurt, but her bloodshot eyes and red nose convinced him she'd been crying. Her hair fell in his face, and its strawberry fragrance calmed him.

"Paul, I'm so glad you're okay." Her voice in his ear—heaven. Thank God they were safe.

He blinked away the fresh pain in his head as she squeezed him. "Sean says I'll be fine. If you can trust him."

Sean winked at him, a protective arm draped around Amanda's shoulders. He gave his head a little shake. Probably still grappling with Dad's message from beyond the grave. So was Paul.

Rachel released him, and he looked her over. "You okay?"

She smiled. "Fine. Better than fine. Great, now that I know you're okay."

"Amanda sort of told me what happened, but my head..." He rubbed the back of his neck. "Do they know who Captain Jim really is, and how he knew about the gold?"

"Apparently Mr. O'Donnell's secretary tipped him off," Mr. Mueller said.

"What?" Beehive-Do was in on it?

"Yeah." Mr. Mueller removed Styrofoam containers and plastic spoons from the bags. "She unwittingly mentioned the gold in the presence of her step-grandson, aka Captain Jim. Jim's mother is an alcoholic, and his dad is in prison, and she took him into her home about six months ago. She let it slip while she was typing up Mr. O'Donnell's notes last night."

He handed Sean a bowl then offered one to Amanda. She turned a little green and shook her head.

"Then this morning, after we showed up at Mr. O'Donnell's, she told Jim about the gold's value. Just flapping her gums. Mr. O'Donnell says she's really trying to get the kid on the right track. She keeps after him, calling home all the time to keep tabs but..."

Paul's pounding head allowed him to perfect his deadpan look. "It's not working."

"No. I guess she called home around the time we were leaving the office with the gold, and he got it out of her that we were headed to the bank without an escort."

Rachel sat on the edge of his bed, popped the lid off her chili, and stirred. "He must've done his homework, though, to know about your dad. I guess you can find almost everything on the Internet."

"Where's the gold now?" Paul asked.

"We finally got our police escort." Rachel swallowed a spoonful of chili. "It's all safe in the bank, and Captain Jim is in the county jail."

"And, our meeting with the state's attorney for the Department of Conservation is on for tomorrow." Mr. Mueller passed around a small stack of napkins.

So, they'd have another day of waiting to find out their fate. Would the state try to prosecute them? Would he and Rachel get any money out of it? Would the Muellers keep their land?

It was becoming a recurring theme in his life—waiting. He hoped he was getting better at it. *Have patience, Paul.* That's what Dad had said. His gaze roved over Rachel perched on the edge of his bed. He was going to need it.

Chapter 30
Life Is A Highway

Mrs. Mueller grabbed the phone from the counter, fumbled with the buttons, and held it to her ear. "Ron, what's the news?" She directed a hopeful smile at Paul and Rachel.

Paul gripped Rachel's hand as they stood at the entrance to the kitchen and listened to half of the conversation. His heart pounded in his chest, and he clenched his jaw.

Rachel squeezed his fingers.

"Well?" Mrs. Mueller's hand flew over her heart. "Outstanding!"

"I'm liking the sound of this," Paul murmured to Rachel.

She squeezed the life out of his fingers. "Me too."

"Love you too." Mrs. Mueller ended the call and returned the phone to the counter.

"Well?" Rachel prompted.

Mrs. Mueller's eyes twinkled, and a huge smile spread over her face. "They'll give us triple their initial offer on the property, and no charges will be filed against you."

Rachel gasped then flung her arms around Mrs. Mueller's waist.

No charges would be filed. Paul blew out the breath he'd been holding. No fine, no record, no jail time. The rest was gravy. He turned to Rachel and hugged her to him.

"One more thing," Mrs. Mueller said.

He and Rachel let go of each other and turned their attention back to Mrs. Mueller.

"You will each receive a finder's fee equal to one half of one percent of the gold's value."

"How much is that?" Rachel asked.

Paul calculated the percentages in his head. "According to the jeweler's estimate, that's about sixty-five thousand dollars each."

Rachel whooped, and Paul wrapped his arms around her, lifting her off the ground.

James bounded in from the living room. He propelled his agile body at them, intruding on their hug and tugging at Paul's and Rachel's arms. "What happened? Do you get to keep the buried treasure?"

"Some of it." Paul set Rachel on the floor and mussed James's hair.

James pumped his fist in the air. "Awesome!"

Rachel laughed, her eyes shiny with unshed tears, and hugged them both.

Life is good.

***

Several weeks passed before the agreement with the Commonwealth was finalized and approved by the necessary bureaucrats. School resumed, and rumors flew about the discovery of lost gold dug up by a couple of students.

There was no news release, no spot on the evening news. The state wanted it that way, for various reasons, until everything was triple-authenticated and the entire area was excavated, and the appropriate commissions were apprised and consulted.

Paul happily complied with their stipulations.

He'd been tempted more than once to let it spill because, well, it was plain, freaking awesome, but the Muellers, Sean and Amanda had cautioned him and Rachel about the ramifications. It was an incredible story, but its revelation would be fraught with a lot of pitfalls. Gold diggers, literal and otherwise, would be at their doorsteps. Trespassers. Thieves. Mr. Mueller had already gotten quotes for fencing in his property. Their encounter with Captain Jim left a bitter taste in their mouths. Paul and Rachel would take their pittance, thank you very much, and get on with their lives.

That's what Paul did a week later when the Commonwealth deposited the cash into his account.

***

The living room was quiet. No signs of Rachel's family in the kitchen or anywhere on the main floor.

Paul's fingers wove beneath the silky brunette waves that fell on Rachel's shoulder. He pulled his lips from hers to kiss her cheek, her neck, and her ear. "Where are your parents?" he murmured.

Rachel turned her head to capture his lips again. It was a full minute before she answered. "In the basement. Something about the water softener."

He considered again the best way to spring his surprises on her.

"I've got something I want to give you." He broke their kiss and allowed his heart and lungs a chance to return to normal rhythm. He would get control of this if it killed him—and it just might.

"I thought we decided you weren't going to give me that until we married." Her eyes teased, and her lips twisted in a saucy half-grin.

The reminder didn't hurt. He'd discovered that strength of conviction was a good motivator, but every time his lips lingered on Rachel's skin, those convictions would be tested.

"Rachel, I want this—I want *you*—so badly." He let out a frustrated groan. "You have no idea. But I want so much more for us. And I don't want to ruin it."

She circled her arms around his neck, planted a kiss on his cheek, and then focused on him, her eyes brimming with love. "What *do* you want for us?"

"I want us to be together, as husband and wife." There. He'd been thinking it forever. Now he'd said it.

Rachel's eyes widened then the corners lifted as she smiled, biting her bottom lip.

"I know I'm young—we're young—but I know what I want. I want us to raise a family together. And I want us to walk side-by-side into heaven where we can meet Mom and Dad."

His chest tightened, and his palms itched. Before he could lose his nerve, he pulled a small gift box from his pocket and held it out to her. "For you."

She lifted the lid and gasped. "Paul, it's..."

At the last second, he realized after what he'd just said, she might've been expecting a diamond solitaire. He hoped she wasn't disappointed. "I would've gotten you a diamond, but I don't believe in long engagements. And I don't think your parents would approve of their sixteen-year-old daughter getting engaged."

She set aside the empty gift box, and examined the ring. She tilted her hand in the light, and the little gems shimmered.

"They, uh, I think they call it a promise ring. The stone is aquamarine, and those are little diamonds along the sides." He pointed to the small stones.

Rachel slipped it onto her index finger and held it up to take a closer look. "It's the stone from Larry's jewelry store, isn't it?"

He nodded and turned the band around her finger. "There's an inscription."

She brought the ring closer and read, "'PRP to RAM—"

"I know a lot of people do the 'love waits' thing, but this is from St. Paul's letter, and it's not like I have to wait to love you. I've been doing that for the better part of two years." He turned the band around in her fingers so that she could read the rest of the inscription. "I just have to wait to express it to you in a particular way. And *that* requires endurance. Hence..."

"Love endures. Oh, Paul, it's beautiful." She rose on her tiptoes and kissed him.

"Not half as beautiful as the girl who's going to wear it. Can we see if it fits? I had to guess at the size."

Rachel held out her hand with her fingers separated, and Paul slid the ring up her finger. He looked forward to doing that at least twice more in his life: when they got engaged and then at their wedding.

"Perfect." He glanced up, eager to see if she looked as elated as he felt.

Tears rolled down her cheeks.

"Why are you crying?" He brushed away a tear with his thumb.

She sniffed and wiped the remaining tears from her cheeks. "I don't know. Just happy tears." She held up her hand and the little diamonds glimmered in the sunlight.

Paul grabbed a tissue from the box on the end table and handed it to her. "There was a time not too long ago when I couldn't say something like this. At least not say it and mean it, but...God's been good to me. He took my parents home, but he brought me to you."

"And I'm so grateful. Thank you, Paul. I love you." She hugged him close, and he relished the feel of her body against his. She was all he wanted this side of heaven. There was more to his surprise, though, so he let her go.

"We could stay here and you could thank me some more, or I could show you what else I got."

She cocked her head. "Okay. That piqued my curiosity. Lead the way."

He took her by the hand and led her to the back door. They walked out and down the porch steps onto the driveway. Paul guided her to the pathway they had worn around the property and onto the little trail that led to the garden room. As summer neared an end, the flowers grew long and leggy but were still bright and lush, bursting with color and life. He'd forever associate the fragrance of wildflowers with this place. A pair of cardinals chirped in a nearby tree as he helped Rachel scale the coal-laden slope near where they had unearthed the treasure.

Parked on the little plateau, which led to the fire road, sat his surprise.

A shiny, cobalt blue convertible Ford Mustang.

Rachel's eyes widened and her face lit up. "Whoa. I don't know much about cars, but I know what I like." She ran her hand along the hood. "You bought this?"

"Yep." It was only a used car, but it was his first, it was paid for, and he loved it. His chest swelled with pride.

"How'd you get it here? You don't have a license."

"Sean drove it here for me. Do you like it?"

"I love it. Oh my gosh, Paul, it's...wow."

He couldn't account for how pleased he was that she liked this car—*his* car. He admired the rugged grill, the shiny hubcaps, and the sexy shape of the hood. He couldn't wait to drive it. Sean had promised to take him to get his learner's permit in the morning.

Rachel's arm slipped through his. "Do you have any money left? This and a ring..."

Paul shrugged. "It's used, and I paid cash for it. I need a car for work anyway. I can't expect my brother and your parents to chauffeur me around for the rest of my life. Besides, I've saved nearly every penny I earned the last two summers for a car, so I added all of that to the pot too. The rest of the money will go toward college. There's still a big chunk left."

Rachel walked around the car, touching the fenders and peering at the leather seats. She gave him a smoldering sidelong glance. "Roomy back seat."

He couldn't wait to see her in it.

"Yeah. I noticed that too." Eventually it would be an advantage, but for now it would be a distraction, at best. "Do you think your parents will let me take you out in this car once I get my license?"

"I don't know, but I think we're going to need a new rule."

Paul grinned. They were learning their limitations. "Probably so."

He rounded the car and opened the passenger side door for her. "Your carriage, m'lady."

She slid in and scooted back in the seat. "Thank you, sir."

He closed the door behind her, jogged to the driver's side and got behind the wheel. With his hands on the wheel, he turned to her. "Where to?"

She shrugged. "Doesn't matter. Wherever you're headed."

Paul smiled. "So you trust me not to get us lost?"

The smile faded from her face. "I trust you with my life—body and soul."

Paul swallowed. Hard. The awesome responsibility she had just entrusted to him didn't escape his notice.

He cupped Rachel's face in his hands. The breeze blew her hair in her eyes, and he pushed it back with his thumbs so that it rested behind her ears. "I love you."

Wanting her to see in his eyes the depth of his feelings for her, he didn't kiss her right away.

After a second or two, her eyes grew watery, and she blinked.

His eyes welled up too, so he closed them and kissed her. If only he could freeze this moment and make it last forever. With a final kiss to her forehead, he reached into his pocket and pulled out the keys. He sucked in a breath then pushed the key into the ignition and started the car.

He gave the engine some gas, and it roared to life. The power it generated gave him a rush.

Rachel must have felt it too. She reached over and squeezed his leg.

He smiled and dug into his pocket for his iPod. He settled it in the dock and pressed "play."

The road stretches out before us,
Wide expanse reflects the light.
Hills and valleys, twists and turns,
I can't see the finish line.

I'll take the wheel, and you take my hand,
Rubber meets road at the horizon
'Til the end of my days, driving away
I only want you beside me.

Epilogue
2017

Rachel lugged the laundry basket through the apartment door and shoved it closed with her foot. She stumbled into the living area, the clean, folded laundry stacked so high she couldn't see over it. Two weeks of clothes from vacation: done. She heaved the basket down next to the couch and gasped.

Paul stood right in front of her.

In a fraction of a second, he grabbed her waist, swung her around, and tossed her onto the couch where he lowered himself on top of her.

"You're pretty sneaky."

He planted kisses along her collarbone, causing her neck to tingle. "I have to be. My wife keeps getting away from me."

"I waited so long for you to call me your wife," she murmured between kisses. "It's never going to get old." Only sixteen days into married life, her heart stilled every time he said it.

In seconds, their clothes were heaped in a haphazard pile next to the basket of folded laundry. After so many years of putting on the brakes, it was such a joyous relief to say with their bodies what they felt in their hearts and what they had promised to each other on the altar.

They'd had a small wedding consisting of a simple Mass and a casual reception, but Rachel would remember it as one of the best days of her life: Paul standing at the end of that long aisle, so handsome he eclipsed even Sean's good looks. The shimmer in his blue eyes when the priest introduced them as Mr. and Mrs. Paul Porter, and he leaned in to kiss her. Then their last moments at the reception, when he'd swung her up into his arms and told her he was the luckiest man in the world, before he carried her out the door.

Their friends thought they were crazy for getting married so young, but they had no doubts. They had only waited this long because Paul thought it prudent to finish school and at least be working at something full time, even if it wasn't his dream job. Rachel would be starting a new semester at college in a couple of weeks. They didn't see a reason to wait any longer. It had been almost five years since she'd accepted his promise ring, and they had finally made it to the altar, as Paul said, "Pure as the driven, but slightly yellowed, snow."

They'd faced plenty of temptations throughout the years, especially around the holidays and the night of Paul's twenty-first birthday—a night that had opened both their eyes to the fact that they should marry sooner rather than later. Over the years, they had stuck to their "rules," although the rules had been adjusted to take into account their commitment to one another and maturity. There had also been more than a few impromptu trips to the confessional for both of them. Still, they had done it—they had saved that most intimate expression of their love for their wedding night.

Seven years of sexual tension and frustration culminated in a night that, to Rachel, seemed like it had ended almost as soon as it began.

Paul had more than made up for it on their honeymoon during lazy afternoons, endless nights, and mornings that were spent entirely in bed, sometimes making love, sometimes just holding one another, talking, and laughing. They were like two kids set loose in an amusement park with ride-all-you-want wristbands.

Already the awkward, clumsy moments were being

replaced by laughter and the selfless kind of total, exclusive love that can lead to holding a baby in nine months, a reality Rachel was pretty sure would be confirmed with an at-home pregnancy test in the morning.

Paul rested his hand on the curve of Rachel's abdomen and placed a kiss on her belly button, causing her to giggle. "I can't get enough of you."

"Mmm...the feeling is mutual." She ran her fingers through his hair; something that, after all this time, she had just learned drove him crazy.

Paul propped himself up alongside Rachel on the couch, continuing to plant kisses on her bare skin as the whim struck him, it seemed. "I've been thinking of my dad a lot lately."

"Because of the wedding?"

"I guess so. I wish you'd had a chance to meet him."

"Me too. I would thank him for giving you life and raising you right." She touched his cheek and rubbed her fingertips over the stubble there. "He'd be so proud of the man you've become."

"I hope so."

"When we have a little boy, I'd like to name him after your dad."

His eyes shone, loving and maybe a little teary. "I'd like that. We'd better not wait too long, though. So far Sean and Amanda have produced only girls, but you never know."

She was tempted to tell him her period was already late but decided to wait for the test in the morning. Paul would be excited about a baby, but he'd already been anxious about being the sole provider for their little family. She was glad he had Sean for support.

Sean was the breadwinner for Amanda and their three beautiful little girls. Rachel was pretty sure he was the one who had given Paul the final push he needed to propose when worry and self-doubt held him back.

Paul eyed their small apartment furnished with hand-me-downs and yard sale finds before he turned his attention back to her. His hand skimmed her bare leg. It wouldn't be long before they ended up back in bed.

"Rachel, do you ever think about the gold? What our lives would be like if we had kept it?"

His question deserved a thoughtful answer, but his roaming hand was making it hard to concentrate.

"Not really." From what she knew, ill-gotten gains were less a treasure and more a curse. They had chosen the honorable path, and it was sweeter because they'd sacrificed for it—for each other. She knew they'd argue and go through rough patches, but with a strong foundation built on integrity, virtue, and trust, they'd make it. "If I could go back, I wouldn't change a thing."

She dug her fingers into Paul's hair again and felt his body tense against hers. Her hand slid through the locks that curled behind his ear, and her eyes caught on the gold band and diamond solitaire that graced her ring finger. "Not for all the treasure in the world."

Acknowledgments

What became *Rightfully Ours* began during National Novel Writing Month in 2010 as my first attempt at writing a novel. People from various writing groups as well as several friends read and commented on early drafts and chapters. I'm afraid in trying to name them all, I would omit someone. Therefore, I offer a simple thank you to everyone who read those early attempts at creating a readable story. Sincere thanks to Don Mulcare, who persevered through chapter critiques, and especially Theresa Linden, who critiqued, edited, and supported me on the path to publication. Special thanks to those who answered my questions regarding emergency medical and hospital issues: Maria Angelo, Tom Buck, and my nephew, Zachary Perpetua. Finally, thank you to Ellen Gable and Full Quiver Publishing. Your patience, courtesy, and professionalism make working with you both a pleasure and a privilege.

About the Author

Carolyn Astfalk resides with her husband and four children in Hershey, Pennsylvania, where it smells like either chocolate or manure, depending on wind direction. She is the author of the inspirational romances *Stay With Me* and *Ornamental Graces* and the coming-of-age story *Rightfully Ours*. Carolyn is a member of the Catholic Writers Guild and Pennwriters and a CatholicMom.com contributor. Formerly, she served as the communications director of the Pennsylvania Catholic Conference, the public affairs agency of Pennsylvania's Catholic bishops. True to her Pittsburgh roots, she still says "pop" instead of "soda," although her beverage of choice is tea.

You can find her online at www.carolynastfalk.com

Published by Full Quiver Publishing
PO Box 244
Pakenham ON K0A2X0
Canada
www.fullquiverpublishing.com

37823410R00184

Printed in Poland
by Amazon Fulfillment
Poland Sp. z o.o., Wrocław